Other books by Kitty Burns Florey

Fiction

The Writing Master
Solos
The Sleep Specialist
Souvenir of Cold Springs
Five Questions
Vigil for a Stranger
Duet
Real Life
The Garden Path
Chez Cordelia
Family Matters

Nonfiction

The Quest for Inez: Two Ways to Find a Grandmother
Script and Scribble: The Rise and Fall of Handwriting
*Sister Bernadette's Barking Dog: The Quirky History and Lost Art of
Diagramming Sentences*

Amity Street

Amity Street

a novel

Kitty Burns Florey

White River Press
Amherst, Massachusetts

Amity Street: a novel by Kitty Burns Florey
Copyright 2017.

First published 2017

White River Press
PO Box 3561
Amherst, MA 01004

WhiteRiverPress.com

ISBN: 978-1-887043-29-8
ISBN: 978-1-887043-30-4 e-book

Library of Congress Cataloging-in-Publication Data:

Name: Florey, Kitty Burns, author.
Title: *Amity Street*: a novel / Kitty Burns Florey.
Description: Amherst, Massachusetts: White River Press, 2016.
Identifiers: LCCN 2016038460| ISBN 9781887043298 (softcover: acid-free paper) | ISBN 9781887043304 (e-book)
Subjects: LCSH: Massachusetts–Social life and customs–19th century–Fiction. | City and town life–Massachusetts–Fiction. | Families–Massachusetts–Fiction. | Interpersonal relations–Fiction. | Amherst (Mass.)–Fiction. | Domestic fiction. | GSAFD: Historical fiction.
Classification: LCC PS3556.L588 A84 2016 | DDC 813/.54–dc23
LC record available at https://lccn.loc.gov/2016038460

Cover images: map, courtesy of the Jones Library, Inc., Amherst, Massachusetts; Mabel Loomis Todd's teapot, courtesy of the Amherst Historical Society, Amherst, Massachusetts; author photo by Turi MacCombie

For Richard

I observed a very slight and graceful hawk... alternately soaring like a ripple and tumbling a rod or two over and over, showing the underside of its wings, which gleamed like a satin ribbon in the sun, or like the pearly inside of a shell.... It was not lonely, but made all the earth lonely beneath it.

Henry David Thoreau, *Walden*, "Spring"

I went to heaven –
'Twas a small town...

Emily Dickinson

The goodly elms, on either side of the large straight street, rise from their grassy margin.... When the great elm-gallery happens to be garnished with old houses, and the old houses happen to show style and form and proportion, and the hand of time, further, has been so good as to rest on them with all the pressure of protection and none of that of interference, then it is that the New England village may placidly await any comer.

Henry James, *The American Scene*

Amity Street is the sequel to an earlier novel, *The Writing Master*, the events of which take place in 1856 in New Haven, thirty-six years before the present story begins.

Cast of Characters

Lily Prescott, daughter of a wealthy expatriate American painter, Orlando Prescott, living in Rome. Eighteen years old and pregnant, Lily was sent in disgrace to America, where she gave birth to a daughter and named her Prudence Ann. When the baby was six months old, Lily returned to Italy and married Basil Felice. She died of malaria six years later.

Elena Zanetti, servant/companion who accompanied Lily to America.

Aunt Julia Tuttle, of New Haven, Orlando Prescott's sister, with whom Lily and the baby lived briefly before they returned to Rome.

Anna Felice, who in 1892 arrives in America from Rome, Italy, in search of information about her family history.

Charles Cooper, the eponymous writing master, who inscribed a birth certificate for Lily documenting the birth of Prudence Ann. He became the founder and director of the Elm City School of Business in New Haven, and eventually enlisted in the 14th Connecticut Infantry. He was wounded at Gettysburg in 1863. After the war, he and his family moved to Amherst, Massachusetts, where he died in 1874.

George Mullen, who assisted Charles Cooper in retrieving Lily's baby when she was abducted. Now living in Amherst, working at a livery stable.

Maud Mullen, George's older sister and Charles Cooper's secretary at the Elm City School of Business—later his wife. Now living in Amherst.

Hazel Cooper, in 1892 the thirty-ish unmarried daughter of Charles and Maud.

Tamsin Cooper Chillick, Charles's sister, who fled her first husband in Ohio, returned to her family in Connecticut, and by 1892 has long been married to Samuel Chillick, a professor of meteorology first at Trinity College in Hartford, then at Amherst College. Their daughter, Lydia, and her husband, Archie Wyatt, have three children.

Davey and Maddox Chillick, Tamsin's twin boys from her first marriage—Hazel's cousins. Maddox is a law professor at Harvard; Davey lives in a cabin behind the Chillicks' house in Amherst.

Amity Street

Chapter 1

O n the afternoon of her second day at the Fifth Avenue Hotel—
it was early April, 1892—Signorina Anna Felice was seated at
a spindly desk in the reading room down the hall from her room
on the fifth floor, which was the highest and, she had been given to
understand, the most exclusive. The desk was directly in front of a
window. Far below on 23rd Street pedestrians shared the road with
carriages and wagons and cable cars and an occasional automobile.

She had ventured out an hour ago, directed by the bellman to
a stationery store at 27th Street, where she bought a notebook with
marbled cardboard covers and a bottle of black ink for her fountain
pen. On her way back to the hotel, she had nearly been run down
by a cable car. A black-bearded man in overalls pulled her out of
the way, leaving sooty handprints on the sleeve of her dress. She
was so flustered she thanked him in Italian: *Grazie, grazie, Signore*—
wondering if she should give him a coin—which coin? But he disappeared into the crowd while she was still fumbling in her purse.

Back at her hotel, she left her muddy shoes to be cleaned. The
filthy sleeve didn't bother her. She had never had to mind such
things. And soon she would be changing to go out. Meanwhile, in
the elegant and nearly empty reading room, she would work on her
English. She filled her pen, very carefully—it was Viennese, and

1

new, and sometimes messy: a parting gift from her friend Nunzia— and turned her mind to the word "donot." She knew "cannot," a very useful verb, but "donot" seemed not to exist, and when she wrote it in her notebook, she divided it in two—"do not"—which of course made sense, but she was left feeling oddly disoriented. Why this and not that?

In Rome, she had thought she knew the English language almost as well as she knew Italian, but, though she had her pronouns and verb tenses well in hand, she knew from only two days in America that her vocabulary was sadly inadequate, and there were subtleties that eluded her. On the desk before her was an Italian-English dictionary, a gift from her language tutor: helpful—indispensable!— but she wished Mr. Banks himself were there to be consulted.

"Excuse me, Signora."

A man approached: quite tall, well-dressed, dark hair worn too long, fussy little beard. Surely not someone who recognized her, who had heard her sing? No. Not possible all these years later in a hotel in Manhattan.

"Yes?" Her voice was frosty.

"Forgive me." He would be handsome if his teeth were not so yellow, and one of them broken. "I could not help noticing you on the street, where you had put yourself in danger as you were crossing it."

"Yes?"

"I heard you speak, and I wondered if you are visiting here from Italy. I am myself in New York from Milano, on business."

She knew that, if she admitted it, he would speak to her in Italian, and she had no wish to hear Italian. Here in her mother's country, she was interested only in her mother's language. "You are mistaken." She tried to enunciate crisply, as the English did, and her smile was as meager as she could make it.

There was a pause, as if he expected her to say more, but she turned back to her notebook. He said, "I regret having bothered you," and added, softly, "*Arrivederci, Signora.*"

What impudence.

On the desk was also the novel *Great Expectations*, by Charles Dickens, which she had found on a shelf in the reading room the day before. The six chapters she had read had yielded half a page of new words. She was familiar with *A Christmas Carol* and was aware that the English spoken by Mr. Dickens's characters was often a kind of dialect, which made it difficult to decipher. But the book also was very funny. The more she read, the better she saw this, though it didn't help her understand some of the words.

Wittles was food: she had gotten that far. Not, it seemed, very nice food. *Rampage*: some sort of disturbance. *Elth* was baffling; maybe Aunt Julia could enlighten her. Tomorrow she would board a train at the Grand Central Depot for New Haven, Connecticut, to visit her American grandfather's sister. She knew nothing of that city, but at least it was not New York.

For one more day, she would have to endure Manhattan, which had revealed itself to her as a chaos of filth and noise. She had left the hotel only twice. On the streets, she coughed, her eyes itched, she was afraid to breathe the air. It was the way she felt when Umberto let her try one of his cigars and she thought she might faint but instead vomited on his waistcoat. They were in the conservatory, she was sitting on his lap, and she was happy that day, at least until the cigar.

Tonight was the opera. Mr. Banks had arranged for Anna to meet his sister, Mrs. Diana Hummerston, who was married to Mr. Morton Hummerston, the owner of a factory that made hatbands. Hummerston Hatbands! Famous across the country! Who could know that one might achieve prosperity manufacturing such items? The Hummerstons were opera-lovers, and had invited her to their box at the Metropolitan Opera House, where Adelina Patti was singing in *The Barber of Seville*.

The light began to fade. Anna closed her book and her notebook, and, back in her hotel room, removed her soiled dress and stuffed it into her traveling trunk: Aunt Julia's maid would restore it to freshness. She washed the fine layer of grime from her face and hands and arranged her hair, something she was becoming used to doing on her own. If she had brought her maid to America, her hair would be done more stylishly and her dress would be cleaned, but part of the price would be the constant chatter. And it would be Italian chatter. The other part of the price would be that Giovannina was a reminder of all she had left behind.

Anna Felice had come to America to transform herself: not completely sure what she meant by that, but hoping the opportunity would present itself, and that she would recognize it when it did.

For now, however competent her English, she was a foreigner. Out on 23rd Street, and in the stationery shop, people turned to look at her, and she knew that, even in this cosmopolitan city, she carried with her an air of the alien, the exotic.

Of course, she was not unaware that she was beautiful. But New York was full of beautiful women, and hers—she had always believed this, with sincerity, and even with some justice—was the kind of beauty that looked best from the stage. She had thick, reddish hair that was hard to keep tidy, so without a maid to arrange it she pulled it back into a tight bun, which showed the round and pleasing open-ness of her face. She would not have agreed that she looked younger than her years, but it was true. Her eyes were large and dark blue, her mouth curly and small like the mouths on Roman statues, and her long nose had a bit of a bump to acknowledge her half-Ital-ian heritage. For a singer, she had always been improbably slender through the middle, though with thicker legs under her skirts than one might expect. And more bosom. She wondered if her evening dresses would be too revealing for America, where she detected a strain of prudishness that was not present in Rome.

She knew little about the island of Manhattan. Her hotel sat neatly in the middle of it. To the west and to the east were rivers, further east the harbor, and beyond it the ocean she crossed on the *Britannia*: a week of nausea that left her thin and ravenous. Now, from her top floor window, she saw a wide expanse of sky turning darker as evening came on. It could be a sky in Rome—or anywhere. The sky was always the same. The world was always big. The speck that was Anna Felice was always small, whichever side of the ocean it was on. For a moment she felt so small as to be invisible. *Do I exist at all, here where I know no one?*

She consulted her little gold watch: time to stop thinking useless thoughts and get ready for the evening. She rubbed on lipstick and a trace of cheek color, and fastened herself into her blue silk, which mercifully buttoned in front: time-consuming but not difficult. Her breasts were pushed into prominence; she hoped that was acceptable but then thought: *Do I really care? I will never be here again, never see these people.* She shook out her cloak and wrapped it around her shoulders because the night would be cool: in addition to its other cruelties, New York in April was as cold and windy as a March day in Rome. She pinned on her hat.

Mr. and Mrs. Hummerston were in the lobby to greet her, very grand in their evening clothes. Mr. Hummerston was short, balding, and merry, with an artful mustache and, buried in his satin tie, a pearl stickpin like one her papa used to wear. Mrs. Hummerston was fat and fair, and her neckline dipped an inch lower than Anna's. The Hummerstons attempted some words of Italian: *Benvenuto, Signorina Felice! Buona sera! Andiamo?*

Anna waved her hands. "Please, may we speak in English? I am so much trying to learn." With obvious relief, they whisked her into their carriage, closed and very comfortable—laughing and making little jokes she didn't quite understand. But they were kind, and proud of their city, driving her down one lamp-lit avenue and up another, pointing out churches and buildings and a park. Anna could see hardly anything, but she exclaimed, at random, "Oh, that is lovely" and "How impressive a place."

Finally the carriage pulled up at their tall, narrow house, where they had invited her for a "bite of dinner" before the opera. Just the three of them, thank goodness. The food was close to inedible (maybe it was wittles!), but the wines were French and very good. The conversation was about opera: the Italian repertory versus the German. Mr. Hummerston, more informed than his wife, had no use for French opera. They seemed unaware of Anna's disastrous career or, at any rate, did not mention it—perhaps Mr. Banks had cautioned them. The Hummerstons were also interested in motorcars and were considering acquiring one. "But who would drive it?" they said to each other, and laughed. Their coachman was terrified of them! Meanwhile, Mr. Hummerston informed her proudly, cable cars had just this year reached Fifth Avenue—a great advance in transportation. "One of them nearly knocked me down," Anna said. (By then she had had two glasses of wine.) Her hosts were mortified—their beloved city had a blemish—and they asked her in detail about her near escape. Mrs. Hummerston patted her hand, Mr. Hummerston refilled her glass. Americans could not roast a leg of spring lamb, but they were kinder than anyone, and, exaggerating only a little, Anna told them how touched she was when the *Britannia* entered New York Harbor at dawn and she saw the Statue of Liberty rising from a mist. There were immigrants on the ship, she told them, and much weeping. Diana Hummerston said that her pet charity was Women's Refugee Relief, and Anna wept a little too, touching a drooping lace handkerchief to her eyes.

Then suddenly, in a flurry, they were off: "We have so enjoyed your company, Signorina, the time has flown!" The carriage dropped them at the door of the opera house, and they pushed their way through the crowds. Even in the dark, Anna could see that the place was unremarkable on the outside. But inside all was gleaming and golden. From the Hummerstons' box, she surveyed it with a practiced eye. She had never sung there, but she liked its sumptuousness, and she had heard much about its impressive acoustics.

They were impressive indeed, and the production was lavish. The hall was a treasure, but the blessing of seeing Mme. Patti in *Barbiere* was a mixed one. Patti was no longer pretty and did not sing well—she was almost fifty years old, how could she not know it was time to stop? But she had grown up in the Bronx, a part of the city of New York, and the audience adored her, applauding even the sentimental rubbish she saw fit to give for her encores. The last, a song called "Home Sweet Home," inspired a standing ovation. Patti had always been of particular interest to Anna because, like her, Patti made her debut at sixteen in *Lucia*. Much too soon for Anna, but just right for Patti. How different their lives. And a part of herself that Anna didn't like was not sorry to see the great soprano in decline.

The Hummerstons applauded until their palms must have ached. They insisted on joining the crowd on stage to shake Patti's hand, an activity in which Anna, pleading fatigue, did not participate. Let the poor old woman go to her dressing room in peace!

By the time the Hummerstons returned her to the hotel, Anna was almost too sleepy to undress and take down her hair. All night, Patti's mutilation of "Un voce poco fa" coursed through her dreams. Or was it she herself who was singing?

When she was awakened early in the morning, the sun had barely risen; the sky out her window was shot through with pink and pale blue. She hurried through breakfast, the hotel sent a maid to help her pack, and a carriage took her swiftly to the depot for the early train. She sank into a seat just in time: with an enormous snort, then another, and another, the train jolted into motion.

In her bag was *Great Expectations*. She knew it was thievery, but she had to keep reading. How else to endure the hours of soot and noise and the whining of the child across the aisle and the chatter of the women in the seat facing hers? *A bad egg,* she wrote in her note-book. *Bunkum. In a fix. Guttersnipe. Plagued to death.* These appeared just below *Bronks, bite of dinner, brownstone.* She studied them all carefully: some made sense, others did not. *A bad egg* reminded her of her brother, Marcello.

They chugged along, past fields, woods, here and there bits of a town, the train shuddering to a stop at depots Anna decided to call *quaint*—not unlike small-town depots in France or Austria. But they grew tiresome. When the conductor announced Stamford station, she took out her book and managed to lose herself. She liked to imagine that, when she finished *Great Expectations*, she would post it back to the Fifth Avenue Hotel with a note saying she had packed it in error. It seemed an American thing to do.

The train ride went on forever. She was stiff and uncomfortable, and she needed a lavatory—why did she drink half a pot of coffee with her breakfast? And the coffee had been weak as water. She already missed the coffee houses of Rome—oh, for a steaming cup from the Caffè Greco. She was feeling grumpy: one of those English words that always made her smile. Until today! But by the time the conductor strode through to announce, over the racket—gusts of steam, grinding of wheels—that they were arriving at New Haven and there would be a fifteen-minute stop, she was lost in the story of Pip and the convict and the prison ship.

There were groans of deliverance up and down the car. Anna woke herself from the dream of the book, shook out her skirts, stretched her legs. The conductor, who was young and handsome, helped her down the iron steps, and she gave him her best smile and said *"Grazie,"* which brought a gleam to his eye, as she knew it would.

Inside the station, Anna visited the ladies' lounge, and then, with her trunk and her leather bag and her cloth bag, she was handed into one of the cabs that waited in front of the station. It was an open carriage, the day had turned warm, the sun shone in. Anna read to the driver from her aunt's letter: the house was in Westville, a half-mile past the park, a turn to the left at the giant copper beech, the last house before the road ended.

New Haven, in the state of Connecticut—which was not pronounced as one would think—was the city where Anna's American grandfather, Orlando Prescott, lived as a young man, and went to college, and owned a house, and where his English wife died after giving birth to a daughter. Orlando and the little girl, Lily, lived in the city from time to time while she was growing up, steaming across the ocean, as people—wealthy people—felt compelled to do, even though in those days it was a trip of two or even three weeks. Now that Anna had made the journey herself, she wondered at their stamina.

Anna settled back against the leather cushion, prepared for whatever the city would give her. In New Haven, at least, one could breathe. Lily Prescott died when Anna was six years old, of *mal'aria*, the bad air, which Anna knew had been combined into one word in English and was pronounced quite differently. Also called the Roman fever. The word had kept coming into her head in New York, where the air was worse than anything she had breathed in Rome, or even in Bellagio the year the disease settled there and they all fled her grandfather's villa on the lake to spend two months at a hotel in the mountains.

The driver provided a running commentary as they drove through the town. This was Chapel Street, a major thoroughfare, he assured her, though parts of it were as rutted as a country road. They passed long rows of townhouses so much alike you wondered how anyone could find the way home—very like the Hummerstons' on Fifth Avenue. And the famous Yale College with its bland red-brick buildings: no beauty there, only utility. And in the middle of town a fenced park, called the Green, with three churches lined up on one side of it. The carriage driver pointed them out, with misplaced civic pride. Anna forgot their names immediately: she would call them Stodgy, Stuffy, and Insipid, three words she was proud to have in her vocabulary. He also informed her that citizens were no longer allowed to graze their animals on the Green. "How civilized," Anna said, thinking: *Gesumaria*! Imagining cows on the lawns of the Villa Borghese gardens.

No wonder Orlando Prescott settled, finally, in Rome, and did not leave it again!

She knew that somewhere in this city was Grandfather Prescott's old house. After he died, it belonged to her and Marcello—sold for them by Papa years ago, the profits dropping with barely a ripple into the mysterious depths of the ancient fund of gold and banknotes and jewels and properties that sustained the Felice family. Anna gave small notice to such things, nor did she ever pay attention to what street the house was on. Perhaps they went by it in the carriage.

When she first made the plan to come to America, she thought she might settle there—her grandfather's native land, the birthplace of her mother who died so young. Now she understood the madness of such an idea. The more she saw of America, the heavier the weight on her heart. But though she had booked return passage for the third of June, she consoled herself—forgetting seasickness and boredom and the terrifying depths of the Atlantic Ocean stretching into eternity on all sides of the ship—with the knowledge that she could go home any time. Next week, if she liked! Refusing to let the idea enter her head that, in fact, she had no home. That she might as well live in one of these drab houses as anywhere.

❧◈☙

Great-aunt Julia Tuttle lived a mile or two outside New Haven proper in Westville, the kind of country village Orlando Prescott liked to paint. A charming image of just such a place, with rustic wooden houses, used to hang on Anna's mother's bedroom wall. On this side of the city, a great rocky brown cliff loomed in the near distance. The carriage driver told her a long and complicated story about it. She didn't understand everything he said—there was something called a New England accent, which was quite different from the way Mr. Banks, her tutor, spoke, and her grandfather too, though he was born in Connecticut.

And she cared nothing for the great rock, or the large park, or the paper mill that rose up suddenly, crossing the sky with black smoke. She was tired; all she wanted was to arrive. And, when at last they turned off the main road and pulled up in front of it, her aunt's house astonished her. It was at the end of a street lined with trees trying to come into leaf, and it was painted an intense shade of yellow, like an egg yolk. Anna was sure this was vulgar, but she had resolved to keep her mind open to new things, and so she said to herself that the yellow house was pretty and cheerful. It had a long front porch, with a great deal of wooden fancywork such as she had never seen, and behind the house a red barn—unfortunately not very far behind it. Chickens pecked on the lawn.

Still, compared to many of the houses they passed, it might be called rather grand. *Everything is relative*: it was one of the expressions Mr. Banks taught her, which infuriated her Papa. Such an attitude, he said, was counter to the teachings of the Church! He wanted to discharge Mr. Banks, but Anna dissuaded him with one of her tantrums. To her, it was a useful way to describe things. Grandfather's villa on Lake Como was not so splendid as Papa's palazzo in Rome, and her darling cat Tosca was insignificant beside the lions on the fountains on the Capitoline.

In spite of the barn and the chickens, she felt easier in her mind as the driver helped her down the step into the sunshine. It was only a small exaggeration to say she was happy to be there. The chickens scattered, noisily, as she approached the porch. When she pushed the bell, Aunt Julia opened the front door herself, as if she had been watching from the front windows, which were sparkling, lightly draped, taller than a man. Her aunt immediately embraced her, which was startling but not unpleasant. Aunt Julia was very fat, with a large, soft bosom and much perfume. Anna could see her grandfather's handsomeness hiding in the flabby folds of his sister's face.

Aunt Julia led the way inside to a sunny entrance hall, where she stood back and gazed at Anna. "I thank the Lord I have lived to see this day," she said in a voice that trembled. Her eyes were brilliantly blue, like Grandfather's and Mamma's, and they filled with tears. She wore a lace cap—because, Anna suspected, her hair had become thin. Wisps of it curled around the edges, as white as the lace.

On the wall inside the front door was a large oil painting, a hazy representation of trees and water and a brilliant sunset sky, that Anna recognized immediately as her grandfather's work. Its presence there gave her the odd feeling, just for a moment, that she was not completely alone in the world, that she had a history.

The carriage driver dropped her trunk and cases on the porch with a scowl. Had she not tipped him enough? Was she not sufficiently respectful of his city? Then a tall black man, wearing eyeglasses and a white shirt with a black vest—or was it a weskit?—carried her things inside. He was the best-looking man she had seen so far in New Haven.

"Burton will take everything up to your room," Aunt Julia said. "The Rose Room, I call it. Long ago, it was where your mother stayed when she visited us. Now it's yours, Prudence dear."

Prudence: the name on the birth certificate Anna found buried in the bureau in her mother's bedroom. She reminded her aunt that she was called Anna, and Julia apologized, saying she still thought of her as Prudence. Then she laughed and shook her head until her bits of white curl bobbed around her face. "And it has been hard for me to stop thinking of you as a baby," she said. Wasn't that silly? She laughed some more. "The last time I saw you, you were a little bit of a thing, no more than six months old. Lily's baby! Not even walking. And look at you now!"

Nothing she said made sense, but Anna was too tired, hungry, disoriented to care. They went up the staircase behind Burton, slowly. Aunt Julia held on to the railing for dear life, her other hand on her heart. Halfway up, she had to pause, breathing hard: "I'm seventy-three." But she did not stop smiling. Anna was touched by her aunt's joy at seeing her, whoever she thought Anna was. "My brother Orlando would be seventy-seven if he were alive. I wish he had lived to accompany you. You must tell me all about him."

She showed Anna to the Rose Room, which was rosy indeed. Pink walls, with a wallpaper garland of roses just below the ceiling. A four-poster bed with a flower-sprigged canopy, a matching coverlet, heavy pink-striped drapes at the window. Another Orlando Prescott on the wall: a gazebo in a rose garden. On the washstand were towels appliquéd with roses, and a jar of rose potpourri sitting much too aromatically on a pink corner shelf. "It's lovely," Anna said, hoping the windows would open.

With another embrace, Aunt Julia said there would be tea whenever Anna was ready, and made her slow way back down the stairs. "Take your time, my darling," she called back to Anna. Another new idiom, and a charming idea: time is something we can take, and use—it is ours! She found her notebook and her pen and wrote it down: *take your time*, along with *a little bit of a thing*.

The house was silent. Anna was glad of the chance to wash her face, reapply a little cheek and lip rouge, brush her hair out and pull it back more neatly. Was this the mirror her mother had looked into? Her beautiful mother, not much more than half Anna's age when she slept in the Rose Room. In the mirror, Anna's own eyes looked sunken, shadowed with exhaustion. At the age of thirty-five, how disheveled one could become on a long, filthy train ride—a dishevelment that, somehow, took in more than hair in a tangle and soot on one's nose. By the time she was forty, she would be casting her eyes down in horror when she passed a mirror.

She pushed a window open and felt the air rush in—not as warm as she might have liked, but it diffused the scent of the potpourri. Then—she couldn't help it—she unlaced her shoes, sank into the depths of an overstuffed chair, and put her feet up and her head back. For a minute or two, she slept.

But the presence of Prudence Ann Prescott was insistent. The mysterious child's birth certificate had haunted her for two years.

It was the reason she had come to America at all. Her eyes snapped wide open, and she put on her shoes and went downstairs.

They had tea in the front parlor: hard horsehair sofa, gilt chairs, blue-and-white porcelain. On one end of the mantel, Grandfather Prescott's sketch of his villa by the lake was propped on a wooden stand. At the other end was a pair of Majolica blackamoors exactly like the ones that used to sit on the mantel of her singing teacher: Papa's mistress, Signora Gismondi. Unfortunate coincidence!

A cluster of family portraits was arranged on a table, and Anna turned to them with relief: who? and who? So with those they began their conversation: Flossie, the daughter, a strikingly beautiful young woman and then, in a more recent photograph, a matron on her way to her mother's plumpness. Aunt Julia herself when young, showing off her tip-nosed profile. Some babies: grandchildren, now grown up and nearly Anna's age. And the low-browed, black-whiskered man was Uncle Henry, recently deceased, proprietor of the Blue Hills Augur and Bit Company. Aunt Julia did not enlighten Anna as to the nature of augurs and bits. Profitable entities, no doubt, like hatbands. Very profitable: Aunt Julia wore too many diamonds for daytime.

The tea tray was carried in by the maid, Sally, dressed neatly in gray, with a white collar and apron. Anna would have preferred coffee, but she was already familiar with the blandness of American coffee, so she settled happily enough to the China tea, also a fresh and delicious raisin cake, with cream to spoon over it.

Her head was stuffed with questions, and asking them was what she had come for, but they had to wait while she ate three slices of cake, forcing herself not to gobble, and drank most of the pot of tea. The prim maid brought another. How did she know when it was needed? Was it the American custom for the maid to stand outside the door and count the number of times she heard tea splash into a cup? Anna tried to imagine training one of her housemaids at home in this custom. The service in America—here, at the hotel, at the Hummerstons'—was greatly superior to what she was used to in Rome. Her father's servants had been with the family for generations, and they knew they would not be let go. In America, you had to prove yourself.

While Anna ate and drank—this was the first time she had been really comfortable since she stepped off the *Britannia* four days ago—Aunt Julia talked. Deeply though she loved her niece, and thrilled though she was to see her, she wanted, like most people, to talk about her own concerns. So: Flossie and her husband, Gerald, in Pittsburgh, their daughter Something, who was engaged to be married, and another daughter, Something Else, who was not, and three sons, the oldest, also Gerald, who would soon be taking over Uncle Henry's company, and who Aunt Julia hoped would marry the young woman he was courting. Another son at Yale College. The youngest at—oh, somewhere....

Aunt Julia was like a faucet that, once turned, could not be shut off. The poor old woman must be lonely. Why did Flossie have to move all the way to Pittsburgh, wherever that might be? An only child had obligations, especially a daughter. No Italian girl would do this!

Pleasantly full, at last, of cake and tea, Anna was beginning to seek a way to direct the flow of the faucet toward the subject of the birth certificate, when, in her impulsive way, Aunt Julia stopped talking and gazed at her. "You were such a dear little thing." She took Anna's hand. "So good, so sweet! And so tiny and pretty. You absolutely melted our hearts! Even Henry. He said, in the end, Julia, what does it matter? Lily is our niece, and this baby is part of the family."

Not knowing what to say, Anna said nothing, sensing that a truth she needed to know was lurking in Aunt Julia's memories.

"You were only here with us for—let me think—oh, it must have been a month or a little more. It was high summer, very hot. Barely enough time for us to get to know you before you sailed to Italy. The sixth of September! How funny that I can recall that date so well, when so much else has flown away." Julia blinked and shook her head at the oddness of memory. "And I remember too how happy Henry and I were to hear that Lily and your stepfather were married. He sounded like a lovely man. The answer to a prayer!"

Stepfather?

"Lily didn't write often. How busy she must have been. A young mother, a new bride, that big house to take care of! But she did write to me about her wedding, and then about the birth of your brother. Marcello! What a mellifluous name. And then—oh, such a tragedy." The tears gathered in her eyes, not quite overflowing. "Our sweet Lily."

Anna gave her aunt's hand an encouraging squeeze. She felt she was just about to hear something important.

One or two tears made their way down Aunt Julia's old powdery cheek, and then she sighed. "After she died, Orlando wrote once a year, on my birthday—what a good brother he was to remember it. He always had news of you and Marcello. Your singing, Marcello's skill on horseback. I remember it all."

"It is pronounced Marcello," Anna said gently. "Like the musical instrument. Not like *sell*."

"No! Well, I had no idea. I've been getting it wrong all these years. It's even more beautifully Italian when it's pronounced properly. My goodness! Is he living in Rome? What does he do?"

"He is a dealer in properties and leases. He has a wife and three children. He—" *He and I speak to each other only through lawyers, I hope I never have to see him again.* "—is well," Anna said. "He has a very good life."

"You must tell me more about him. And about yourself, what you've been doing all these years. I'm surprised a lovely girl like you didn't come with a husband and babies trailing behind you."

"I did have a husband, for a mercifully short time." Anna paused, savoring the look of alarm on her aunt's face. "His name was Umberto Crescenzi." She waited for alarm to become enlightenment, but it did not. "The Crescenzis are an ancient and respected Roman family. Papa had a friend at the Vatican, so, after three brutal and difficult years that you will forgive me for not describing, some money changed hands, and the marriage was annulled."

"Annulled!"

"Yes. Due to a technicality. Gone. Removed from church records."

"Well, my goodness!" Aunt Julia pressed her hand to her chest again, as she had when climbing the stairs. "I have never heard of such a thing!"

"It is not uncommon in Italy. I once again became Anna Felice, as if Signor Umberto Crescenzi had never existed."

She said nothing about the settlement awarded to her by the lawyers or the providential technicality that smoothed the way to the annulment: the mysterious absence of any record that Anna Felice had ever been baptized in the Catholic Church. Nor did she mention Liliana, her child, who came spilling in a gush of blood, dead, from Anna's twisted insides.

As if for reassurance that there were happy stories in this world, Aunt Julia's eyes slid toward the picture of Flossie and the grandchildren. The word *stepfather* was still ringing in Anna's ears, and with it the sound of something crashing down around her.

Her aunt changed the subject, being tactful. "Now Marcello. He's four years behind you—is that right? So he would be thirty-two. Imagine that. I recall so well Lily's letter saying he had been born, how happy they were to have a boy, what a delight it was for you to have a brother."

Anna set down her cup. There was a misunderstanding that had to be dispelled, and she could not wait. "Aunt Julia." She stood up, scattering crumbs. "Forgive me. I must—I will be back in one minute," and, leaving the old woman gasping, she ran up the stairs. Sally had unpacked her clothes and hung them in the closet. The birth certificate was still in her leather bag. Of course Sally would not have unpacked it: Sally dealt with clothing, not with large pieces of foolscap—was that what it was called? Anna unfolded it. There was the name, elegantly inscribed: *Prudence Ann Prescott*, and the date of birth: 9 March 1856. Exactly hers, except for the year.

He is four years behind you, and so he is thirty-two. Prudence Ann Prescott was thirty-six, and she was born in New Haven, Connecticut.

Who was this Prudence? Why did she and Anna have the same birthday but a year apart? Why did her aunt say *stepfather*?

Anna returned to the parlor, spread the document out on the tea table, and, with much weeping, Aunt Julia told her.

&ເ⯑

At midnight, Anna was still sleepless. She got out of bed and tied her silk wrapper around her. What a *zizzania*. Or a *muddle*—

the American word was more suited to this murky confusion. Her window was still open, bringing in too much cold air and doing little to remove the scent of potpourri. She pushed the jar to the back of the wardrobe, with a pillow over it, and closed the window. Better. Outside, she could see nothing but the hazy half of a moon and an opaque darkness: street lamps had not yet made their way to Westville.

She pulled the rosy drapes shut and turned up the gas lamp. On a clean page in her notebook she wrote the numeral 1. She had always lived on the edge of her nerves, but she could sometimes quiet the agitation of her mind by making a list—she liked the word *itemize*. She wondered from time to time—almost with serious-ness—whether instead of a singer she might have been happy as a clerk in an office, using her polished script to copy things from one piece of paper to another. How calmly one would go to work every day!

After the numeral 1, she breathed deeply and wrote: *I, Anna Felice, was born Prudence Ann Prescott in New Haven, Connecticut, in 1856, not in Rome, Italy, in 1857. I am a citizen of the United States.*

Under this startling fact, she wrote a 2 and counted again on her fingers. Could she have been wrong? No. It was the truth. She had to grip the pen tightly and concentrate to keep the words legible: *I am not 35 years of age but 36.* A blot accompanied the 6, and she wrote it again. Six. She was thirty-six.

There she paused. This fact alone was enough to keep her from sleeping for a week. She went to look at her face in the mirror. Yes, there were wrinkles between her brows, at the corners of her eyes, and creeping down from the sides of her nose. Faint still, but deeper every day: since her thirtieth birthday, she had watched their slow progress. Now suddenly three hundred and sixty-five days had been added: the lines had become deeper, more determined. In a few hours, she had aged a year. Was she seeing white hairs as well? The light was too dim to judge, but they had to be there—if not today, then tomorrow.

Under the blot, after the number 3, she wrote: *My father was not Papa but some other man, about whom nothing is known. This man and my mother were not married. That is why she was sent away to America to bear the child. Me.*

This was what, over the tea table, Aunt Julia (handkerchief to eyes) had called the painful truth, and, when it was revealed, Anna knew she was probably expected to call for smelling salts or collapse into a heap of sobs. But it was Julia who wept. Anna bore the news in silence, sitting very straight in her chair and keeping her eyes fixed on the drawing of her grandfather's villa on the mantel—the lake and the knot garden, the square tower, the massive mountain behind it, and then the white expanse of sky. *I am not who I thought I was.*

The sentence echoed and repeated in her head like the phrases did in Handel's English arias. Besides shock and dismay, they brought with them a clarity she had never known. Her life, after all, had been a sequence of subtractions: over the course of it she had become motherless, grandfatherless, voiceless, husbandless, homeless—a long list of new words, some of them not in dictionaries. And now another: was there a word for it? Mere fatherlessness was not enough; her Papa had never been much of a refuge, much of a comfort. He had done his duty, but there was no doubt that he preferred Marcello, the male heir, a carbon copy of his Papa. Even on his deathbed, it was Marcello he asked for, Anna hovering in the hallway with the servants while her father groaned his last and Marcello sobbed loudly enough for them all to hear. And why should Basilio Felice not prefer his son to his dry-eyed daughter? But now she saw a deeper truth: Marcello was his flesh and blood; his daughter was his wife's bastard, imported from America.

I am not who I thought I was. Aunt Julia's revelation also answered a question Anna had never been aware she was asking. Since her mother's death—for almost as long as she could remember—she had stood outside the family, always different, always detached, as if looking at her father and her brother over a wall that got higher every year. Eventually she had come to despise Marcello. And Papa? She had not despised him, but she had not loved him either. When he died it was as if the big umbrella pine at the edge of the garden had blown down. *Dio!* Such a shame! It had been there so long. But once it was taken away and the garden was cleared—what space, what light...

"Anna? I'm so sorry. Maybe it wasn't my place to tell all this ancient history."

Her aunt was ready to sink again into the pool of tears that was always at her service. Anna reached out to squeeze her hand—two large diamond rings digging into her palm—as if it were Julia who needed comfort and not herself. And maybe that was true. "There was no one else to tell me. And I have wondered about this certificate for a very long time."

The old woman picked it up. "I remember this." She smoothed a crease, touching the florid *P* in *Prudence*, another in *Prescott*. "It was made for Lily by a nice young man named Charles Cooper. He was a penmanship teacher in New Haven—what was called in those days a writing master." She smiled, pleased that this inconsequential detail had come back to her, and then she put down the paper, stricken again, wringing her hands, eyes brimming. "Oh goodness, the day I met him—how could I have forgotten this? I have not thought of it in so long, but now it's as clear as yesterday."

Anna thought: *What next? What now? What else?*

The story was that Lily had not traveled alone from Italy to America; she had brought a servant with her, a sort of companion—the sister of the baby's nameless father. An Italian woman. She and Lily moved into Orlando's house on York Street. And one day this woman had simply disappeared, taking the baby with her! Charles Cooper—he of the birth certificate—had come to the rescue and plucked little Prudence Ann from the arms of her abductress. And when mother and daughter were reunited, Julia had insisted that the two of them come home with her to Westville, and here they had stayed until they left for Italy.

"What a day that was! Your mother was nearly crazed with worry."

"I don't understand. Why did this woman take me away? What happened to her? What was her name?"

"I cannot remember." Julia stared toward the window as if the dimming of the day might help her bring back the past. "Alas, it has fled. But oh! You poor darling. How you were screaming. That I cannot forget. And Mr. Cooper was so good."

Her aunt's wild tale was almost too much for Anna, like the final course of a dinner that has already been varied and rich and sometimes unpalatable. She had been up since dawn, she had endured a long and uncomfortable train ride, the jolts and shocks of her aunt's revelations had rattled her—no denying it—and the hands of the dainty mantel clock were moving toward seven.

She needed to be alone, to think. To digest, somehow, this incomprehensible plate of wittles. Could she even trust that the implausible account of abduction and rescue was true? She knew Aunt Julia Tuttle, Grandfather's sister, only through a few letters, a few hours in her parlor. Why should she not be a fabulator, as deluded as Miss Havisham in *Great Expectations*?

Anna begged her aunt's pardon: she was so tired, so in need of rest, the day had been so long. She could not possibly stay up any longer. Might she just shut herself in her lovely room for the evening and come down again in the morning, refreshed?

Aunt Julia said, "Oh, my dear, dear child," and clutched her in another fragrant hug. "How upsetting all this must be for you. You do look exhausted. Shall I send Sally up with some supper later? A decanter of wine?"

Yes, yes, and thank you, *grazie tanto*, you are too good, all will be well, please do not worry about me....

❧

Now, at half past midnight, Anna poured herself two inches of claret from the decanter and wrote the numeral 4 in her notebook: *My real father's sister came to America with my mother, from Rome. Also there was a New Haven penmanship teacher: Charles Cooper.*

Minor characters in the drama that was Anna Felice's life. She entered them into her notebook out of a desire for completeness.

She sipped at the wine and thought about the new world that had opened up. Her father was a Roman—or was not: Aunt Julia's grasp on the events of thirty-six years ago was shaky. About his sister nothing was known: why she fled with baby Prudence, where she took her, how the improbable rescue took place, what happened to the woman afterward. Even her name was a blank. And why was she in America while her brother—the baby's father—remained in Rome? If, in fact, he did. The tangle always came back to Aunt Julia, who was now the only witness to these strange occurrences.

Except perhaps Charles Cooper. Could he still be a penmanship instructor in New Haven, Connecticut?

She was inspired to write one more numeral, 5, and after it the words that she had begun to find so stirring she wished she could sing them—words that summarized everything this strange day had given to her: *I am not who I thought I was.*

She had come to America with the aim of transforming herself, and here was the beginning of a more immense transformation than she could have foreseen: the discovery that she was someone else. But who?

She finished the claret and, when she turned out the lamp, a long-ago summer came into her memory—suggested, maybe, by the drawing she had seen on the mantel downstairs. She and Marcello, ten and six, were standing with Grandfather Prescott on the stone steps leading down to the great lawn of the villa at Bellagio. A hot-air balloon was being launched on the opposite shore of the lake. The town there was Tremezzo, which the children had visited many times, crossing on the paddle steamer and eating lemon *sorbetto* on the terrace of the Grand Hotel. Now, holding the old man's hands, they watched as, straining against the ropes holding it, as if it were a living creature, the balloon rose up from the beach—an enormous crimson magnificence, like the glass baubles from Germany that decorated their Christmas tree. It was the largest object Anna had ever seen, the brightest and most beautiful. But what had stuck in her mind most vividly was the moment when the balloon was loosed from its moorings and began to ascend, like something in a dream, slowly, as if it wasn't sure it wanted to go, but then faster, until it was higher than the roofs of the town, higher than the mountain, a serene and tiny globe floating free, free against the blue sky.

❧❧

At breakfast, Aunt Julia appeared in a simple house dress, no diamonds. Her cap was plain cotton, and askew. Her embrace was unscented. She reminded Anna of her grandfather more than she had in all her splendor: a handsome, bright-eyed woman.

She watched Anna uncertainly, as if afraid of the effect of the revelations of yesterday. Had she slept well? Anna repeated something she had heard on the train: "I feel like a million dollars," hoping it would prompt a smile, and it did.

Sally brought tea, cream, eggs both scrambled and boiled, fat sausages, a bowl of fruits, buttered toast, and two glistening jams, one red and one purple. "And you, dear aunt? Did you also sleep well?"

Her aunt said she hardly slept a wink, their conversation had been so unsettling, had brought back so much, such sadness. The loss of Lily, half the family in Italy all those years, Orlando's empty house in New Haven—oh, how she missed her brother....

"I'm sorry my visit has stirred it all up." Anna felt she had to say this, though it was true only on her aunt's behalf: not on her own.

"Oh no no no. I would not have missed your visit for anything. It's almost like having your mother back again." Aunt Julia dropped two cubes of sugar into her tea. "Life goes on, and there is no use in crying over spilt milk, is there?"

Life goes on. Had Anna ever been more conscious of it? She spread jam on her toast, took a sausage. Everything was delicious. The sun was shining. She was optimistic, full of curiosity—a new person, floating above her old world, on the verge of great delights. She must find her father—her second father—her real father. He could be anyone! A great singer who passed on his gift. A humanitarian who devoted his life to helping people. An artist, a writer.

She had awakened full of determination, with a need to know that was more urgent than her hunger for toast and eggs. If she asked the right questions and itemized in her notebook what she learned, surely the truth could be comprehended. She set down her fork. "I must ask you, Aunt Julia, if you remember anything more about this strange event of my abduction. It is odd to think that that helpless child was myself. I wonder if I have the memory of it stored somewhere inside my head. Maybe a vision of the face of that mysterious woman as she carried me away through the streets of New Haven."

"What a funny thought. A hypnotist might help you reach in and find it. My friend Lucy Marshall consulted one, a Mr. Jorgensen, when she lost her emerald ring, and after only one session she remembered that she had taken it off when she had her bath. She found it on the floor beside the tub!" Aunt Julia laughed and touched her napkin to her lips. "But, you know, another memory has come back to me about that extremely hot day when you were taken away. Very late in July, it was, or early August. It was quite dramatic, you know. I thought of this during the night, and I sat bolt upright in bed when it came to me that the Italian sister had taken you all the way to Fair Haven!"

"And where is that?"

"It's a part of New Haven on the river." Julia gestured in the direction of the fireplace. "Somewhere over there. It's where they do oyster fishing, and the streets are paved with oyster shells—or so I have heard. How anyone discovered you were hidden in a place like Fair Haven I have forgotten. But when I remembered that, the whole scene came back to me—George and Mr. Cooper banging on the door and shouting, 'Here she is! We have found her!' And poor little you, crying like a lost soul. Oh, what a moment that was."

"George?"

"George Mullen. That funny Irishman." Anna stored the name away for her notebook. Aunt Julia brightened at the thought of him. "Always wore a bowtie. A small problem with the drink. But George could charm the wings off a bee."

It seemed George Mullen had been the driver of the wagon in which Mr. Cooper set off on his mission of rescue. Why George, Aunt Julia did not know. Her memory skipped ahead to later, when he came to work for the Tuttles, doing what Burton—he of the straight back and the noble mahogany profile—did now: fetching, carrying, "seeing to things," Julia said. And driving: George drove Henry to his augur and bit company every morning and returned him to the yellow house every evening. He worked for them on and off for many years. And then—Julia couldn't recall exactly when, maybe twenty years ago—he had left New Haven and gone to live in Massachusetts with his widowed sister, whose name Aunt Julia did not know.

"Massachusetts is another of the United States?"

Her aunt nearly choked on her toast. "What a darling you are! Fancy not knowing what Massachusetts is! But then, why would you? It is the state just north of here, where the city of Boston is."

Ah: Anna assured her she had heard of Boston, and stored this fact away as well. "And the name of the town?"

"Andover? Amesbury? Gone with the wind, I'm afraid." She looked sharply at Anna. "You're not thinking of making inquiries about this father of yours?"

"It has crossed my mind." Anna wondered why she felt in the wrong.

"The man who deserted your mother. Who left her to bear her child alone."

Anna's thoughts skittered away from these questions: why he disappeared, why Lily was sent away in disgrace. "Ah. Yes. But we don't really know that."

"And your poor stepfather. Lily's husband, who raised you as his own. What about him?"

He did not raise me as his own. But all she said was, "The man I called Papa is dead. He can no longer care what I do."

"Well, we don't know that, either, do we?"

"I suppose we don't." Anna fetched up a smile. "But Aunt Julia— what harm can it do if I ask a few questions of people? You can imagine how great is my curiosity! Maybe I should go to Fair Haven and knock on doors. I have never walked on streets paved with oyster shells."

Aunt Julia didn't respond; her gaze was abstracted. Anna had never seen anyone quite so visibly thinking: she furrowed her brow, looked down, looked up, nodded her head, frowned again. "Or you could go to Massachusetts."

"I could, if I knew where to look. Is it as large a state as Connecticut?"

"Larger. But you would know where to look. You would look in a town called Amherst."

"You have remembered?"

"I had not forgotten, Anna. But I thought I should not encourage you to—" She gestured vaguely. "To open a can of worms. The past is the past. Is it right to delve into such a sad story? You don't know what you will find."

"I will find myself, Aunt Julia."

"You may find more than that, child."

"It is something I want to risk. So thank you, dear aunt. Amherst, in Massachusetts, is where I shall look for George Mullen, and I hope he can enlighten me."

They clasped hands, and when he brought in the post Burton found them that way, smiling at each other, talking of the merits of a carriage versus a train to Amherst. He told them there was a train three times a day from Union Station. Then Sally came in to remind Mrs. Tuttle, with a curtsey, that she had to decide what they would have for supper so it could be shopped for. Julia stood up and straightened her cap. "I must see to things, Anna dear. Perhaps in an hour you would fancy a walk? Westville has some charming streets."

Anna would like that very much. And meanwhile, would her aunt have a dictionary? And an atlas? She would like to look at Massachusetts.

"Burton will bring you both of those things." Aunt Julia paused in the doorway. "I wonder if George Mullen will be much help. He's a dear fellow, but he has probably been drunk these past twenty years."

Anna remained in New Haven for the week that Aunt Julia let her know was the barest requisite for a visitor from abroad. On her third day, Flossie presented herself, with her husband. They came on the train from Pittsburgh to get a look at the grown-up version of the famous Prescott baby who had been there so briefly and then whisked off to Italy when Flossie herself was just a girl. Prudence Ann's well-remembered infant beauties were endlessly enumerated—the Prescott chin, the precious fingers and toes, the rosebud mouth. At one point, Aunt Julia leaned over, disarranged Anna's hair slightly, and crowed, "Yes! I remembered right. We all noticed that you and Flossie have precisely the same ears!"

It was true: her rather large but (she hoped) well-shaped ears were very like Flossie's. Anna managed to greet this revelation without undue excitement. But later, as she and Flossie sat talking in the drawing room, she had been touched almost to tears. Her closest living relative was Marcello (who may very well have shared those ears, she did not remember and did not wish to), but here in New Haven, Connecticut, she belonged to a family.

Since her mother died, and then her grandfather, since the fiasco of her marriage to Umberto Crescenzi and the humiliating end of her life as a singer and then the death of her distant and preoccupied *Step*-Papa, Anna had not belonged anywhere. Even Marcello, as it turned out, was only her half-brother: something she realized on her second night with her aunt, as she was dropping off to sleep, and the thought so pleased her that it was another hour before she became calm enough to close her eyes again.

Despite her sentimental feelings for Julia and Flossie, however, a week in their company was a very long seven days. Flossie's husband, Gerald, a big, lumbering man with a waxed mustache, was involved in the manufacture of steel (or iron?) and hadn't an idea in his head besides business dealings and what time the next meal would be served. During their three days in residence, Gerald went downtown to some club every day, where he met other iron (or steel?) magnates, and came home at suppertime smelling of cigars and bourbon. Flossie was earnest and religious, determined to find the good in everything, with an occasional endearing flash of humor. Very like her mother. As if to celebrate the return of her long-lost second cousin, Flossie dressed every day as if she were going to a ball, with her waist painfully corseted and her dress cut to reveal the deep divide between her matronly breasts. She wore great dangling gobs of diamonds and emeralds clipped to her Prescott earlobes. Flossie was fifty years old. Anna could see herself in her soft, wrinkled face: oh yes, it was not just the ears. And now that Anna was thirty-six, officially middle-aged, that softness and those wrinkles were not so far off. Or so she said during her communications with her mirrored self.

It was a relief that no one asked about her singing career—no doubt feeling that, at Anna's age, it would be natural for it to have ended. They were helpful about words—though *elth* and *farden* remained mysteries—and talking to them she learned new ones: *scatterbrained, tuckered out, flabbergasted, frippery*. She added them to her notebook.

On a Thursday afternoon, the three women squeezed into Aunt Julia's carriage, and Burton drove them to York Street, where they stopped in front of a tall and narrow townhouse, statelier than those that surrounded it, or so Anna liked to think. This was the house Lily had been sent to from Rome, the house from which Anna was abducted and returned. She leaned past her aunt's caped and bonneted bulk and looked at the place hungrily, as if she could will herself to remember it: black shutters, creamy drapes at the windows, a graceful pedimented door with a brass knocker shaped like a fish. How often must she have been carried up and down the stone steps. How often must her mother have stood with her at one of the high windows, the two of them looking out on this busy New Haven street from which, now, she was looking up. The world whirled around her. *Oh, how life is strange!* No. *How strange is life!* Neither sounded right. But Anna knew it was the truth, however you were supposed to say it.

They drove on, to the city's downtown, where Burton located the Elm City School of Business, on State Street: a gray stone building with glossy, varnished wooden doors. Aunt Julia waited in the carriage while Anna and Flossie went inside. A woman behind a desk—a small plaque proclaimed her Miss Betty Wellington—was intrigued by their inquiry. Mr. Charles Cooper? The name was familiar, but—well, she had been there only a month. Certainly he was not a teacher there at the moment, but—wait, she would ask Mr. Twemlow.

Anna and Flossie were shown to a bench, and Miss Wellington disappeared down a hallway. Flossie, of course, knew the story of Anna's birth, and something about her abduction too. The two of them had gone over it several times as they sat over tea in the afternoon or sherry in the evening. It was Flossie's opinion that Anna's lost father must have died, after he and Lily were secretly married, and that Lily had come to America not under duress but to get away from the scene of her heartbreak. Flossie also remembered that she and Lily had played duets on the piano during her brief stay at the Tuttles' and that Mr. Cooper had visited Lily more than once at their house. Flossie had seen him kiss her hand.

Miss Wellington reappeared. "Mr. Twemlow will see you. I feel very silly. I knew that name was familiar!"

They followed her to the office of Mr. Twemlow, a middle-aged man wearing steel spectacles and a melancholy expression. "Ah, Mr. Cooper," he said. "He was one of the founders of this school." Mr. Twemlow had arrived there as an instructor just before the war began, and a year or two later Mr. Cooper had enlisted in the Union Army, with the 14th Infantry. He was wounded at Gettysburg—quite badly, but details forgotten—and eventually he and his wife had moved away from New Haven. The school was notified that their beloved Mr. Cooper had been called to the Lord—again, he was not sure when. Maybe as long as fifteen years ago. Elm City School of Business had declared an official day of mourning, greatly regretting that there was no official portrait of such an innovative leader. Where had Charles Cooper died? A town in Massachusetts, he would know the name if he heard it, he could of course look it up. Perhaps … Amherst? Why yes, Amherst it was!

Like New Haven, the town of Amherst had a Green in the middle of it. But here it was known as the Common, as Anna learned from the droll old fellow who transported her and her luggage from the railway station to the hotel. (Were there no young, handsome carriage drivers in this country?) He also pointed out the home of a deceased spinster poetess, which was painted the same yellow as Aunt Julia's house in New Haven, and the new Town Hall, made of alarming orange bricks swagged with granite. It was clear that notions of what was ugly or crude or garish or dreary were not universal. A New Englander in Rome might find the basilicas too elaborately ornamented or the fountains too grotesque!

It was dusk when they pulled up at the Amherst House Hotel. Anna was stared at as she crossed the lobby, as she had expected she might be—a woman not only foreign in some obscure but unmistakable way, but also traveling without a husband or a maid. So long as her buttons were done up and she didn't have spinach on her teeth, Anna had never minded being stared at: one did not choose to be a singer unless one could, at some level, bear to be looked at.

The Amherst House, though recently rebuilt after a fire, was the oldest such establishment in the town: the desk clerk assured her that Mrs. Harriet Beecher Stowe had stayed there after the publication of *Uncle Tom's Cabin*. Anna was delivered up to the third floor in a rattling elevator and shown to a spacious room, which, aside from a fitted carpet blotched with large, purplish flowers, was charming and comfortable, with lace curtains, green-shaded incandescent lamps, and a marble fireplace. On the wall was a brass speaking tube through which she could order food and drink from the kitchen; an ornate menu with a dangling gold tassel hung on a hook. Two large windows looked across to the Common to a row of shops on Main Street, each with its own bright awning. On the Common she could just make out a great heap of old snow piled in the middle of it, as high as the heads of pedestrians. She had never seen anything like it. It would not melt completely until May, the carriage driver had said.

Unlike the prospect of 23rd Street from her hotel in New York, the view from these windows was pleasing, and she felt an instinctive liking for the town. Or maybe it was simple relief after the over-coddling and stretches of tedium at Aunt Julia's. She had promised to return after her Amherst adventure, for another sojourn in the rosy bedroom before she sailed home. But she need not think of that now.

In the morning, rested and breakfasted (three eggs, a rasher of bacon: soon she would put back the flesh she lost on the ship coming over), Anna walked in her cloak across the sunny Common, under the trees—chestnuts and elms—and looked in the windows of the shops at pyramids of canned vegetables, bags of chicken feed, a display of new novels, flowery spring hats. The town was busy: carriages, people, horses, dogs, the clang of the blacksmith, a wagon loaded with squawking chickens in crates. Amherst was home to a college, she had been told: she had never seen so many handsome young men. They paid no attention to her—a hag of thirty-six—but she didn't mind not being looked at any more than the reverse. She had much to think about besides young men. And maybe this was the beginning of old age: not to care.

From New Haven, she had telegraphed to her banker in Rome, and she stopped in at the First National Bank to see if the draft she requested had arrived. Mr. Hills, tall and pear-shaped in a pin-striped suit, assured her warmly that everything was in order. A relief: Signor Morelli at the Banca Italia, whatever else he might be, was punctual. Bank notes found their way into her purse along with a receipt as beautifully inscribed as her birth certificate. Mr. Hills made a low bow, conveyed his delight that she had come all the way from Italy to their little town, and asked to be allowed to express his gratitude for the privilege of doing business with her. All bankers, she supposed, were alike.

With the agreeable sense of security that money provided, Anna continued her walk. But the sun disappeared, and a cold wind came up, and she turned back to the hotel. Coming to a cemetery, she went through the iron gates, thinking of the opening pages of *Great Expectations*, half expecting something terrifying to leap out at her from behind a gravestone.

But there was not a living soul in the place. She walked up and down the rows, huddled into her woolen cape, trying to make out names and dates. The lettering on many of the stones was unread-able, carved into some substance that crumbled away in the weather. How short our lives, how insignificant—always true, Anna thought, but it seemed truer in this American cemetery. She contrasted the moldering gravestones with the elegant marble mausoleum where Mamma was laid, and Grandfather, and now Papa, and she was washed with homesickness. If she should die during her stay here, would she be buried under a stone that might not last fifty winters?

Did they not have marble in America? Must everything here be new, and raw, and flimsy?

If the cemetery was not melancholy enough, on the corner near the hotel half a dozen soldiers from the American Civil War huddled against the cold. *Veterans*, they were called—sometimes *vets*. A bucket with a printed sign saying PLEASE HELP. All of them in rags insufficient against the sudden shower of snow that came up. One man without a nose, just a horrid scarred crater. One with an empty sleeve pinned to his chest. Two on crutches. Anna scooped all the coins from her purse and dropped them into the bucket, not knowing if she should, or if this was too much money, or too little. There was no one to whom she could ask a question like that.

They thanked her with mumbles that only made her feel worse, calling her *Miss*, smelling of death and rot.

When she got to the hotel, shivering and damp, the bushy-haired and bushy-eyebrowed desk clerk, Mr. Hatch, made her laugh: "If you don't like the Massachusetts weather, just wait a minute"—because, sure enough, the sun had come bursting through the clouds again. The elevator man said the same thing: obviously a time-honored witticism.

Still, it seemed to be true. The afternoon warmed up enough for her to sit on the veranda, her Kashmir shawl around her shoulders, and leaf through magazines, including one in which she read a curious story that purported to be diary entries by a woman going mad, seemingly because of the wallpaper in her room but really because of her stupid and overbearing husband. If Anna had kept a diary during her marriage to Umberto, it might have been the one in the story, though with frescoes and tapestries instead of wallpaper. She couldn't decide if it was a good story or not, but she was sure she wouldn't forget it quickly.

At suppertime, she was ushered by an unctuous headwaiter to a seat in the ornate dining room under a crystal chandelier and opposite her a wall lined with mirrors: surely the apex of loneliness, to eat dinner with no companion but your own reflection. Next time she would bring Dickens. She was deep in the poignant chapters about Pip and the heartless Estella, whom Pip loved for no reason except that he found her *irresistible*—another new word that seemed useful. Not that she had ever known anyone to whom she might apply it.

She sat up in bed, propped on pillows, and read until the end of Chapter 29, then turned out the lamp and lay in the dark, trying to work out what was troubling her. It had been a day of disturbances: the cemetery, the ragged men, the madwoman in the story, the lonely meal....

But the source of her distress was simpler: it had been a day of idleness. She had done nothing to further, by even a casual inquiry, the search for George Mullen—by which she meant the search for her lost father. She had never viewed herself as deficient in courage or determination, but she knew it was dread that blocked the way, the fear that her father, should she find him, would not want to welcome into his life the child he cast out of it—that she had come all this distance to find someone who never wanted to be found.

Or—more likely—he had been a scoundrel and a cad, an unsavory character like Estella's father in *Great Expectations*. Some lowborn Italian Magwitch!

As for finding herself, as she put it with such grand vagueness to her aunt, all she would find was a more solitary Anna than before: the Anna whose best companion would always be her own aging face in a mirror.

But she awoke the next day with renewed pluck, even a dash of hope. Light poured through the windows. The Common below was greener than ever, spring hats in abundance, the college boys dapper in their light jackets. Beside the mountain of snow, borders of daffodils glowed in the sun.

Anna laced herself into her corset, braided her hair and tied it up—the only time she missed Giovannina was when she had to do her corset and her hair. The hotel maid had pressed her brown-checked morning dress. The breakfast eggs were perfectly poached. Somewhere in her sleep she had faced her fears and disposed of them. She would find George Mullen, he of the bowties and the Irish charm, and be ready for anything he flung her way.

Aunt Julia had suggested she might inquire at the post office. Anna had no other ideas, and after breakfast she set out. Mr. Hatch at the front desk greeted her with a beaming smile. He called Anna "Signorina," pronouncing it wrong, and his teeth were too gleaming and perfect not to be false. But he was truly kind, and so, on a whim, she stopped and asked him if by chance he knew anyone in town named George Mullen.

His eyebrows shot up like living things. "But you have met him already, Signorina. It was Mr. Mullen who drove you here in the hackney from the railway station."

The grizzled old fellow who rattled on about Miss Dickinson and her white dresses and her yellow house? Well! Anna told Mr. Hatch that George Mullen used to work for her aunt's family in New Haven, and they had asked her to pay her respects. The desk clerk looked dubious. Did she have the right George Mullen? Irish fellow? Yes, definitely an Irish fellow. Well, that's him, then. He was employed by Paige's Livery, directly around the corner on Amity Street, but at the end of the day, maybe around five in the evening, he could often be found right here in the hotel saloon bar or the billiard room. Unless he was down at Blodgett's Tavern, on East Street.

Anna asked if a note might be sent to Mr. Mullen at the livery, requesting that he come to the hotel to meet her after his work day. She was not sure how he did it, but Mr. Hatch conveyed to her without words—with eyes and eyebrows and gestures—that he considered it improper for a lady, even one from Europe where people were no doubt shocked at nothing, to meet someone like George Mullen at a hotel, much less send him a note requesting such a meeting. Anna shrugged, her own eyebrows not ineloquent. Mr. Hatch flashed his accommodating smile and let her know that, if that was what she wished, he would see that her note was delivered.

Then she hesitated. Was this a foolish idea? She wished she could consult Aunt Julia, or Flossie, or Diana Hummerston. "Let me think," she said. She had walked by Paige's the day before as a crowd of college boys came roaring out in a carriage with high wheels and two wild-eyed horses. A man on the sidewalk shook his fist at them and shouted, "Rascals! You think this town belongs to you?" to which they replied with one voice, "Yes!" before they turned the corner— on two wheels, she would swear it—and made off toward the hills. Anna had smiled in spite of herself.

Knowing where Paige's Livery was, even having an anecdote about it, was oddly reassuring, and so was the knowledge that she had in fact met Mr. George Mullen, who had seemed amiable enough and knew something about poets. What a small and funny world it was. And really: What did it matter? *What is Amherst to me, or me to Amherst?* She would be remembered in local history as the eccentric Italian woman who invited a livery driver to her hotel. But perhaps she would find out what she needed to know. After all, what else was she doing in this place?

Mr. Hatch gave her a piece of hotel stationery, and she wrote, as directly as possible, having no idea whether it was proper or not:

> *To Mr. George Mullen:*
> *I am a niece of Mr. and Mrs. Henry Tuttle, by whom you were employed some years ago in New Haven. I have a particular wish to meet with you in the hope that you can provide information I am seeking. I will be grateful if you come to the Amherst House Hotel this evening at five o'clock. If this is not a convenient time, please let me know by return. Otherwise, I shall await you in the lobby.*
> *Yours sincerely,*
> *Anna Felice*

Chapter 2

With Owosha on his arm and a sack over his shoulder, Davey Chillick crossed the meadow and the railroad tracks, went down a little slope, and stopped just before he reached the birch thicket. It was early on a chilly April morning in Amherst, a gentle wind blowing from the north, the sky lightened to luminous gray. This was the kind of day he had waited for.

He told himself not to make much ado. He released the hawk, just as he always did. But this time she wasn't tethered. She spread her great wings and flew, leather jesses dangling, from the gauntlet to a high branch. Could she feel it already? The breaking of the connection between herself and the food-provider who stood far below watching her? And would the need for it return?

He could feel his heart jumping, and he pressed the palm of his ungloved right hand to his chest. Sometimes he hated it that this was so important to him: this bird who had become the center of his life. *Please*, he whispered to no one. Not taking his eyes from the bird, he removed from his sack the bloody leg of a pigeon.

Rising from the branch, her beautiful ruddy tail like a hand of cards, Owosha beat her wings once, twice, caught a breeze and rode on the wind in a wide arc across the sky until, with uncanny speed, she hovered in midair and then dropped to the meadow and disappeared. In two heartbeats she soared upward again, a small creature caught in her beak. Chipmunk. Davey stood with his arm extended, and she made her descent, tail furled, and glided to the gauntlet with a shudder. Her wings trembled, her breath stirred the markings of her belly as he tethered her. The chipmunk was limp in death, the stripes down its back wet with crimson.

Davey dropped it into the sack. Owosha took the pigeon leg, and he watched her eat, gore on her feathers, a gray tendon hanging from her beak. He had to beat back his own disgust. It didn't matter. It was the making of the bond between them that was important, and the bond had held.

Billy Fox had brought her to him at the end of February—a young red-tail he had trapped last year and named Owosha, the Pequot word for *hawk*. However American the world had made Billy Fox, however far he was from his people, he was a Pequot still, and he conducted ceremonies Davey knew nothing of. Billy had planned to keep the hawk only until her first molt. A young hawk's tail feathers were not yet red but banded in two shades of foggy gray, and those were what he needed. Davey persuaded him not to release the hawk after she molted but to let him have her. In return he gave Billy a haunch of dried venison.

On cold winter evenings, before the hawk arrived, Davey made a gauntlet from heavy deer hide, which he sewed with coarse black thread, and then the thin leather jesses that would tether her. The most time-consuming was the creance, the long lead that allowed the hawk to fly and also brought her back; Davey worked on the braiding, huddled in front of his woodstove, until the lead was fifty feet long. The hawk had taught him patience. Where had it been hiding when he was at the college learning Greek? Or reading the essays of Mr. Emerson?

Not far from his cabin door, he had made an enclosure from birch saplings and covered it with a piece of the tarpaper roof from the old tool shed, pieced with chicken wire to let the sun in. Two perches, one high, one low, and a coyote-proof latch. Not fancy, but cleverly built.

First he had to train her to trust, and to submit: days and nights of walking, the hawk tethered and clinging to the gauntlet on his arm with her strong talons—three in front, one in back, exactly like the feet of the chickens in the coop on the other side of the barn, but far more beautiful and terrifying. She was not a pet, she was a killer, with the eyes of a mad assassin.

But there was nothing about her, Davey thought, that was not perfect. As they walked, he sang. Because that was what tamed her: his voice. The song that made her calm and still was the old ballad "Ar Hyd y Nos." Their Welsh father used to sing Davey and his brother to sleep with it—maybe their only good memory of the man. He knew he didn't have all the Welsh, but it was good enough for Owosha. And when he called her for food, he whistled a tune of his own devising. The singing was to make her feel comfortable and secure on his arm, but the whistle always meant supper: the bodies of mice, chunks of fresh-killed squirrel, the breast of a pigeon—horrible stuff, but how she dug into it, making sharp mewing noises and from time to time a kind of grunt. A hawk eating was a hawk's pinnacle of happiness, except maybe when she was soaring on the wind. Or so it seemed. All this was something no one could know.

Singing, whistling, he would walk her past the barn, through the orchard and the meadow, around the pond and across Walt Oakley's cow pasture, down to the railroad tracks and back, repeating the same reassuring route, sometimes in snowfalls and freezing rain, watching the sun's rise and the moon's changes, hearing the coyotes and the fisher cat and the owls, the scream of a small animal being murdered, the midnight howl of the wind.

After a few weeks the hawk had lost her fear, and he took her out on his arm every day, to hunt and return, fastened to the creance, perched on the gauntlet: hot, that glove, even on a winter day. And filthy. The gauntlet was where she had her food, and where she returned from flight, not to Davey but to the glove on his arm: her home.

When they were not hunting, she perched in the enclosure like an old bishop in the pulpit—big-chested, dark-robed, stern. He would stand and watch her until the brown-and-white pattern on her breast began to look like print, a secret language he was trying to learn. Hawks needed little—just food and safety. When they were contented, they slept, or they stood on one leg and fluffed up their feathers and chirped softly. When they were not, they screamed. Davey found it unbearable to hear her scream.

Contentment seemed to rule her days. But Davey imagined, always, that he could sense her straining toward flight. He thought often of a letter the poet Keats wrote to a friend, about a sparrow he saw out his window: "I take part in its existence and pick about the gravel." He dreamed he was flying and woke up in a panic, not sure if he was relieved or disappointed to find himself lying in his narrow cot with the four walls of the cabin around him.

❧

Soon after dark on the evening after the hawk's free flight, Ida Schmidt knocked on Davey's door. He closed it quietly and kissed her: Ida in her turban and her cape, eyes shining. She was the barmaid at Blodgett's Tavern, and also worked in the kitchen. She handed him a parcel. "Pork pie, still warm. That's for you. I have had my supper, but I would accept a glass of George's rhubarb wine if you have some."

"I do. Did you walk on the tracks?"

"It's the quickest way. And the goods train had just gone by. There will not be another train until five in the morning."

"You don't know that. And rattlesnakes, Ida. They like the railbeds."

"And I could fall on the gravel or catch my foot in the gap between the ties or a giant eagle could carry me away. I forget what else. You have so many fears, Davey. Anyway, I'm here now."

He cut a slice of pie and poured two tumblers of wine. Ida lit a candle, and they sat by the stove. He wanted to tell her about Owosha's flight, but Ida was not interested in his hawk: passing the enclosure, she would turn her head away. Only once did she say, "She should not be held captive to your needs." It was something Davey knew they could not talk about.

38

He took a bite of pie: it had onions and raisins mixed in with the meat. "Thank you for this, Ida."

"It's my pleasure to give you pleasure. Of various kinds."

Ida unwound her turban while he watched, and her hair fell to her shoulders—brown, streaked with gray. In candlelight, with her hair down, her angular face had a kind of distinction. He knew she loved him but also that, if he ever asked her to marry him, she would say no. Or so she had declared once, years ago, laughing at him: "Never have I seen such relief on a man's face!" Ida was a suffragist—married, she said, to the cause. "You know I don't like men."

"But you like me."

"No, I don't like you. I love you. It's very different."

He finished his pie, and she sipped her wine until it was gone, and then she held out her hand.

After they made love, he sank into a heavy sleep and woke in the morning alone. He was used to it: Ida always left as silently as if she were not German but Pequot. When he asked her to stay, she always said, "I sleep better at home." Home was two rooms above Blodgett's. Davey had never seen them.

When he got up, he found a bag of gumdrops tucked into one of his moccasins, and under the tea tin a copy of A. Conan Doyle's *The Sign of Four* from the lending library. Leaving him secret small gifts was another thing Ida always did: "To surprise you," she had said when he mentioned it. "And to make you remember me."

&~&

Davey was helping his sister Lydia's husband, Archie Wyatt, design a new sheep barn, and his table was a chaos of lambing rooms and feed cupboards. He knew he would have to visit the site, something he did not look forward to, but he managed to spend a profitable morning with graph paper and rulers. At noon he cooked three fresh eggs with a bit of fried cornbread.

Then he went for a walk. As he neared the orchard, he heard singing: Valentine, his niece, visiting the big house where his parents lived, gladdening the lives of her grandparents. He traced the sound to one of the gnarled apple trees—perfect for climbing—behind the henhouse. She was perched like a bird among the blossoms, and singing her heart out like one too. No Welsh ballads. What Miss Valentine Wyatt knew were mostly the bits of light opera she was learning with her teacher—in this case, one of the better ditties from *The Pirates of Penzance*, which Miss Finchett had taken her to see at the music hall in Northampton. There was no denying that Val could sing, but even Davey could hear how the high notes strained. When she was older, she should go to Boston. There must be a dozen teachers there who were more competent than poor Miss Finchett.

He stood listening but stayed out of sight—Valentine, the oldest in a lively family, probably cherished her solitude as much as he did. He set off south across the meadow, to the tracks, and walked along the cinderbed as he had scolded Ida for doing; it was daylight, and he had his wits about him, and maybe Ida was right, he had more fears than he should have. He walked until he was too exhausted to think about sheep, or Ida, or the other subjects that preoccupied him, and, when he returned, Archie's new carriage was just pulling away down the drive, taking Valentine home.

Davey built up the fire, pulled his chair close to it, and wrote a letter to his twin brother, who was a professor of law at Harvard:

> *25 April 1892*
> *My dear Maddox,*
>
> *I must tell you that Owosha has flown free. She flew, circled, dived to earth, and returned to my arm with a chipmunk. There is, no doubt, something amiss in a man whose heart leaps at the sight of a dead and dangling chipmunk. I make no excuses for myself.*
>
> *Owosha aside, my life is as devoid of adventure as ever. I rarely see Hazel, and when I do she is much too quiet, even with me, and she wears a frown, as if there is a distant voice she is straining to hear. Since you ask, Ida stops by from time to time. But that is not even in the category of Minor*

Adventure. If it has to be filed somewhere, put it under Comfort. She brought me more Sherlock Holmes stories, which I'm sure are beneath your dignity, but maybe not the dignity of Tobias. If he has not yet met the famous detective, it's high time he did. Also, I have a squirrel skull for him.

Every day I feel more bungling and absurd—fit, no matter what I might wish, for no one's company but my own. I did sit on the porch steps with Mother last week when it was so warm, but I didn't stay long. I fancied I heard Owosha screeching. But when I rushed back, she was peaceful on her perch, making her noise of contentment, a sort of mew, like a kitten. I put on the glove and whistled her tune and gave her the back end of a stoat, and we were cozy together, like an old married pair.

Mother would be glad if you visited—you and Caroline and Tobias or any combination of these. This is merely a report, not a reproach.
Your loving brother,
Davey

Chapter 3

The letter from California arrived on a cold spring afternoon. In the little house on Amity Street, Hazel took it to the sitting room, poked up the fading fire, and curled herself into an armchair.

> *The midday sun is already hot, the bull calves are frolicking, the apricot trees are in full bloom, the roses are budding, and the monkey flowers along our road are thick with butterflies....*

She raised her eyes to the window. Amherst in the spring: the muck of the back garden, leafless trees swaying in the wind. A stubborn wall of snow, hard as cement, was banked against the north side of the shed. And then there was Calvin in Sacramento:

> *Luisa has an ambitious scheme to plant an acre of grapes and become a winemaker. The children have put in their own vegetable garden this year. I still spend most of my time smoking my pipe and making up preposterous plots about people who, if they existed, would scorn me as a lazy lout.*

Calvin Jessup was her father's cousin, the youngest of them, but Calvin and Hazel had been friends since she was a little girl in New Haven and he was a student at Yale who came for Sunday supper bearing books. By the time she was old enough to read them, he had graduated from college and was wandering up and down the Pacific coast, working when he could and writing odd, appealing scraps of stories—a dreamy, gifted, worrisome drifter who had surprised them all, finally, when he was well into his forties, by settling down with a Mexican wife in the fertile Central Valley of California. He now owned a modest but thriving beef cattle ranch with an apricot orchard attached, and wrote popular novels about an adventurer named Alonzo Woodley.

The letter went on to say that they had acquired a pony called Gracia and a collie dog called Goldie, and that Luisa and the children sent their love, as did Calvin, to Hazel and Aunt Maud and Uncle George and anyone else in Amherst, Massachusetts, who might welcome it.

And then, under Calvin's flamboyant signature, a postscript:

> *You may remember my orchard manager, Stefan Dubrowsky, who traveled east with me last year. As I write this, he is supervising the planting of a new hybrid apricot he has devised, crossed with a peach. He can turn his hand to anything, from keeping the books to fighting the codling moth blight with a bag of tiny wasps he got from an entomologist at the State Fair! He is a brilliant orchard man and a good friend as well. He would like to write a letter to you, and insisted I ask if that would meet with Miss Cooper's approval. We both look forward to your reply.*

Her cheeks burned; the room was suddenly very warm. *You may remember Stefan Dubrowsky.* She remembered him only too well, a widower with a young son. They had talked for nearly an hour at her aunt's house, where he and Calvin had been invited for supper.

After he had left Amherst for New York—he had a sister in Brooklyn—Hazel thought about Stefan Dubrowsky constantly for a week, then regularly for another month, then occasionally and painfully as summer turned to autumn, until finally, whenever his face came into her mind—the sensitive mouth, the unusual light-gray eyes that had looked into hers with such interest—she had to force herself to acknowledge that the tiny flame of hope should be extinguished. She had meant nothing to him. He had probably enchanted pathetic spinsters all over the East Coast.

Hazel stuffed the letter into her pocket and went to the kitchen to start supper, peeling potatoes in a daze and putting them to boil, catching herself staring at the wall or out the window with her mouth open. *What does it mean, what does it mean....*

That night, after she turned out her lamp, she lay awake until she heard the bell chime midnight, and when her uncle George came banging through the back door, home from Blodgett's, singing "I'll Take You Home Again, Kathleen" in his melodious tenor, she was still awake.

❧

The next morning she rose late, and went downstairs to find her mother measuring tea into the pot and her uncle standing at the front door squinting out into the sunshine, scratching his armpit. "I hate this bloody weather. The kind of day that makes me wish I was back in Ireland."

"Where you've not been since you were nine years old," Maud reminded him.

"I ain't forgotten it. We never had this kind of weather."

"A beautiful morning like this? No, we didn't. What we had was rain, George."

"Better rain than tropical heat, which is good only for camels."

George had come to Amherst to live with the Coopers after Hazel's father, Charles, died, but, as Maud put it, her brother had never really been domesticated. He slept in the storeroom off the kitchen. He roamed around in his undershirt, suspenders flapping around his skinny hips, and he preferred the outhouse to the modern toilet behind the pantry.

"You know what our Mammy used to say: *There's nothing like the rain to invigorate the brain*."

"Don't be ridiculous. She never said any such daft thing."

"You just don't remember."

"You just wouldn't know the truth if it leapt up and punched you in the eye."

After George left for the livery stable, Hazel and Maud went out to the front porch with the tea tray and a plate of Hazel's currant scones. Hazel sat on the swing, her mother in the creaky wicker chair.

"Isn't it amazing, how George never shows any ill effects the next morning?"

"He has the constitution of an ox."

"A strange kind of ox with a taste for whiskey." Maud beamed over at her. "And what are you doing today, my Hazel?"

"I'll be spending the best part of it trying to teach Amy Osborne enough mathematics to get her admitted into Smith College."

"Oh dear. She's the one who has such trouble with her x's and y's."

At their last session, Amy, after much agony and lamentation, had managed to solve $2x + 5 = 10$, but had balked at $2x + 11 = 9$, declaring it an utterly nonsensical impossibility, calling Hazel a torturer, and flouncing out of the room, leaving Hazel to the task of persuading Mrs. Osborne that, although Amy had cut the lesson short, Hazel expected to be paid in full nonetheless.

"Yes. I do not look forward to it."

The sun was absurdly warm. Hazel concentrated on a Vermont-shaped puddle on the front walk, which shrank as she watched it. If she sat there for half an hour, it would gradually vanish before her eyes. Maud poured out a cup for her. "Hazel?"

"Ah. Tea. Thank you."

"Are you all right?"

"I'm fine, Mother."

"You are very quiet."

Hazel poured milk into her tea. She had meant to tell her mother about Calvin's letter. For all Maud's unorthodoxies—the suffrage meetings, the anti-corset and anti-feather and anti-war letters to the Amherst *Record*, the clouds of curly half-gray hair that billowed behind her when she bicycled around town in her bloomer suit—for all that, Hazel knew it was a disappointment that her daughter, at the age of thirty-one, had never had a serious suitor.

But what was there to tell? If Maud knew about Calvin's post-script, her eyes would gleam with hope, her hair would stand on end with joy: *Here is Hazel's last chance!* And then what if Stefan Dubrowsky only wanted her advice about teaching mathematics to his little boy?

"Suppose I said I've been quiet because I am pondering the wisdom of chopping off all my hair and running away with Isaac Paige down at the livery."

Maud raised an eyebrow. "You would tell me, Hazel, would you not? If something was really troubling you?"

"Yes," Hazel lied. Her mother's conception of women's rights sometimes failed to include a respect for her daughter's right to privacy. "How are the scones? The currants were a bit dried out, so I soaked them in whiskey."

"No wonder George ate three of them for breakfast." Maud took a bite. "You have a beautifully light hand with such things."

Hazel knew her mother believed, earnestly, that women should be independent and should not shrink from a solitary life. But her parents had had a blissful marriage. Maud wore her husband's image in a locket around her neck, slept in his old nightshirts, went to the cemetery on Triangle Street nearly every day to visit his grave. Hazel knew that was what Maud wanted for her daughter—not the sad ending that came too soon, but the happiness, the devotion.

Faintly, from the grammar school down the street, came the voices of the children singing: *Rally 'round the flag, boys, Rally 'round, rally 'round....* The stagecoach to Northampton drowned them out as it clopped past, the sun glinting off its windows. Two college boys in striped blazers cycled along behind, followed by a pair of dogs and a man in overalls leading a goat: old Mr. Shaxter, addled ever since he came home from the war.

Maud crossed her legs at the knee—she was wearing her striped bloomers. "Mother."

"Oh—I'm sorry, darling, I really did forget. Front porch. Yes. Of course." She arranged her skirts neatly. "But you know, Hazel, running away with poor Isaac is one thing, but chopping off your hair—well, don't think I haven't considered it myself."

Especially when she smiled, Maud Cooper at sixty still had the kind of face that made people turn around on the street. Hazel had inherited her father's small chin and narrow jaw and his short, broad nose. In her lowest moments, she thought that, if she looked more like her mother and less like a rabbit, she would be a different kind of person. Maud was fearless: it was because of her beauty, Hazel was sure, that her mother was freed from caring what anyone thought about her. Hazel, being plain, cared too much. Her cousin Davey had told her once: "Pretty is so ordinary, and beauty is so rare. You are neither pretty nor beautiful, Hazel, but there's a wonderfully pleasing logic to your features—one would not want to change a thing."

Hazel remembered his words almost every time she looked in a mirror, but given a choice she would take ordinary prettiness over pleasing logic.

"I'm quite serious, my darling. If you ever did want to cut your lovely hair short, I'd not try to stop you."

"I appreciate that, Mother. You will be the first to know."

The bell of Grace Church interrupted with nine booming strokes, and then the singing could be heard again: *Gallant lads, fire away, and fight for the flag....* Maud sat up straight, her eyes blazing. "Why do they inflict such stuff on those poor children? It is nothing but a glorification of war."

"The children pay no attention to what they're singing. It's just words. All they're thinking about is when will it be time to go out into the sunshine and play."

"But this patriotic nonsense becomes engraved on their hearts. Why can no one see the stupidity of it—of killing and killing until someone is forced to give in. How barbaric! Here we are, creeping up on the twentieth century—imagine that: the twentieth century! And still we have not found the will to outlaw war."

A man and a woman, passing by, slowed down to get a look at her over the hedge: the beautiful Widow Cooper, raving on.

Hazel reached over to touch her mother's arm. "You're right, of course, but do we need to talk about it on the porch?"

Maud subsided into her chair and sipped at her tea. "It will do people good to hear some sense for once." But she lowered her voice. "You do know—do you not?—that we are in the process of embroiling ourselves in the Caribbean, that there is a ridiculous movement to add Cuba to our list of possessions, to protect it from Spain!"

"Mother."

Maud exhaled loudly—more of a snort than a sigh. "All right. I know I talk too much about all this. And that you do not need persuading. And I also know I'm not being logical—the war your father fought in had to be fought. All those young men had to die. Didn't they? Your father had to come home so terribly wounded and ill, had to be taken from us in the prime of his life—" Her voice shook. "Sometimes I wonder, why was there not another way?"

Hazel never knew what to say when her mother expressed despair, beginning with the state of the world but often narrowing to the death of her husband. Hazel wondered: If Father were still with us, what would Mother be like?

She offered the plate of scones, and Maud waved it away. "I'm going in. I can't bear that dreadful singing another minute. The suffrage meeting is at noon. I'm giving my temperance talk. Wish me luck."

"You will be terrific."

"Terrific? Does that mean frightening?"

"I got it from Amy Osborne. It means very, very good. Frighteningly good, perhaps."

The talk, called "Don't Tarnish the Cause," summed up Maud's raging objections to linking suffrage advocacy to the temperance movement—a sentiment that made her unpopular in certain reformist circles. She was a stirring speaker, with a clear and musical voice that held a trace of her Irish origins, and the force of her character was evident in the flashing blue of her eyes. Sometimes she would bang her fist on the podium, sometimes raise her hands to the heavens as if calling on a god in which she didn't believe. No matter how firmly she pinned her hair up, it always came down. When Mrs. Cooper was scheduled to talk, on whatever subject, she drew crowds—men as well as women.

"I hope I will not bore my audience."

"The only time you're boring is when you rant at them, Mother."

"I do try not to. And I've put in some grand, cheerful bits about New Zealand, where people actually seem to understand that, if the two causes are joined, votes for women are doomed. Temperance is all very well, but universal suffrage is vital!" She gathered up the tea things and looked down hopefully at her daughter. "Would you like to go with me this time? It's always so interesting. So many opinions. It leaves one with much to think about."

"I have the x's and y's."

"Ah yes." Maud bent to kiss her daughter's hair as she passed. The door banged behind her.

Hazel closed her fingers around the letter in her pocket. She had it by heart—not the parts about the monkey flowers and the pony, but the end: *You may remember Stefan Dubrowsky.... He would like to write to you....We look forward to your reply....*

The words that might constitute that reply rattled around in her head. *Dear Cousin Calvin. I have not forgotten Stefan Dubrowsky and am intrigued by....*

No. No no no.

Of course I remember Mr. Dubrowsky very well, and I would be....

No.

But yes: even after a year, she remembered Mr. Dubrowsky very well indeed. Too well: straight dark hair, slightly overlapping front teeth, hands brown from working outdoors, the tender way he spoke of his son.

She went inside and up to her bedroom. Her favorite sprigged petticoat was sprawled across the foot of her bed, waiting to have its torn hem repaired. She tried, but her hands were too unsteady to thread the needle. The envelope in her pocket was like a living thing, demanding attention. She could almost hear it murmuring: *Well? Well?*

She flung the petticoat aside and went to her desk: Write the letter, get it out of your mind so you can mend underwear and think about algebra. It means nothing, nothing, less than nothing, a bottomless pit of nothing, zero plus zero times zero divided by zero. Her clock said quarter past ten. Was she going to torture herself all day? She was well aware that it was a possibility.

She took out a piece of flowered stationery, reconsidered, found a piece of plain white paper, uncapped her pen, and wrote:

> *Dear Cousin Calvin,*
>
> *Thank you for your letter, though it is painful to read about your sunshine and flowers. It has been raining and wintry here for a week. Today is warm and bright, in the precarious way of early April. But you no doubt remember what the weather is like in New England. I enjoyed hearing all your news. Luisa is enterprising indeed. And a pony! Do you remember how I used to badger my poor parents for a pony...*

Drivel, drivel, drivel. She wrote another page of it, with news of Maud and George and the various cousins and aunts and uncles, and a note about the dedication of the new Town Hall. Her shaky scrawl improved as she went along. At the end she paused, chewing on her pen before she added, in a firm hand: *And of course Mr. Dubrowsky may write to me. Why ever not? Love from your cousin Hazel.*

When she left for the tutoring session, Ella, their maid-of-all-work, had arrived and was kneading bread in the kitchen. They were nearly out of whole-meal flour, she said, and Mr. George had eaten all the raisins. Would Miss Hazel stop at Jackson's, or should she go herself? Miss Hazel said she would stop on her way home.

The Vermont-like puddle on the walk had dried in the sun without a trace. What kind of life was this, that she would notice such things? Her world was made of trifles. A puddle. A petticoat to mend. Raisins and flour. A long dreary morning with a lazy student. Who would Miss Hazel Cooper be in ten years? A peevish old spinster.

She walked down Amity Street to the post box in front of the bank and dropped the letter through the slot.

సౌ

Because she'd loved being a student herself, Hazel assumed when she graduated from Smith College that she would enjoy teaching others. But she had found that only students with lively minds provided any kind of satisfaction, and they were precious few. There was Selina Harper, who, despite her woeful incompetence at Latin, at least had the sense to love the language once she had stumbled her way through it—even Caesar's *Commentaries*, which she deemed "crackerjack." And James Clay, the sickly boy, facing death from some kind of brain fever, who had wept over an ode of Horace when he came to the lines *Quis scit an adiciant hodiernae crastina summae tempora di superi?* Which he translated, almost flawlessly, as "Who knows if the gods on high will add a tomorrow to today?"

Hazel saw them both on a Monday morning and, as she walked home from the Clays' house on Sunset Avenue, she counted in her head for the dozenth time: it was more than a week since she had replied to Calvin. Four days out, four days back: there could, plausibly, be a letter in the box.

There was not. It was empty except for one of Maud's suffrage magazines and a bill from the grocer.

George was at work, Maud at a meeting. Ella had sent a message to say her daughter Peggy was ailing, which meant Peggy's husband had beaten her again and Ella had to tend to her and the children. Hazel hung her coat and satchel on the hooks by the door that her father had put up, and she tidied her hair in the mirror over the mantel where his photograph presided in a wooden frame he had made himself. Hazel was fourteen when her father coughed himself to death in the big back bedroom, but his presence was still potent: his carpentry tools in the shed, the portable writing desk where Hazel stored her drawings, his old clock with its noisy tick.

She asked herself for at least the fifth time: What would her father say about the letter?

The letter: it was all she could think of. Impossible to settle down to a book or a drawing, so she raked out her flower beds, turned the compost with a pitchfork, dug the weeds out of the herb garden, made a barrier around the baby lettuces with the crushed eggshells she'd been saving. Then she tried to bring some order to the clutter of the back parlor: inks pots, stacks of books and letters and magazines, an overflowing basket of mending, and the wobbly easel she no longer used. She lugged the easel out to the shed, then darned the holes in two pairs of stockings and mended the hem of her petticoat and patched a rip in the elbow of one of her uncle's shirts.

That was Monday. On Tuesday she helped Ella in the kitchen, mixing up molasses bread and bringing up the last of the apples from the cellar to chop for sauce and listening sympathetically while Ella talked about her good-for-nothing son-in-law. After Ella left, Hazel retrieved the post—a bill from Cadwell the iceman, a letter from Maud's sister in Boston—and then scrubbed the kitchen floor, blackened the stove, washed the upstairs windows with water and white vinegar, and shook out all the rag rugs.

On Wednesday morning, she walked down to East Street, where Joe Blodgett and her uncle George made wine every year from the rhubarb they grew in a field behind the tavern. She cut forty pounds—four half-bushel baskets—and hauled them to the barn where Ida Schmidt and some of the Blodgett girls were chopping it, and went home at noon to find the letter box empty. She had a cup of tea and a sandwich, then swept out the attic and scoured years of cobwebs and dirt from the fan-shaped window.

By suppertime that day, she had managed to make herself so weary she could hardly eat. Her mother and her uncle were both in contentious moods, Maud buzzing on about the exploits of the suffragists in England who were making the Americans look like ninnies, and Uncle George raving about how, if the damned suffragists were going to force their husbands to become household drudges, they had best be prepared for armies of savage men taking to the streets. Hazel was used to their bickering, and she knew too that they depended on her—as they had on her father before her—to build the bridges between them, to steer the conversation to, for example, the new pond that was being dug at the agricultural college, a project they all approved of.

But she was too tired, and when supper was over and George slipped out to Blodgett's, Hazel was glad to see the back of him. Maud put on her eyeglasses and went into the parlor to mess it up again with her papers and pamphlets as she worked on an article. Hazel swept the floor and was washing the dishes when the *clackety-clack-ding* of her father's old typewriter stopped and Maud rushed in from the other room. "Hazel, dear! I forgot. Mr. Mackey came with the post as I was leaving, and I was in such a hurry, I just stuffed it away." She reached into the deep pocket of her skirt and brought out an envelope. "I'm sorry, darling. My absent-mindedness has probably ceased to be one of my endearing qualities and instead has become an annoyance. Tell Calvin I send my love when you write to him," she said and disappeared again.

Hazel stood gaping at her name and address in her cousin's familiar scrawl. Why Calvin and not Stefan Dubrowsky? *I apologize for the false alarm, Stefan has returned to Poland ... has died ... has gotten himself engaged to ... has decided to remain a bachelor because ...*

She tore it open: a scrap of paper folded around another envelope.

> *Dear Hazel, Please find enclosed a letter from my slightly mad friend and colleague, Stefan Dubrowsky, who swears this is the proper way to do things. When he is in his right mind, he is quite a delightful chap. Cal.*

And on the envelope, in a hand she vaguely recognized as European: *Miss Hazel Cooper.*

It was hard to breathe. She went out to the chilly air of the porch. Maud's old crocheted shawl was on the chair, and Hazel wrapped it around herself. In the fading light, she could barely make out her name on the envelope: the M with its long tail, the beautifully flourished H and C. Whatever he thought of the letter's contents, her father, the writing master, would approve of the script. Where had Stefan Dubrowsky learned his graceful hand? Maybe it was taught in Poland. Or he had learned it here, had had ambitions to be a clerk or a banker. What had taken him to Calvin Jessup's fruit farm in the Sacramento Valley of California?

The light dimmed, the air grew colder. Hazel sat watching the golden glow of the gas lamp across the street vibrate in the near-darkness. The envelope was a white square on her lap: *Miss Hazel Cooper*, her name for thirty-one years.

She was thinking about kissing. She had had three kisses in her life from people she was not related to. One from Merwin Booth, which had ended with her pushing him away in disgust and panic. And two lingering ones from Edward Fletcher that she had spent years trying to forget. She remembered them now and closed her eyes, thinking of Stefan Dubrowsky and wondering.

It was nearly dark by the time Maud poked her head out the door and said, "Hazel, you will catch your death. What *are* you doing?"

Hazel jumped. "Enjoying the night air?"

"You're shivering. Come inside and I'll make you a cup of tea."

"Cocoa."

"Cocoa, then."

So that it was curled up in the chair by the kitchen stove, with a cup of cocoa beside her, feeling as warm as she might on a sunny day in California, that Hazel opened the envelope and read the words:

> *Dear Miss Cooper, I know this is an unusual request, and I hope you will forgive my presump-tion, but I would be greatly honored if you would consider becoming my wife.*

❧

Nearly three weeks later, Hazel walked out to her cousin Davey Chillick's with a loaf of bread and a jar of applesauce.

She had now received three letters from Stefan Dubrowsky and had slept badly since the last one, so the scant mile out South Pleasant Street seemed long. The air was chilly despite the April sunshine, but, as she walked, the morning rose out of a white mist, and the sky turned blue, streaked with cirrus clouds. The hopefulness of spring was all around: trees with tiny new leaves, frogs croaking in the pond, pansies in pots outside the shops. And baseball: a boisterous crowd of boys in their flannel uniforms crossed College Street in front of her on their way to the ball field.

Professor Todd, her uncle Samuel's colleague in the Department of Astronomy, was already wearing his summer straw, which he tipped to her. Ida Schmidt in a lilac turban waved from across the Common. Hazel bowed to them both, but she didn't slow down. Her walk was purposeful. The need to visit her cousin was frequent but erratic, prompted by she knew not what: if she took the trouble she might figure it out by charting what she had eaten, the phases of the moon, the temperature of the air. That morning Davey had come into her mind like the answer to a riddle: he would help her decide what to do.

Her uncle Sam Chillick's big farmhouse, not far past the college buildings, was set back from the road in a hollow, with wide fields behind it stretching away to a cow pasture on the south and the railway tracks to the east: the whistle of the morning train from Belchertown sounded as she walked down the drive. Except for Heloise the cat, asleep on the bench where Hazel had sat last summer with Stefan Dubrowsky, no one was around.

Davey, of course, would be at home. Apart from an occasional visit to the big house, he could almost always be found in the cabin behind it, or nearby. He had gone into town for his uncle Charles's funeral and again for his sister Lydia's wedding. There was a time when he had still walked over to the ball field to watch a game, but he had given that up when, he said, people insisted on asking him questions. Hazel knew that he walked the streets of Amherst late at night when the town slept. Once, he told her, he had walked up Amity Street, seen a light burning in her own window at three in the morning, and stood watching until, toward dawn, it finally went dark—a confidence he had made to her shyly, his head half-turned away. Years ago now.

55

Davey described his life in the world as a tightrope on which he could never really find his balance; the cabin, by contrast, was a sturdy boat on a turbulent sea. A confusion of metaphors was not something that ever bothered Davey, or Hazel. She always understood what he meant—or almost.

A ribbon of smoke rose from the cabin chimney. She skirted the long border of daffodils and the chicken yard where her aunt Tamsin's hens muttered among themselves, and went around the back of the barn to the cabin Davey and his twin, Maddox, had built nearly twenty summers ago, when Davey was fresh out of Amherst College and unable to live either away from his family or with them.

Hazel was twelve when the cabin was going up—an enchanted place, a playhouse. It was a foursquare shingled structure Davey designed himself: fireplace at one end, heavy door on the other, sash windows on the east and west to catch the sun coming or going. The shingles were painted a dark green that blended into their surroundings: woods, orchard, garden.

Davey had taught Hazel how to cut pine shingles and nail them over the cladding, how to putty glass into the windows and smooth plaster walls with a trowel—she could still almost smell the wet, chalky lime. He was kind to her—everyone was kind to her—because her father was so ill. But Davey was her favorite from the beginning. Maddox, she always said, was her cousin. Davey was her brother.

Hazel had been cutting shingles on the day that Davey came leaping across the meadow waving a pair of deer antlers he had found in the woods, to be nailed up over the door for good luck. Years later, it had occurred to her one day to ask him if their magic had worked: had he had good luck? He waved his arm to embrace his one room, the view from the windows, the heavens beyond: "Do I not have everything I need?"

"Only you can answer that." Hazel loved her cousin's little cabin, but it was hard to see it as enough. "Do you, Davey?"

"I try to follow Epicurus, as you know."

"Oh—Epicurus. *He who is not satisfied with a little is satisfied with nothing.* What utter poppycock. Do you really believe that?"

"I will admit that there are ways in which my life does fall short." What they were, what he needed and did not have, he did not tell her.

Perhaps it was only a fierce bird of prey. Now, since January, he had had Owasha. The hawk was sitting on a perch in her enclosure. The sun, still low in the sky, lit up the red fan of her tail where it poked between her gray back feathers and the fluff of her hindquarters: it was her one improbable blaze of color. Hazel would have liked to draw her in ink, with a color wash.

"Good morning, Owosha."

At the sound of a voice, the bird swiveled her head and glared with murderous fury, then turned away again, as if in disdain. Davey had said that disdain was not something a hawk was familiar with— or malevolence, either. Those feelings were for humans. Owosha, he said, was pure appetite, a mind with but one thought in it. She had no interest in anyone who was not a small scurrying creature that looked like a meal.

Hazel walked around the enclosure, and Owosha's head followed her. The impression of fierceness, Hazel decided, came from the bold black-rimmed eye and the downturned, sneering hook of the beak— accidents of biology, like beauty or plainness, curly hair or bad teeth, which reveal nothing about their possessor but greatly affect how people see them. The hawk reminded her of a long-ago schoolmistress, Miss Ingleby, whose heavy dark eyebrows gave her a perpetual scowl that terrified her pupils until they discovered her particularly kind and tolerant heart. But a hawk, her cousin had assured her, did not have a kind and tolerant heart.

The approaching train rumbled on and, as it neared the Amherst depot, gave another hoot. For years, Hazel had registered the noise of the railroad without attending to it. Now it had become poignant: the sound made her imagine herself in a berth in a Pullman car, gazing out the window into the dark and watching the sun come up on forests and mountains and fields and sky. Seven days, Stefan had said: maybe eight: the Boston & Albany, then the New York Central to Chicago, then the Union Pacific. He would meet her in Sacramento.

And then what?

Hazel banged the knocker: a leaf Davey had carved from a hunk of butternut from the south slope of Mount Norwottuck. He opened the door. "I've been watching you out the window. You and Owosha seem fascinated with each other, as indeed you should be. But do come in where it's warmer. This is fine weather for hawks, who don't care one way or the other, but not for humans."

It was cozy in the cabin, and on the hearth stove, a kettle was steaming. Davey said, "I hoped someone might stop by to enliven my poor, piddling life, and so there's hot water for tea."

"You complain mightily, Davey, but for a recluse you always seem quite cheerful."

"Ah. *Seem.* There is the crucial word."

"If you're asking me to sympathize with the poor, piddling life you have chosen of your own free will, you're asking it of the wrong cousin." Hazel set down her basket. "But I did bring gifts. A pot of mint for your garden, applesauce from the last of the apples, and a loaf of Ella's rye-and-Indian bread."

"Who could not be cheerful with Ella's bread on his table? Shall I give us each a slice?"

She was ready with an automatic no, but realized that she was hungry. And tired: she could probably stretch out on the floor in front of the stove and sleep until suppertime as she hadn't been able to in her soft bed at home. Being with her cousin made the world settle down: its pieces fell into their grooves, like something neatly carpentered—like her father's old portable writing desk with the leather strap. Sometimes, when Davey went suddenly silent in the middle of a sentence, or confessed he had eaten nothing but eggs and apples for a week, he was as foreign to her as a zebra, but the next minute it was as if she, not Maddox, were his twin.

"What's the state of your butter supply?"

"Mother left me some yesterday," he said. "And I have jam here somewhere. No—drat. I've used it all up."

"Double drat. Jam would be good."

"But not really necessary. Ella's rye-and-Indian does not stint on the molasses."

The cabin's determined austerity, so unlike the untidy abundance of the house on Amity Street, always charmed her. A long shelf of books, and a short one holding the speckled halves of a finch's egg, Davey's collection of arrowheads, and a rickety model he had made of the ship their great-grandfather served on in 1812. In one corner a hand pump on a stand, with a toothbrush, a can of tooth powder, and a towel. Davey's narrow bed in a corner, a pair of beaded moccasins tucked under it, a bright Indian blanket folded at the foot—gifts Calvin had sent years ago from a silver-mining town in Nevada. A stack of Cal's Alonzo Woodley novels with their colorful covers: on top, *The Curse of Rattlesnake Dick*. Two chairs, one on either side of the woodstove facing the mantel, a plain maple beam that the heat had slowly singed to a deep brown on its underside. Davey owned two knives, one large and one small, and a bread board made from a crosscut slice of maple when a tree came down in a storm. He set the bread on the board, cut two pieces with the big knife, and slid them onto a green plate with a crack in it.

"We'll have to eat by the stove. The table is all about sheep."

Among rulers and a protractor, templates and triangles sheets of graph paper, Hazel picked up a rough sketch of what looked like a platform worked by a pulley. "I assume Archie will be satisfied with nothing less than the grandest barn in Hampshire County."

"That would be simple enough. But it also has to be the most modern and ingenious. Archie has become enamored of the word *gadget*. So we're working on a new way to water the sheep. Depending on its size and what it's eating, a sheep can consume as much as four gallons of water in a day—I'm sure you already knew that, Hazel—so this contraption has to be quite large. And easily filled. Archie also likes the word *automatic*."

"Just your sort of challenge, I should think."

"It does occupy me, I admit. When my mind isn't consumed with Owosha, it's trying to imagine what it is like to be a large, thirsty ewe."

Hazel settled into a chair and watched him move about the cabin. He seemed happy enough as he measured tea into the pot, and she was relieved to see he had spruced up. There were times when Davey retreated from them all—further than his usual distance—times when he might have been mistaken for one of the vagrants who loitered on the Common near the frog pond: scruffy, sad-eyed men who smelled of desperation. Davey could wear the same clothes for weeks, until they were stained and stinking. One memorable winter he had let his beard grow halfway down his chest and put his long hair in a braid.

But today, though he could use a haircut, his hair was freshly washed, he wore a clean shirt, his cheeks were pink. Hazel had often tried to find the proper adjective for Davey's strange radiance. Radiance with a comfortable touch of squalor: she could find no word in English or Latin to describe it.

"You're looking well," she said. "Have you put on weight? It suits you. You were too thin over the winter."

"I like to think of myself as lean and sinewy. But yes, I seem to be expanding a bit." He handed her a slab of buttered bread and set the teapot on the floor between them, with two thick mugs. "Since I adopted Owosha, people bring me more food than usual. Lydia sees me as a skeleton close to death from malnutrition. And Ida brought a meat pie that I ate in one day—breakfast, dinner, and supper. I need to keep my strength up to deal with a wild bird. Speaking of whom—"

"Ida?"

"Owosha. She has flown without the creance. And returned with a chipmunk."

"Congratulations! But please tell me that was her supper, not yours."

"It was nobody's supper. I have to calculate her appetite carefully. If I could, I would weigh her. She has to be hungry enough to hunt, but not so hungry that she hasn't the strength for it, and so, just as she is about to eat her catch, I have to be quick to snatch it away and replace it with a carefully calculated morsel of something equally delicious."

Hazel stared. "She's not allowed to eat what she catches?"

"Eventually. I pop it into a sack and take it home and save it for the next time." He smiled. "A strange kind of hunting, isn't it? It's as if Archie went out and shot a pheasant, but I grabbed it away from him and gave him a chicken sandwich. Then we do the same thing the next day, only this time I give him a pheasant sandwich. And so on."

"And Archie would keep performing this charade because you have forced him to trust that you'll give him the sandwich."

"Something like that."

"But what if Archie took it into his head not to come back? That he would rather be free than fed?"

"I don't know about Archie, but hawks don't have such preferences. They operate purely on instinct, and Owosha's instinct says: a chipmunk in the sack is worth two in the bush. At least that is the wisdom of Billy Fox, and it's what I reassure myself with."

"So you stay home, she goes out into the world."

"But just far enough to swoop on her prey. She won't be going down to Main Street to the shops."

"She is missing some glorious spring hats."

He poured tea into the mugs and handed her one. "I would like to make a table that would just fit here between the chairs. Or would that be the beginning of evil? Isn't that what Thoreau called a doormat when someone offered him one?"

"He said he didn't want to take the time to shake it out. Surely that was a joke."

"I hope so. With Thoreau, you never know." He looked over at her. "Tell me how you've been faring. You seem a bit mumpish."

"You're too good at noticing things. I'm confused, I'm feeling hopeless, and I want your advice about my life."

"My advice? I don't know anything about life."

"Why? Just because you're a hermit?"

"I prefer troglodyte."

"Call it what you like, it doesn't mean you don't have great powers of imagination and empathy."

"My imagination is failing me right now. What does that mean—hopeless? What is it about your life that you could possibly need advice about?"

She spoke testily. "If you think my life is perfect the way it is, then you're being willfully obtuse."

"All right." He sipped at his tea. "Just tell me what it is. If something is wrong, I want to solve the problem, quickly, like Sherlock Holmes. I can't bear to see you confused and hopeless." He shifted in his chair, found a handkerchief in his pocket, and handed it over. "It's clean, believe it or not. In case you cry during the telling."

"I'm not going to *cry*, for heaven's sake!"

"I know it's part of your religion not to cry. But if you need to, go right ahead."

The tea was very hot. She wished there was milk to put in it, but Davey had milk only in cold weather. For a summer or two, he had kept the bottle cold by putting it down the well with a rope around its neck, but the well was too close to the house, so he foreswore milk in the summer months—"It will make a man of me," he said— and for winter had invented a "milk cozy," a box within a box, with straw packed between the two and the bottle of milk inside, wrapped in a knitted blanket to keep it from freezing. He knew his ascetic routines were not lacking in absurdity—he could walk two hundred yards to his mother's kitchen and help himself to milk. Or acquire an ice box. But he did not do such things; his version of a hermit's life was flawed, but it was entirely sincere.

"Hazel?"

"It's actually very difficult to talk about, even to you."

"Do it anyway."

"I'm being courted."

His eyebrows shot up, then came down again in a frown. "Courted."

"Yes."

"I think you are going to have to tell me more. Confusion I can perhaps understand, but being courted doesn't seem to warrant hopelessness."

"It's just that it's so humiliating."

Outside somewhere, a blue jay screeched. A dog barked. One of Oakley's cows called loudly, then another joined in. Inside the cabin, all was silence. Hazel studied the lettering on the stove: GARLAND. WORLD'S BEST. The stove could use a blacking.

She could sense Davey watching her patiently, then the patience getting thin. Finally, he said, "You are either going to tell me or you are not. Please make up your mind. Take a deep breath."

She inhaled and exhaled twice, noisily, looking him in the eye. "I am nearly thirty-two years old. I have never been courted by anyone before except Edward Fletcher, who broke my heart when I was nineteen—"

"Fletcher was not worthy of you."

"And that dreadful Merwin Booth, whom you may recall."

"The one who—"

"Yes. I still have nightmares about him."

"Are you joking?"

"Not entirely." Merwin Booth's narrow eyes and foul breath had in fact visited her in a dream not so long ago. "That's the history of my romantic life: one tragedy and one comedy. We don't have to say any more about it." She sat with Davey's handkerchief in her fist, squeezing it to death. "The fact is that I am a spinster with no prospects. I am what is probably called *desperate*."

"A hateful word."

"That's how people see me, I'm sure. And it's how I see myself. And that's why I'm considering an offer of marriage from a man I met once and scarcely remember."

"Ah. Now we have a story." Davey stood up and maneuvered another log into the stove. "Who is this enterprising fellow? Presumably he remembers you well enough."

"That Polish man who came on the train from Sacramento with Calvin last summer. He manages the orchard."

"Yes." Davey turned from poking the fire. "My mother invited them over here for supper. Stefan something."

"Dubrowsky. He only stayed a day, then went on to New York, where he has a sister. Calvin is very fond of him. He's like a member of the family."

"He and I had a rather interesting talk about the best way to lay a stone foundation." Davey slammed the door of the stove and sat down again. "As I recall, he built himself a house on Cal's property and lives there with his little son."

"His wife died when the boy was born. Kasia, her name was. Katarzyna, I think. She came over with him from Poland." *My Kasia left my life when Victor entered it.* What could it be like, Hazel wondered, to raise a child whose birth had caused the death of a beloved wife? Did the boy look like his mother? Did they ever talk of her? Was she beautiful?

"So the two of them are alone."

"Yes. That is the point." She took another deep breath, released the handkerchief and smoothed it out on her lap. Telling it to Davey was meant to be a relief. Why was it so difficult? "He needs a wife, the boy needs a mother, and he has asked me if I will fill the roles."

"And why is this so dreadful? Did you dislike him that much?"

"No, I did not dislike him."

"And so—he has proposed marriage after an hour together at a luncheon party?"

"I have had three letters from him and have written back two. The letters are quite long, and so in some ways we are beginning to know each other. In others, we are still strangers."

"I recall a rather mild young man, full of ideas. I had half a thought that I'd trot him out here and show him my cabin—he was intrigued—but we never got around to it."

"I'm surprised you'd want a stranger to see this place."

"Could be that's why we never got around to it. So one of the things he knows about you is that you have a peculiar cousin."

"My cousin the troglodyte."

"Is that what he said?"

"You may find this hard to believe, but he hasn't mentioned you at all."

"There! You made a cheery little noise that people who didn't know you might interpret as a laugh." Davey looked at her expectantly. "Now explain to me, please, what the difficulty is. Here is a man you do not dislike, and he has asked you to marry him. Why are we not opening a bottle of champagne? Not that I have any champagne. A bottle of your uncle's rhubarb wine is more likely."

"Because—well, he doesn't love me, he just needs me. I'm feeling like a mail-order bride."

"Ah." Davey shifted his gaze to the east-facing window. "Has he not written, then, about love?"

"No. He writes about the ranch and the apricot trees. The weather. His family's orchard in Poland. And about his little boy. The horrible sadness of his wife's death. The difficulties of raising a child completely on his own. He is obviously a doting father."

"You are seriously considering this offer?"

"I've told him I need to know him better, I cannot make a quick decision, I need time to think. But I like him, Davey, and he is my last resort. So yes, I suppose I am." Hazel followed his gaze to the window, the closer one, where she could see the crack that bisected one of the panes into two right triangles: how had it happened? She'd forgotten. Against it, her cousin's neat, somber profile was as still as a face on a coin. "Davey? I want to know what you think."

"Well." He turned back toward her. "At least he is not lying to you. Don't you think many attachments begin that way—with need, which turns into love? And he knows how to dote. That is something! Why should he not eventually dote on you?"

"I knew you would make a joke of it."

"Is that what I'm doing? Hazel, forgive me—I don't mean to."

"No—a joke is good for me. I've been so befuddled."

Hazel leaned back and stretched out her legs. Her black boots, Davey's scuffed brown ones, the teapot between them on the faded rag rug: a pleasantly homely composition. She had half a wish for her sketch book. Over the years she had made dozens of idle sketches of the objects in her cousin's cabin, but she had not opened her drawing case since the letters began arriving from California. Maybe she should start again: begin with Owosha, end with the boots. Making the world into images always created a magic space somewhere between distracting her and concentrating her mind. She could take a sketch of Davey's boots with her to California.

"You would go there," he said as if he'd read her mind. "You would live on this ranch."

"I suppose I would."

"And what about his people? Does anyone know them? Was he born in Poland?"

"Yes, his family is there, except for the sister in New York. Stefan lived there before he went out west. Calvin has known him for a while, of course."

"How long?"

"I don't know, really—two or three years."

They were silent another moment. This cabin, she thought: what would her life be like without it? Before she left, she would draw—not just hawk, boots, teapot, but everything. Or no—this was 1892, after all. She would make photographs. Her aunt Tamsin had acquired a camera and a tripod after they had gone to see an exhibit of photographic still lifes at the college museum. Black and white and gray. Flowers and pottery and statuary. Why not a ship model and a cracked window pane?

"And so will you accept?"

"Ah. Reality. A decision." She pulled her legs back and shook out her skirts. "What would you do if you were me? A female, past the age for marrying, who suddenly, like a brick thrown through the window, gets a proposal from three thousand miles away."

"Even aside from the female aspect and the age aspect—though of course you seem like a child to a grizzled old codger like me—"

"Nine years."

"Half a generation. But all that aside, I may be the wrong person to ask, since I cannot imagine traveling to Boston to visit my own brother, much less to Sacramento to live on a ranch. And then there is this emotion called love. My direct experience of that sort of thing is slight."

Hazel wondered at the word *direct*. And also *slight*. Everyone knew her cousin had some kind of friendship with Ida Schmidt, her mother's fellow suffragist who was also the barmaid at Blodgett's, but whether that was based on love, or need, or something else entirely, was a mystery.

"Your opinion is important to me."

"Really? The opinion of the troglodyte cousin?" It took her a moment to understand that he was angry. "I'm sorry. I cannot dredge up an opinion. You're talking about a dream of a future world, one that you want to live in, Hazel, but it's a world that to us—to the ones you leave behind—to me—it's just a world without you in it. How can I give you anything so cold and studied as a judgment about such a thing? How can you ask it of me?"

"I just meant—"

He held up his hand. "Don't." They stared at each other. Hazel felt the strangeness of the moment: Had he ever raised his voice to her before? Had they ever had an argument? Was this an argument?

Davey set down his mug of tea and stood up. "Come outside. I want to take a look at the sap buckets. Right now, they're just about all I'm capable of having an opinion about."

In the yard, the smells were of wood smoke and blossoms. Red-winged blackbirds made their racket down by the tracks. Owosha sat immobile, one-legged, on her shadowy perch.

Davey stomped across the meadow to the row of maples and the brick-lined pit where the sap was boiled every spring. Hazel pulled herself up onto the mossy wall that bordered the property and took it all in. The rich grays and ochers of the old rocks. The sky opaque as felt. A noisy formation of geese overhead sailing toward the North Amherst pond. Davey in his blue shirt moving among the trees. At the base of the wall, tiny white stars that would be wild strawberries in June. The acrid earth-scent from the cow pasture. Everything so familiar, and now her life in the midst of it so suddenly uncharted.

And how could she tell her cousin that her vision of a future world was mostly about having a man beside her in bed?

Davey came toward her empty-handed, his hair gold in the sun, his fine-featured face restored to amiability.

"Nothing?"

"Not a drop." He hoisted himself up beside her. "That warm spell pretty much did us in. But we got plenty this year. I'll fetch you a jug before you leave."

"Thank you. And Davey—"

"What."

"Please don't think that having to leave the people I love is not part of the swamp of confusion filling my brain." Hazel laid her hand over his, where it rested on the rough stone.

He turned his hand over to clasp hers quickly, then withdrew it. "I'm sorry. It was not fair to get angry. But you know this will be hard for me."

"It's not done yet."

She leaned against his shoulder, feeling him tense, then relax. They didn't return to the subject of Stefan Dubrowsky. Softly, Davey hummed one of his Welsh songs. His voice, the sun, the soft twittering of the birds.... Hazel stopped resisting the fatigue that was plaguing her. Her brain clicked into a doze, and for a quick moment the sun slanted through the window of the workshop behind the New Haven house, and her father was saying, "Never use paint without stirring it first...."

The noon whistle shocked them both: had they sat there so long? She rubbed her eyes with the heels of her hands. The paint had been a light tan, she had been wearing her embroidered apron....

Davey brought a jug of syrup from the barn and walked with her up the gravel drive to the street. "I don't know what to say about your suitor, Hazel."

"Maybe I just wanted to tell someone about it."

He was taken aback. "You've not told Maud?"

"She would be naming the grandchildren before I finished talking."

"Or reminding you not to give up your rights when you become a wife." Hazel was glad to see him smile. "I appreciate your confiding in me."

"Thank you for listening."

She wanted to embrace him and thought, fleetingly: Why do I not? There would be comfort in having Davey's arms around her. But she feared it would embarrass him, and so she just handed him his handkerchief. "Unused, you see."

"I know: Thou shalt not weep." He stuffed it into his pocket. "But the offer remains. My shoulder is there to be cried on. Even if only figuratively."

Walking home, the pint jug heavy in her basket, it occurred to Hazel that what was perhaps true of Stefan Dubrowsky was true of herself as well. Why should he love her? She did not love him. She felt something, but it could not yet be called love. Need: she had never thought about need before. There was something sad about the word, incomplete; it took a certain humility to admit to it. But maybe Davey was right: if there was need, equal need, on both sides, could it not, in time, be as powerful as love?

Chapter 4

They sat in the saloon bar at the hotel, drinking whiskey, scandalous indeed: the foreign *signorina* in her pearls and silk, and the small gray livery driver in a morning coat that had seen better days and a bow tie the startling green of absinthe. At the end of two hours and half of a bottle of Irish whiskey, the two of them were calling each other *George* and *Miss Anna*, and Anna had heard the story of her life.

She listened, questioned, drank more whiskey. She shed a shocked and bitter tear or two into her handkerchief. Finally, she excused herself and found her way to the ladies' room, where she reclined for five minutes on a chaise longue and let the room spin. Then, somewhat restored but in no less a state of confusion, she returned to the table, where George apologized for the distress he had caused her, and sometimes wasn't life a godawful confounded mess, if she would pardon the expression.

He escorted her to the elevator. She took his hand in both of hers with a tremulous *Grazie*, and George uttered a soft, hushing noise that sounded like *Eeyou wa*: "That's the Irish, Miss Anna, and it means: A good night's sleep will set you to rights." He was about to leave when a thought struck him. "I'll tell you what. You come over to tea in a day or two and meet my sister, Maud Cooper. And young Hazel, my niece, if we can corral her. I think you'll find it a comfort."

When she returned to her room, Anna ordered a pot of coffee and resorted to her notebook. A new page, a deep breath, and she picked up her pen:

> *I am the daughter of Tomasso Zanetti, a boy who worked in my grandfather's stables. He was killed in a fight in a tavern. And my mother was packed off to America to give birth to his child.*

Then she had to lean back in her chair and close her eyes. For the first time since her arrival in America, she understood the depth of her solitude. It was something like being on a stage when the set was being struck, the familiar world pulled away bit by bit, leaving emptiness. She had come here to find out who she was, and she was no one. Had not Aunt Julia cautioned her?

And yet even Aunt Julia could not have imagined this. Flossie's romantic notion of a secret marriage and a tragic death, the stuff of opera and melodrama, had been closer to the truth. She imagined telling the two of them what she had learned—telling anyone! Imagined the news filtering back to Rome. Marcello discovering she was his half-sister, the daughter of a peasant. Umberto—married for three years to the granddaughter of his father-in-law's cook. Mr. Banks, her tutor, with his reverence for the Roman nobility—what a disappointment she would be to him. And Nunzia Colluci, her best friend, who would perhaps cease to be a friend if she knew the truth—or might equally well break down in giggles and say, in her practical way, "At least your inheritance was not imperiled!"

And what a miracle that it had not been. Her father—not her father—her stepfather—her *patrigno*—her mother's husband—Signor Basilio Felice—O Dio, what a conundrum! He had been as generous to her as he was to Marcello. Did that mean he had loved his wife's bastard daughter after all? Or—more likely—had he made a promise to Lily when they married? Probably a legally binding one known to half a dozen people, among them certainly the man who advised her papa about his wealth, Signor Carognesco—not his name, she had mercifully forgotten what it was, but that was how Anna thought of him: *Signor Rat*, the verminous monster who pulled her into the cloak room off the grand hallway and groped under her dress with his fat fingers. And said if she told her Papa she would be sorry. Knowing it was a peasant's daughter he assaulted.

Anna went to the window to push aside the curtain. There was the dark Common. A gas lamp lighting up one slow-clopping horse and wagon. The deep blue night sky, with a slice of moon over the church. She could just make out the bank, the Bonnet Shop, the grocery, and in the other direction the ungainly town hall and the main street that led to the railway depot and the yellow house of the poetess.

She poured cream into her coffee, opened her notebook again, and continued:

> *Tomasso Zanetti was the son of Angelina, Grandfather's cook. The kind, wrinkled, garlicky old woman who held me on her lap and gave me sweets and let me stand on a stool and stir the risotto. Who sang in a creaking soprano that I knew, even as a child, hit perfectly the heart of each note. And whose delicious way of making suppli, with tender chunks of meat tucked into their middles, was handed down to her daughter, who became Papa's cook: Lorenza, my aunt, dead just a year ago of the mal'aria. And there is more. It has taken me all these days to let the idea into my head that Giovannina is yet another Zanetti—my first cousin. This makes my maid my closest relative on this earth, closer than Flossie's children, who are my second cousins.*
>
> *No wonder Angelina loved me. I was all that remained of her son.*
>
> *It is not too absurd to be believed. I have only to look in the mirror. If I have Flossie's ears and*

Mamma's eyes, I also have the high brow and modest widow's peak of the Zanettis. And Lorenza's nose. All this I can see now—just as I can see that Papa's nose and brow were quite unlike mine. We see what we expect to see.

The Zanetti family was part of my childhood. Angelina the cook always came to the villa at Bellagio, where I spent so many summers with Grandfather Prescott. We all knew that Angelina, mother of daughters, had also had a son, Tomasso, her youngest, and that he had been killed in a fight in a tavern. Long, long ago. What had it to do with me?

There had been some talk about the eldest daughter, who had gone to America and not returned. This was the mad aunt, who had come here with my mother and spirited me away to raise as her own child, because to her I was as much a Zanetti as a Prescott. She hung on to me, weeping, George said, and would not let me go. Her name was Elena. Is. George says she married an Irishman, and he is confident they can be found. He knows Fair Haven, where the streets are paved with oyster shells. Another improbability: and yet that is also true. George Mullen swears it.

This I cannot think about. All I can think is: My father was a boy who worked in Grandfather's stables, a boy of seventeen who rubbed down the horses, fed them, cleaned their stalls. I don't suppose he hauled the droppings off to the manure yard himself, but he probably shoveled them into a cart. A handsome boy—why not?—bare-chested, sweating, forbidden. And my young and spirited and very, very foolish mother. Children, the two of them. Scarcely knowing how babies came into the world. And then Mamma, sick in the morn-

ings with me in her belly, hearing that her lover was dead. The fury of my grandfather. Mamma packed off to America with the sister of the dead boy to accompany her. And finally a baby with a name that—I cannot help it—makes me laugh. Prudence indeed. Oh, Mamma!

Anna dozed off, pen in hand, and woke abruptly to find the last words obscured by a blot. She put the notebook aside and turned out her lamp, feeling like Pip when he learned that his benefactor was not Miss Havisham but a convict: he was speechless, his blood ran cold, he thought he was suffocating. How well Mr. Dickens understood the human soul.

༄

She woke late the next day and dressed with care to go down for breakfast. The thought crossed her mind that she might be looked at askance after her evening's debauch with George Mullen. But as she stuck a pin in her hat she thought: Which Anna Felice would mind about such a matter? The signorina who was so wealthy her reputation was secure no matter how outrageously she behaved? Or the peasant *bastarda*, whose reputation mattered to no one?

Her long sleep had indeed set her to rights—a phrase she had jotted in her notebook. She ordered an omelet with herbs, a double ration of sausages, and biscuits. Coffee with cream. Honey in a silver beehive pot. The sun shone brightly through the window. The New England spring had arrived, her waiter was pleased to report: in a week she would be breakfasting on the veranda.

In a week. Well. Her return passage had been booked for the third of June, four weeks off: New York to Naples, aboard the same *Britannia* on which she arrived. Home to Rome! To the huge and terrible apartment on the Corso, which Papa had left to her so Marcello could have the palazzo. Fine: she would not pass through the doors of that place again if an army of angels carried her there. Her residence would change, but otherwise she would resume her old life. Suppers at the homes of the few friends to whom she had not become an embarrassment. The risk of running into Marcello—or, God help her, Umberto—in someone's drawing room. Agonizing evenings at the Teatro dell'Opera to show the world her wounds had healed. Long wearisome days. Even longer solitary nights. Flirtations with unsuitable men and rebuffs from suitable ones, assuming she met any. The sight of her face in the mirror as time laid waste to it. The beauty of the city all around her like a reproof.

She would have a cat, maybe two. No more Toscas. Give them names that didn't evoke shame and sorrow: Stella and Salvatore. She could imagine the cats becoming her hold on life. If they were waiting for her to come home, she would not throw herself into the Tiber.

It was at this point in her musings that she began to laugh at herself.

She spent the day with *Great Expectations*, falling into and out of a doze, dreaming of Miss Havisham's houseful of stopped clocks, waking disoriented, reassured by the sight of her lace curtains and green lamps. No, she was not in Rome. She was safe—odd thought, but there it was.

She ordered supper through the speaking tube, and it arrived along with a note that had been delivered to the front desk:

> *Please come to tea with us tomorrow afternoon at five. Our house is just down the way, number 7 Amity Street, scarcely a step from the hotel. I should love to meet you and have a talk about the status of women in Italy, which is of burning interest to me. My brother George will call for you. I look forward to welcoming you to Amherst. With warmest wishes, (Mrs.) Maud Cooper.*

The cloudy day was darkening to gloom as she and George crossed over Amity Street, which was thronged with carriages and buggies and wagons driven by more of those loud young men, who she was beginning to learn were the lifeblood of the town. The colleges, George told her, offering his arm as they crossed, did not allow students to bring their own horses with them, so there was a brisk trade in rentals. Paige's was only one of half a dozen thriving livery stables. George said, "I do not look forward to the summers, because I dislike warm weather, being Irish, but I do find it is restful here when the students go home in June and leave the horses and the taverns and the streets to the real people."

They approached the Coopers' cottage: flowering bushes, a rickety front porch, curtains tied back at the windows. Maud, it seemed, gave speeches on the subject of women and the right to vote. Her daughter, Hazel, tutored private pupils in Latin and mathematics. George had come to Amherst to live with them after the death of Maud's husband, Charles, the writing master and baby rescuer. "They needed me to take care of them, though Maud would never admit it," he said, then stopped short on the sidewalk in front of the house. "Here I must confess to you, Miss Anna, that my sister knows all about that little Prudence—that is, about you, and your complicated history. We always thought of it as a family story, because Charles and I were the ones who brought her home to her mother. Never thinking we'd ever lay eyes on that child again." George took off his hat and held it over his heart. "I hope you don't mind being the object of gossip. It was all meant in kindness. And what might be called human interest."

She was surprised by the little leap of her heart at the news, and assured him she did not mind in the least. What had she to lose by being known for who she was? This was America!

Maud met them at the door: an aging beauty with untamed graying hair and George's brilliant blue eyes. She was wearing a divided skirt. "The only practical choice for bicycling," she said, and put her hands in her pockets to spread out a rather startling pattern of green and violet, which were the colors of the suffragist movement. Anna knew nothing about the movement, least of all that it had its own unfortunate colors, but she admired the logic of the skirt. Maud promised to give her a pamphlet on the Rational Dress Movement. "I could teach you to ride a bicycle, if you were interested."

"I must confess, Mrs. Cooper, that I have never seen a woman ride a bicycle."

"Not even in Rome, Italy? That does surprise me! Well, wait until you have been in Amherst for a while. There are quite a number of us, and more every day."

George snickered. "At last count, there were exactly four."

"You may well laugh, George. The rumor is that Ted Paige is going to start a line of women's bicycles at the stables. And who knows? Anna may be his first customer." She broke off to ask, impulsively, "I hope I may call you Anna, and you will call me Maud? Leaving off the Signorina and the Mrs. I'm thinking lately that the world doesn't gain from so much needless formality. And George may have told you that we've always thought of you as part of the family. To think that you are that kidnapped baby we all marveled over! George said you were the sweetest little thing."

Maud led the way through the cramped and cluttered house to the back parlor. A wall of disorderly bookshelves. Between the windows, a piano heaped with music. A basket of mending. A square of carpet before a fire burning in the grate, and on the mantel a vase of dried flowers and a photograph of a man Anna took to be Charles Cooper: gentle face, droopy mustache, kind eyes. George had told her Charles came home from the war badly wounded—he had lost an arm—and harboring consumption, of which he had died not many years later. Hard times for all of them.

Maud cleared the table of a tottering heap of something called *The Woman's Journal* and brought in a pot of tea so strong it might as well have been coffee. The Irish way, she said: put plenty of milk in it. There was also a plate of what was called rye-and-Indian bread—brown and sweet, eaten with butter. Maud passed it across the table.

"I apologize for the absence of cake. Our cook has problems at home—her daughter is married to a brute—and she didn't get to the baking today. I am hopeless at such things, and Hazel—well, Hazel is an excellent baker but is lately preoccupied." She sighed. "Have you noticed that, George?"

He nodded. "She is not herself." He set a bottle on the table: Old Bushmills, the label said. "And, as for the absence of cake, we can perhaps compensate with a bit of whiskey in our tea."

Maud ignored him. "You will meet our Hazel, Anna. The dearest girl. Perhaps the two of you will be friends. She could use a pick-me-up."

She asked Anna about the position of women in Italy. Had she heard of a suffragist named Maria Mozzoni in Naples? Someone else in Venice. Anna said such things were not talked of in Italy, and George said he was glad to hear it. George said the movement was nothing but a crusade against men that encouraged women to neglect their duties. "My question is: who will mind the babies?"

"George, you are being ridiculous."

"You see? That is what they never talk about. Who will cook the supper?"

The idea of voting in elections was unclear to her, but Anna did not understand why casting a vote would prevent supper from being cooked. It sounded like an argument George and Maud had had so often that, by now, he was only half serious and she only half outraged.

"I fear I know nothing of the position of women in Italy," she said. "Only the position of myself."

"Which was?"

An unfortunate marriage, she told them. A dead child. Other, smaller tribulations. The wish to start over. Where? Somewhere. These new revelations about her family had thrown everything into turmoil.

"Ah, you poor lamb." Maud gave Anna's hand a motherly squeeze, then let it go to pour more tea. "What a series of shocks, and you not even in this country a month."

George raised the bottle of Bushmills over Anna's teacup with a questioning look. She nodded. He poured. "Shall we tell Miss Anna what we were wishing to talk about, Maud?"

"It's your wish, George, not mine." Maud set down the pot and leaned back in her chair. "You know I think it's a daft idea."

"Well, we don't agree on that, and I'm inclined to give it a try. That is, if Miss Anna will allow me."

Anna took a sip from her cup: tea, milk, whiskey—a delicious combination, and unknown to her until this afternoon. "Allow you?"

"It's Maggie McAlmond, down in Connecticut. I thought I might write her a wee note and see what she remembers about that aunt of yours."

George had been searching his brain since their talk, he said, and out of the blue he'd remembered Maggie, an old friend of the family who had been living in Fair Haven at the time of Anna's kidnapping. She would know what had become of the Elena Zanetti who married an Irishman whose name George was unable to recall—Duffy, he thought. Or possibly Donovan. "I can see him as clear as day," he said. "Big fella. Hair black as pitch. Everything but his name, which has flown up the chimney, I'm afraid. But Maggie will know it."

Maud raised her fine eyebrows skeptically. "George doesn't even know where to address a letter to."

"I do, Maud. She lives on Pearl Street, right by the water, where all those oyster houses are."

"It's been more than thirty years! Why should Maggie McAlmond even be alive now?"

"And why should she not?"

Maud looked at him in exasperation. "What kind of world do you live in? She must be nearly eighty years old."

"Those tough old Irish birds go on forever." George poured a tot of whiskey into his teacup and sipped it. "Now that's the way to drink tea."

"George."

"Maybe it's the booze, Maud, but I feel optimistic about this. And if Maggie doesn't know the truth of it, there are folks in that part of the world who do."

Maud threw up her hands. "It's Anna's decision, not yours. This aunt is maybe not someone she wants to meet. Besides, it will be like dropping a stone into the river."

"Or a baited hook. I'll bet you a dollar we catch something."

Anna imagined a woman in a hovel—now elderly, very likely insane, and with who knows what ideas in her head. Would she claim kinship? Would she want money? Would she plague and harrow her and make this new world into a place of dread, as Rome had become? And did Anna really need to know any more about her origins than she knew already?

"Last time you saw this aunt, Miss Anna, she was stealing you away, passing you off as her own child." George winked. "We'll not let that happen again. You're safe here with us."

His words were half a joke, but at the same time oddly reassuring. What a comfortable world it was in the back parlor of Maud Cooper's house: the clutter of books and papers, the fire, the concern for her welfare. When had she ever experienced this warmth and goodness?

"And you know—" Maud's face brightened. "She may not be mad at all, so many years later. Think of it. An immigrant from Italy married to an immigrant from Ireland. She may be a complex and fascinating woman you will be glad to claim as a relation."

George took a bite of bread and washed it down with tea. "Or she may be a suffragist with bobbed hair and a bicycle."

Anna found that she was able to smile. "I will take a chance." After another sip of whiskey tea she said, "All I really want is to know the truth about things. That's why I came to America. It's why I am here in Amherst. And so I would indeed be grateful, George, if you wrote that wee note to Mrs. Maggie McAlmond."

Chapter 5

D avey was working at the table with his rulers and compasses when he heard voices in the drive. Finding solutions to the problems of Archie Wyatt's new barn was not without its satisfactions—today he was tackling the watering system—and he didn't welcome an interruption. He had delivered his plans for the feed-storage contraption, which worked on a pulley, and it was the talk of the sheep community—or so Archie said. Davey's only innovation was the way the rope was attached, but Archie made him feel like Archimedes. Davey should design such things for a living.

Davey had a feeling his brother-in-law was in cahoots with his sister: Lydia had nagged at Davey for years to use his training—that was how she summed up four years at Amherst College playing baseball and cutting his classes to go climbing in the hills with Billy Fox—to get out into the world and make something of himself. *Like you did, eh, Lydia? Did you go to Smith College so you could devote your life to babies and bonnets and butting in?* This he did not say, of course: he was fond of his overbearing sister—the Mighty Lydia, he and Maddox called her—and of her babies too. And he did not need to earn a living, thanks to the Pennsylvania Dutch branch of his mother's family. Davey barely remembered them: the large, scolding Legenhausen aunts. Their white-blond hair was one legacy; a modest but sufficient income was another.

He heard George's voice, and that of a woman—unfamiliar. And Tilda flitting by with the eggs. There was a laugh, not far from his door. Damn it! He was in no mood for company. He went to the door and flung it open. George stood there in an acid-green bowtie, holding up two bottles. "Last year's vintage, Davey me lad. A good one, I think. If you like it I'll trade you a couple of cases for a footstool like the one you made for Sam. I've reached the age where I like to put my feet up."

"It's a deal before I even taste it. I have a great partiality to your rhubarb wine, whatever the vintage."

"That is gratifying. Maud is not so enlightened. She says Blodgett's vegetable garden is encroaching on the rhubarb and making it taste of cauliflower."

"Your sister has many fine qualities, but she is no wine connoisseur."

David could never stay angry at George: just looking at his twinkling blue eyes and curious taste in neckwear could make anyone cheerful. As for the apparition at his side, it had to be the Italian woman who was staying at the Amherst House—someone, according to Tamsin, whom George had saved from a gang of kidnappers many long years ago in his incarnation as a jack of all trades in New Haven. Could this be true? George was a master of the ancient Irish art of embroidery. But here she was, and no doubt there were nuggets of truth buried in the story.

"I am pleased to introduce you to the latest member of our family." George removed his hat and bowed: "Signorina Anna Felice." He pronounced her name with relish, making it as Italian as he knew how, though with the inevitable Irish twist, and Davey saw a smile hover around the signorina's lips. "We have just been paying a call on your mother, and Miss Anna professed a desire to see your hawk."

Davey said he was happy to meet her, hoping it sounded convincing. She replied, in barely accented English, that she was equally happy to meet him. The quality of her voice was unusual: not quite hoarse, and not unpleasing, but rough at the edges, as if being gently forced past some minor obstruction. "It was not only the hawk I wanted to see. I am familiar with hawks. But George said you built this cabin yourself, and I have never seen a cabin—not one built by anyone."

His curiosity got the better of him. "You are familiar with hawks?"

Back in Rome, she said, her Papa had kept a regiment of birds. Hawks and peregrines. He employed a falconiere, an Arab man named Hamid. Anna had had her own leather *guanto*, embossed with the family crest. "I wore it only once," she said, with an air of disgust, and didn't hesitate to add that she did not approve of dispatching large birds to kill smaller ones for people to eat, which is what her father did.

"That is not what I do. She hunts only for her own food."

Anna Felice moved nearer to the enclosure to get a look at Owosha, who stared into the distance, oblivious of a woman in a large hat. "She is so much more beautiful than a bird in a hood with a gold finial and feathers. Our birds wore blue feathers, taken from who knows what other creature. Blue feathers and gold on birds who were perfect as they were!"

"Gilding the lily, you might call it," George put in.

"That is it exactly." Anna looked a minute longer at Owosha, knitting her brows with what Davey knew was disapproval—at what, he couldn't guess. Probably, like Ida, at the idea of keeping a wild bird captive at all. Or maybe she was just finding fault with the length of the perches or the shabbiness of the roof. While she stared at the bird, Davey stared at her. She was dazzling, with her reddish hair and dark blue eyes and Italian nose. She radiated a combination of keen intelligence and florid warmth. He wished she would leave.

But she turned her attention from the hawk to the cabin, exclaiming about the butternut knocker and the antlers over the door, and he knew his mother would not forgive him if he didn't invite her inside. George stood in the doorway with his thumbs in his waistcoat pockets, rocking back on his heels and beaming—no doubt wishing to be offered a drink, something Davey had no intention of doing. He pushed the chamber pot further under the bed with his foot. Then he showed the signorina his hooks and shelves and contraptions and the plans for a puppet theater he planned to make for Lydia's twins. Anna took an interest: she was once a singer, she said, always fascinated with sets, with how things were made. He had a sudden premonition of her offering to help with the toy theater, and immediately began thinking of an alternative: he could make them hobby-horses, a chess set, a miniature farm.

For a foreign woman, new in town, hardly acquainted with him, Anna was—thought Davey—uncommonly garrulous. She talked of theaters, of the pleasures of solitude, of Davey's view over the meadow—and was that where the railroad passed by? She talked of railroads. It occurred to him that she might be trying to prolong the visit. Was she one of those women who fancied him? He had met a few. This one was perfectly agreeable, in fact charming, but when she and George left, he was exhausted. The last thing George said was, "We'll be seeing you at the party." The signorina added, "Your mother was kind enough to invite me." Davey had forgotten that his parents' anniversary party was on Saturday, that Maddox would not be present, and that therefore the burden was on Davey to behave like a civilized son of the family, including proposing a toast.

He had to make an effort not to groan.

George's wagon rattled down the drive to the road. Davey answered his jaunty wave with a wave of his own. Then he went back to his cabin and opened a bottle of rhubarb wine.

❧

In Davey's student days, he had belonged to a group called the New Thoreauvians, who had revered Thoreau's preference for a simple, self-sufficient life, separated from humanity and close to Nature. When Davey was at last set free from Amherst College—it was the way he thought of his graduation—he was convinced that becoming a hermit was the only way to live: maybe in Hadley, in the flats by the river, or in one of the caves near the summit of Mount Norwottuck.

Maddox had graduated with honors and was already courting Caroline Vandermeer when he went off to get a law degree at Columbia College in New York. His future was planned in a line as straight and logical as a roof beam. Davey's was more like a ramshackle hut.

He had always been slightly worrisome. The upheavals of his early childhood—Ohio to Connecticut to Massachusetts—had affected him as they hadn't his brother. Even as a weedy little towhead in overalls, Maddox seemed to thrive on everything: separation from their father, their mother's remarriage, various resettlements. When he fell out of an apple tree and broke his arm, he turned it to advantage and taught himself to write with his left hand.

Maddox had thrived, Davey had managed. He turned inward, becoming solitary and bookish, and when one day he quoted Thoreau ("There is some of the same fitness in a man's building his own house that there is in a bird's building its own nest") and announced that he wished to build himself a little house out behind the orchard, his mother's worrying didn't subside, but it shifted, and over the years it had faded away. Davey was never an adventurous eccentric—not even as adventurous as Thoreau, whose mother did his washing as Davey's did his. Davey needed to be by himself, but with comfort nearby: people there when he needed them, willing to retreat when he didn't. He was amiable, bothered no one, content enough to be his own best friend. He contracted his world to a meadow, a few broad fields, a railroad track, the distant low mountains that bordered the town, and he didn't live in a cabin for two years, as Thoreau did, but for what was now going on twenty. He was as much a fixture as the henhouse.

And why? If he ever knew the answer, he had forgotten it, but he was satisfied with his life. The only complication was his cousin Hazel, with whom he had been in love since she was sixteen. Hazel with her broad little nose, her narrow hands and graceful fingers, her honey-colored hair, straight as a pin until a humid day released wispy feathers around her face and gave her the Botticelli angel look that woke him in the night and sent him out roaming the town until he came to Amity Street and stood under her window, willing her to come to it and see him and—then what?

Davey knew she was fond of him—but as if he were an older brother, nothing more. That was the way it was, had been for all these years. Would always be. She was not his, but at least she was there, a mile down the road, in all her lovely goodness. Her Hazel-ness.

For years, Maddox had been urging Davey to declare himself. His theory was that Hazel loved Davey as deeply as he did her, but was not aware of it. Or was too timid to think such a thought. Or was abashed by their first-cousinship.

"Or too much in awe of my magnificence."

"Or put off by the fact that you're a jackass."

They had had similar conversations a dozen times. Davey had written to Maddox about Hazel's California suitor, and Maddox's latest letter said what he had always said, but with more vehemence:

> *I have been thinking about the Hazel situation, and I will say it one more time, Davey, before I close up shop and devote my energies to something more promising, like finding an honest Boston politician: stop being a fool and ask her yourself. Save her from this mad scheme! Her last resort? Why are you not her last resort? At least she's used to you. Propinquity is all—I'm sure that's somewhere in Shakespeare. What has this Polish apricot-raising California jasper done to deserve a gem like our Hazel? You are a dull and muddy-mettled rascal, my brother, if I have the quote right. Pigeon-livered (I suppose you would know about that) and lacking in gall. I may be mixing up my Shakespeare, but screw your courage to the sticking place, if you have one. What have you to lose?*

The next morning, early, Davey put on his broad-brimmed hat and walked along the tracks toward Northampton. A smudge of yesterday's moon rode in the sky above the dark silhouette of the Pelham hills. The landscape Davey lived in was a perfect one for thinking—beautiful, calm, predictable. *Solvitur ambulando*: it is solved by walking, one of the few bits of Latin that had stayed with him. He knew the phrase had some philosophical nuance attached to it, but he'd forgotten what it was. It didn't matter; for him, walking was always medicine and antidote and inspiration.

Davey needed to think about Hazel—specifically, about Stefan Dubrowsky. Hazel's savior, her happiness. Who could have known that, behind her sweet face, her wry humor, her love of poetry and mathematics and Chopin and the Latin language, her competence in the kitchen and the garden, there was a deep and wretched loneliness not so different from his own? A desperation, she had called it, so unbearable that she was willing to give herself to the first man who asked for her.

Davey had always assumed that of course Hazel would marry, and that when it happened their long friendship would not end, it would just be altered: he would move farther to the edge of her life, see her less often, learn to find pleasure as well as heartache in the existence of her children. Uncle Davey. But, if this happened, the lucky man would be local. A young professor at the college seemed likely. At worst, someone from Hadley, Northampton, even Springfield: this could be borne. And then, as the years went by, he had stopped thinking about it. Hazel remained unmarried, still lived a mile away. She was not his, but she was not anyone else's either.

Now his unhappiness was overpowering, and deep at the heart of his misery was an idea he'd concocted that he couldn't shake: to write to his cousin Calvin Jessup in Sacramento for some kind of reassurance that Hazel wasn't making a mistake. What troubled him was that doing so would mean a failure of what everyone knew was the supreme test of love: to wish, more than anything, for the happiness of the loved one, even if that meant losing her. And it was impossible for Davey not to admit to himself that what he hoped, desperately hoped, was that Calvin would write back saying Stefan Dubrowsky, while an excellent chap in many ways, was unworthy of their cousin, and that—Davey tramped on, the sun climbing in the sky and sweat dripping into his eyes—someone should sit the poor girl down and talk her out of it.

He stopped in the shade of the big copper beech that marked the halfway point to Northampton, took off his hat, and dried his face and neck with a handkerchief. He had walked four miles and solved nothing. Of course Cal would sing the praises of Stefan Dubrowsky, and declare Hazel lucky to have him. All the letter would accomplish would be to prove Davey Chillick a monster of selfishness.

Still, when he arrived back at the cabin, he sat at his table and wrote to his cousin.

> *Dear Cal,*
>
> *I should have told you sooner how much I enjoyed* The Curse of Rattlesnake Dick. *I wonder where you picked up the knack of bringing rascals and reprobates to life—certainly not from your genteel New England upbringing. I trust you're deep into the next Alonzo Woodley adventure and will let us know when it will be published. Did you know that Spear's had a large window display of* Rattlesnake Dick *with its sensational lurid cover? It was the talk of the town. What joy you must bring to the coffers of the D.C. Heath Company!*
>
> *You are aware of the letter-writing romance between Hazel and your ranch manager. Hazel has told me about it but I think has told no one else—this for reasons of her own. You know how inscrutable she can be: she is nothing like Maud or, God knows, George. And so she has no guidance. It is troubling to me that Stefan Dubrowsky did not approach her through her mother, or maybe Sam, as head of the family. It's troubling that we don't know who his people are—though Hazel says everyone is in Poland, so I suppose he can't be expected to trot them out. There is a sister in New York, apparently. I wonder if you have met her, or know anything else about her. And what is*

his position with you? Is his place secure? Can he support a wife?

I hope these questions don't put you off. My impression when I met him was a good one, and I know you value him. But Hazel has always called me her unofficial brother, and she has confided in me, and so I thought I had better write. You know what she means to me. To us all. If we are going to pack her off to Sacramento, we need to know what awaits her.

There seems to be so much news, but, when I gather it up, it amounts to very little. An Italian signorina has joined the family, my hawk has learned to hunt and return, Archie's sheep barn is the delight of us all. I lack the heart or the gumption to write any more at the moment. I look forward to your thoughts, cousin to cousin, on Hazel and her suitor.

With best wishes to you and to Luisa and the children,
Davey

He read it over: maybe it didn't sound so bad. Maybe, buried in the mountain of selfishness, was a nugget or two of real concern for Hazel's welfare. And if Calvin could remove all doubt about Stefan's character, at least simple anxiety would be removed from Davey's complicated tangle of torments.

The immediate and surprising effect of the letter was to cheer him up. He stripped down, washed, put on a clean shirt, found a decent hat, walked into town, and dropped the letter to Cal into the postbox on the Common, thinking: When was the last time I did this?

From across College Street came the cheers of the crowd, a sound he'd been aware of from time to time since the new baseball field opened the spring before. Occasionally he'd been tempted to wander over and see the college team play, asking himself what on earth was preventing him from walking half a mile, mingling with the town, watching a small leather-covered sphere being thrown, hit, fielded? If someone recognized him, he would do what anyone would do: smile, chinwag, yes, it is a glorious game, and now I must be off.

This time he did not resist. When he got there, Amherst was ahead of Brown 9–4. Davey paused inside the fence. The new field was a marvel: rows of ranked bleachers, cleanly laid-out baselines, and a tall scoreboard. In his student days, they had played in a scrubby vacant lot behind the chapel. His last game had been a loss to Williams, himself in right field, Maddox pitching. Amherst had been outhit by a powerful Williams nine; their own best hitter was sidelined with a bad ankle. Davey had had one unforgettable moment when a drive was hit to right field, so high and deep he thought it was a goner, but he stayed with it, and it sank into his glove like a bird into its nest. Out! To no avail: in the last inning that same batter—Nate Hubbard, he would never forget his odious name—hit the ball into left field and away, with two men on base.

Sometimes, on a sleepless night or a long walk, Davey entertained himself by reliving a game. His memory of Latin conjugations was spotty at best, but he was sure that, if pressed, he could recall every inning of every game he had ever played. God, he had loved baseball. The geometrical logic, the silences, the waiting—a game of bated breath, he often thought. And in the outfield a curious kind of isolation that had been congenial to him. In the broad stretches behind the bases, very little happened: a fielder could roam over the grass almost at random, lost in a dream of blue sky, sunshine, the distant whack of wood on leather, until the sudden, intense thrill when the ball came his way and set up the rhythm of chase, reach, catch, return.

Like being a hawk. He remembered a write-up in the college paper, *The Student*—his mother must still have it somewhere—that had referred to him as "David Chillick, strong of arm and fleet of foot, ballhawk extraordinaire in right field."

He had not meant to stay to the end, but the game was compelling. The gangly, light-haired pitcher reminded him of Maddox: a watchful stance, a speedy windup, a confident smile when he let go of the ball. Amherst won 12–7, the final out thanks to an impossible catch by the third baseman that Davey felt down to his boots.

He walked home exhilarated, wishing Maddox had seen it with him: there was much to be said for having someone to pound on the shoulder when your team won. And how easy it had been to walk to the Common in the sunlight, mail a letter, watch a ballgame, walk back home. Not only easy: it had been more than that, something that resembled a pleasure so much it was tempting to call it that.

Maybe, when you had lost what was most precious, it was not so difficult to give up a few other things as well.

Chapter 6

Five letters from California, and still she had told her secret to no one but her cousin Davey. On the day the sixth arrived, a fine May afternoon, she and Maud were sitting on the porch when Mr. Mackey handed two envelopes over the railing with a "Good day, ladies." Maud set them on the little porch table: on the top one, Hazel's name in Stefan's script.

But Maud had just returned from her suffrage meeting, and was thinking only of the plans being made for a "woman's club" in Amherst, where women of the town could not only congregate but simply rest, read, escape the cares of family life.

"Mabel Todd was there," Maud said. "And she said something that really warmed my heart: that because we love the world so much, we should try to make it better. Perhaps she's not the flibbertigibbet I thought her—though you'd never know it from her *chapeaux*." Maud took off her own plain straw hat and flung it down. "But there is still so much controversy about the temperance issue, it's disheartening. If Miss Marjorie Cowls says one more time that women would not need the vote if men were not drunkards, I shall be forced to strangle her."

"I should think your lucid explanation of the question would have settled that for good and all."

"Are you laughing at your mother?"

"How can you say such a thing? And should we have something to eat?"

"I haven't eaten all day. I completely forgot Ella would not be here."

"Lately it seems Ella is never here. We could have jam sandwiches. Yesterday's bread, but I could toast it."

"It sounds lovely. The perfect midday meal, rivaled only by an onion sandwich."

"We are out of onions."

"So I assumed."

Hazel told herself: If she sees the letter and asks me, I will tell her. But Maud was not wearing her spectacles. Hazel pocketed the mail as she went inside—the letter from Stefan and one from her old college friend Bessie Bell, who had married an Army captain and moved to Connecticut. She made two jam sandwiches, and when they had been eaten Hazel took the letters to her room. She forced herself to read the one from Bessie first:

> *So pleased about the new addition to our family.*
> *Jeffrey was born three weeks ago, he is fat and*
> *happy, and I've nearly returned to normal. Martin*
> *will be stationed here at Fort Trumbull for another*
> *year, and he and I both hope you can come to visit*
> *soon—it's so long since we've seen you! We want to*
> *show off our children, and of course hear your news.*

Martin and I: the eternal "we" of marriage. Maud always said that one of the hard parts of widowhood was learning to use "I" again instead of "we." *We want to hear your news.* Bessie, along with everyone else, had surely given up any hope of real news from Hazel, meaning any change in her romantic prospects. But Bessie meant well—why did that phrase always imply a criticism?—and someday Hazel would go to New London and see the ships and the whaleboats and Bessie's perfect babies and handsome husband....

She opened the white envelope from her own possible husband. It was short:

As always, Hazel, I think of you often as I go about the daily round. My newest project is an addition to my house, which is becoming too small for Victor and me, and which I continue to hope will soon be home to three people. You and I have known each other—if I may put it that way—for two months now, and I welcome your letters. Nothing has changed my mind about wishing you would become my wife. The time has seemed long, and yet you say in every letter that you need more of it, and I wonder when the day will come when you feel you can give me a definite answer. With every day that passes, I am more sure that I want to marry you, and I hope it's the same for you. I would like to know sometime soon. I think you owe me this.

She read it over once, then again. Two months! An addition on the house! A definite answer! And when? When? When?

The tone of the letter was disturbing. Could she call it peevishness? Or a natural impatience? And how was it possible that she could both want something to happen urgently and also want it to happen—someday? Was her hesitation unreasonable, as Stefan seemed to think? Would her caution end in her losing him to some California woman who was bolder, more decisive—more like a hawk than a rabbit?

She fetched her drawing materials and fled to the garden. The best antidote to a troubled mind was drawing, which opened to her a bountiful and mysterious world, endlessly rich, endlessly absorbing. And all her own.

Perched on the metal seat, she had a view of the gate that needed repairing, the woodshed, the twisted old pear tree. As she began to sketch out the lacing of the branches against the sky, Stefan's letter was gradually pushed to the back of her mind.

But she woke the next morning in the cold dawn with a dim memory of a dream about Stefan and Victor in the little house. As the day lightened, the spring peepers started up and accompanied the ceaseless noise in her head: *I have never done anything. Never taken a chance, a risk. Never surprised anyone. Never kicked out at life or grabbed at it hungrily. This is the last chance.*

She wanted to see Davey. Her excuse would be Owosha: she would ask Davey if she could make a drawing of the hawk. The prospect soothed her again. She pulled the covers around her head and slept until Maud called up the stairs to remind her of an early tutoring session.

After an hour with poor James Clay, who seemed closer to the end each time she saw him but whose enthusiasm for the intricacies of Virgil and Horace burned bright, she packed her basket (sketch pad, pencil case, half a rum cake) and walked to the cabin.

She found her cousin reading on the bench outside his cabin, Heloise curled beside him, Owosha on her branch. Cat and bird had learned to coexist, Davey said, simply by ignoring each other: humans could learn much from animals.

When Hazel sat down, he closed his book: a volume of Shakespeare with a hawk feather for a bookmark. "Which play?"

"*Hamlet.* Indecision has been preoccupying me."

"What are you indecisive about? Have you had an offer of marriage from a woman in Saskatchewan?"

"Ha ha. No, I've had a piece of advice from my brother. I'm trying to decide if it's wise or foolish."

"Maddox is probably not capable of folly. I would take his advice." Hazel set the basket at his feet. "I came to draw the hawk, with rum cake as a bribe. I'll give you the drawing if you want it."

"You are a beacon who lights up my tiny, miserable existence."

"Like the new gas streetlamps on Amity Street. Not that you've ever seen them."

"You might be surprised at what I've seen."

He reached into the basket, broke off a hunk of cake, and took a bite, leaning forward to let the crumbs fall between his knees. Hazel would have liked to draw Davey, in just that attitude, but she had asked half a dozen times over the years, and he always refused. Nor would he agree to have his photograph taken, even by Tamsin. "I am too flimsy a creature to be spread around like that," he had said once. "I could disappear"—which sounded like a joke, but Hazel was almost sure it was not.

Owosha hunkered, a mere six feet away. At close range, the hawk was a magnificent creature. Hazel took out her pad and pencil. She began with the intricate pattern of the breast feathers, like neat rows of arrowheads surrounding the white bib—filling it in with sharp strokes, working quickly, before Owosha could change position. Then she turned her attention to the fan of tail, the downy under-feathers, the black talons like commas at the end of each scaly yellow foot.

Davey sat silently beside her, eating cake and watching the drawing take shape. "You really are amazingly good."

"I don't usually work so fast. It's crude."

"So is Owosha. You should draw her with blood on her beak and a mouse in her claws."

The hawk moved suddenly on the perch, shook her wings and half-spread them, turning her mad stare toward the sky where a pair of buzzards reeled with the wind before they dived toward the earth out beyond the tracks. Owosha gave a hoarse, muted scream. "Oh, to be a buzzard, she is thinking. Flying free. Nobody puts buzzards in cages."

"She is not capable of such a human emotion as envy."

"Lucky bird." Hazel sighed. "Just return to your pose, Owosha. There. Thank you." She wanted to catch the black overhanging beak and the concentrated glare of the hawk's round eye, which was, she realized, only a shade darker than the amber of Davey's eye. She decided not to point this out.

"Hazel." His voice was abrupt, and she looked up from her drawing. "Are you going to tell me what's happening between you and Sacramento?"

"Oh. That." She returned her gaze to the bird, filling in the malevolent black beak and adding a glint of gray along the ridge where it met a band of white. "That's what I really came here about.

Again. If you don't mind." He started to speak, but she held up her hand. "Wait. Was that a raindrop? I just want to finish this."

With a few more lines, she darkened the overhanging eyelid and sketched in a few jagged feathers. "There. What a subject she is."

"You have captured her soul."

"Or whatever it is that burns behind those eyes." She held it out and looked at it. "That will have to do. I definitely felt a raindrop, and there—that was another. Can we go in? Then I'll tell you about Sacramento."

"I will bear it better with another piece of cake."

Inside, Hazel set the cake on the breadboard and cut slices with the big knife while Davey made tea, and they settled down on the two chairs by the fireplace. The day had darkened quickly; rain drummed hard against the roof.

"How often have we sat here like this?"

"Not often enough." Davey took a piece of cake. "Do you remember the blizzard?"

Of course she remembered the blizzard: winter before last. The storm came up quickly, but they could have gone up to the big house to wait it out with cocoa and coddling. Instead they had sat for hours, first in the dark—as dark as the inside of a sheep, Davey said—and then, as evening fell, by the light of two tall candles. They wrapped up in Indian blankets, feeding the stove and watching the candles burn down, while the world outside whitened and then darkened.

"Nothing existed but this cabin."

"And now our existence must include Sacramento, California."

"I suppose." She sighed. "Stefan feels that, after two months, I should have made up my mind. That was just about all he said in his last letter."

"An ultimatum?"

"I don't know. Written in a letter, words can be different from the way they sound in person with a face and a tone of voice attached. I'm trying not to be affronted. And not to be a spiritless creature who bolts into its burrow, squeaking in fear if anything should be demanded of it beyond making scones or translating Latin."

"For a rabbit, you have a superlative gift for exaggeration."

"No—it's true. Another kind of person would just stop thinking and get on the train. If this is my last chance, then why not grab it? And who can blame this man for being impatient? Life is passing quickly, for all of us." A peal of thunder, then a shaft of lightning that lit the apple trees out the window. "You see? Excellent timing. The gods are angry with me for dithering. *Fortis Fortuna iuvat*, if I have that right."

"Just because it's Latin doesn't make it true."

"The only way I'll find out is to give it a try. Be one of the bold ones and see if Fortune favors me."

A moment went by while they watched the rain pound the glass. *I don't want to be bold,* Hazel thought. All she wanted was to sit there in Davey's cabin until the storm was over and then walk home and read a book. *What is wrong with me?*

"I want you to be happy." His voice was unsteady. "And so I shouldn't say this, but I wish you would not go."

She had put off thinking about how diminished her life would be without her cousin. They would write letters, he would send news of home, she would give him news of apricots and children. Maybe a visit now and then from one of them or the other. From time to time she would pull out the drawings she had made of the objects in his cabin and remember those long-ago days, a different life....

The memory of the snowstorm brought with it her awareness—familiar, suppressed—of the confusing closeness between her and Davey. The way his eyes would sometimes meet hers and then look quickly away at something else. Her frequent desire—she had it now—to touch him, even if it was just to take his hand.

The silent noise of his distress filled the room. "I know how you feel," she said finally. "I know you think it's mad to think of leaving the civilized world of our ancestors and travel for long, filthy days through hostile territory to become the wife of a farmer in California simply because nobody else ever asked me."

"That's not true."

"If anyone asked me, it has slipped my mind."

"I mean it's not true that you know how I feel."

"Oh." She sipped her tea: too hot, as usual. "Well, you could tell me. I would like to know."

"I don't think you would. But no: it's hard for me to say so, but I do not think you're mad for considering this offer of marriage." She watched him stand up and go to the window. "The rain is letting up. There's Tilda, going out to the barn. Heloise coming out from under the porch. Owosha on her branch, unperturbed by the roaring of nature. I wonder what she makes of thunder and lightning." He raised his head. "And listen. Here it comes, with perfect timing. The horrid hooting of the Belchertown train."

"I wasn't aware that you are an admirer of Miss Dickinson."

"I'm often not her admirer at all. I don't approve of her calling the railway horrid in one breath and comparing it to a docile horse in the next. Speaking of indecision."

The train rattled past, down below the apple orchard and the big field, subsiding into the distance with a lingering wail. Hazel wondered about the source of Davey's indecision, and what Maddox had given him advice about, and how he might answer if she asked him. But she didn't ask.

"The sound of the railway seems more dismal than horrid," Hazel said. "Melancholy."

"Melancholy is a romantic word for a very real and unromantic state of mind. *The mass of men lead lives of quiet desperation.* If you call it *quiet melancholy* it sounds almost appealing."

"Your Henry Thoreau has a tendency toward generalization. How many of that mass of desperate men did he know?"

"He is not *my* Henry Thoreau. I am nothing like that character. I'm not interested in political things, I don't travel, I'm not a devotee of Buddhism, and I don't write books. Just because I live in a tiny cabin and take long walks and fritter away my time in idleness, people compare us. I wish they would stop."

"Consider me stopped." Hazel studied his lean frame, the silvery-gold curls gathered at the nape of his neck. "Davey? What are you thinking?"

"How Owosha's enclosure could be improved if that back wall was open. She always faces this direction, but if she had something to see, she might look north instead of south. Enlarge her world."

"You should have been an architect. Or an engineer."

When he looked at her she wished she hadn't said it. "So Archie and Lydia tell me repeatedly. And Sam, and my mother, though not in so many words. I should have done many things, Hazel. Most of all, I should have grown up."

"I didn't mean—"

"You're right, of course. How different my life would be if I had an office in town that I went to every day like a real person. Or learned to play the trombone. Or grew alfalfa. But I've done nothing but pursue my peculiar brand of solitude." She waited for him to say more, but he ran his hand over the rough wall by the window frame and gave a short laugh "This wretched bit of plastering was your first attempt."

"You should have made me do it over."

"I'm glad I didn't. It reminds me of you every day." He smiled at her. "I'm sorry if I'm being curmudgeonly this morning."

"You should be nicer to me. I brought you cake."

He walked over and picked up the sketch pad. "And you made a drawing of my hawk."

"It's not really finished. It's just stopped. But you can have it if you want it."

"The likeness is remarkable." He detached the page and propped it against a stack of books. Owosha glowered into the room. "This is not just a hawk, it's my hawk. Maybe you'll return to Amherst someday and finish it."

"Maybe I won't like him. Maybe I'll be back home in a week."

"Don't, Hazel. He is a perfectly nice man. You and I will cripple poor Mr. Mackey with letters. I'm used to getting used to things. And I am very slowly enlarging my own world."

"What does that mean?"

"I don't know. Not very much. But every now and then I ask myself why I'm still living in this cabin, even as an old man of nearly forty."

She stared at him. "You're thinking of leaving it?"

He picked up the basket and held it out to her. "That's a topic for another day. Thank you for your visit, dear coz. I suppose I'll see you at Sam and Tam's anniversary party."

"A herd of wild rhinoceros could not keep me away."

"I don't think the rhinoceros, wild or tame, travels in herds." At the door he looked up at the sky. "Stratus nebulosis. The rain is still lurking, ready to pounce. Would you like to borrow an umbrella? Or wait by the fire for sunshine? Or chance a wet walk across the meadow with Owosha and me?"

She would not. There were Latin exercises to be graded, petulant girls to be tortured with algebra.

A light rain started up again before she reached the Common. A poem by Emily Dickinson nagged at her: *I cannot live with you, that would be Life—And Life is over there behind the shelf....* How it went on she couldn't recall, but she matched her quick steps to the rhythm of the line, and she was hurrying down Amity Street when a truth came to her, as if she'd looked through a window pane just washed: *feeling.* That was all she wanted. That was what she meant by *life.* Maybe Miss Dickinson did too. Love, anger, frantic weeping, bliss, anguish, passion. When had she last felt anything passionately? Her father's death? Nearly eighteen years ago. Eddie Fletcher's treacherous kisses? Ten years. In a decade, had she felt anything stronger than placid contentment, mild irritation, minimal pleasure, the occasional short, glum blur? A spring day or a page of Chopin might bring a flicker of joy. Was that all?

She stood in the drizzle with her hand on the gate, hardly hearing the bustle of Amherst as it passed her on the road, until Isaac Paige, returning to the stables in a red carriage drawn by a white horse, called, "You're getting wet, Miss Cooper!" She came back to life, waved, opened the gate, and went inside.

No one home: sometimes she loved isolation as much as her cousin did. She shook the rain from her hat, took off her muddy boots, and changed into dry stockings. The quiet settled around her, broken only by the noisy ticking of her father's old clock. She hadn't been indoors ten minutes when the sun came pouring through the windows, lighting up plates on the table, an apron hanging from a hook, a lampshade painted with ivy. She had looked at these objects for much of her life, a life that was as seemingly small as Emily Dickinson's had been—another spinster daughter—but unredeemed by poetry. She thought of Lydia's life with Archie and the children. Her own parents and the delight they had taken in each other. Her aunt and uncle in their big, cheerful house full of visiting grandchildren. Bessie Bell in Connecticut with her brood of chicks.

Life: she would reach up to the shelf and take it down. Write the letter. *Yes, I will be your wife*—or some approximation of that. Then she would tell Maud when she came in, and George. She would tell Tamsin and Samuel and the whole Chillick family, write to Bessie and Cousin Sarah and the Legenhausen cousins in Pennsylvania. Let her students know she would not be teaching them in the fall. Get herself some new summery dresses, a pair of open shoes, a thin nightgown, a light bonnet. Her mother's wedding dress fetched from the mothballs. Congratulations, tears, champagne toasts. *I will arrive on the train at the end of June, I look forward to seeing your house, meeting Victor, I will go to the depot tomorrow and arrange about a ticket, I will be your wife.*

But when she sat down at her desk, it was James Clay's *Aeneid* translation she picked up, his ten lines of Virgil at the close of Book III, when Aeneas ends the story of his journey with the death of his father and then, in James's translation, "At last he stopped talking and took his rest."

Chapter 7

Driving back with George after the encounter with Davey Chillick, Anna tried to think if she had ever seen anyone whose appearance had so affected her: she, who had lived all her life among Romans. But all those men were remarkable in the same way—Umberto was one of them, Marcello another. They were the statues in the piazzas, the gods and warriors. They were the saints and martyrs and angels in the paintings in the Corcini palace.

But Davey looked like no one else. Anna wondered how the rest of them could have become so used to his appearance that the maid coming up from the henhouse didn't even glance his way, and his mother called to him, irritably, to remember to close the gate behind him. He was not young, he was not tall, and there was an unexpected plumpness to his face that gave him a slightly angelic look. He had curling blond hair streaked prematurely with silvery white, but his eyebrows and lashes were dark, and his eyes were the gilded brown of topaz. The combination was strange and beautiful.

"Davey Chillick is certainly very handsome," she said to George, feeling the inadequacy of the word—of the whole English language, perhaps.

George chuckled. Our Davey? Yes, he was a fine-looking lad, and a smart, good-hearted one too, once you got beneath the nonsense.

Astonishingly, Davey was half of a pair of twins: there was another one of him in Boston, named Maddox, a professor at Harvard Law School and a grand personage indeed. Did they look alike? They were not quite identical, but they used to look more alike than they did now. Maddox was taller, had become a bit stout, had lost much of the hair on his head and grown it on his chin. He also had a wife and a child—and no, Davey had never had either. The twins were Tamsin's sons by her first husband, a Welshman in Ohio, long dead—a bit of a beast, the story went. Davey and Maddox graduated from Amherst College and built the cabin together almost twenty years ago, and Davey had been living there ever since. On what? George (who never minded such questions) said there was a small inheritance from his mother's mother's family, the Legenhausens— a German clan no one ever saw but, as George put it, "When those old Huns die, they do their duty."

Davey didn't need much in the way of money because he never went anywhere—never even went into town. Never? Never—or not in the daylight. He had been spotted at odd hours of the night. And George knew he took long walks into the Holyoke hills. But he didn't visit people, and he didn't go to the shops or the library or the post office or the taverns. The womenfolk brought him things, or he did without. He seemed to like doing without. He had always been an odd duck. But, George hastened to add, a grand lad for all that.

As they approached the hotel, Anna could not resist asking: Does he do without female companionship? This made George laugh outright. He said, "You would not be the first woman to come up against the great closed door that is Davey Chillick."

Back in her room, she used the time before supper to write a note to her aunt:

> *Forgive me for not writing sooner. I hope you*
> *are well and that Flossie and Gerald are safely*
> *back in Pittsburgh after their visit. I am still*

> *here in Amherst, where I have found Mr. George*
> *Mullen, who is as bow-tied and mustachioed as*
> *you described him. He remembers you and Uncle*
> *Henry with great affection and sends greetings.*
> *He was able to give me some information about*
> *my parentage, but there may be more forthcom-*
> *ing, and so I remain here for some time longer*
> *while Mr. Mullen makes inquiries. I will write*
> *again when I am able to be more definite about my*
> *traveling plans. The Amherst House is an excellent*
> *hotel, though it cannot compare to the delights of*
> *the Rose Room.*

This was not quite the truth. After the aromatic rose bedroom, the Amherst House was a haven of simple comfort. Anna had become used to her purple-flowered carpet and had pulled a comfortable chair over to the window that overlooked the Common. She liked the gleaming, starched tablecloths of the dining room, which at her request stocked a very good Amontillado and had a standing order for the sausages Anna was fond of, from a farmer in Shutesbury who raised his pigs on buttermilk. Mr. Otis, the black headwaiter, had lost his awe of her and become fatherly. Even the mirrored walls no longer distressed her; the eccentric signorina now brought a book to the dinner table. One of the hotel maids had become adept at doing Anna's hair—better than Giovannina—and Mr. Hatch at the front desk had said, at least twice, "You are becoming quite a fixture, Signorina Felice!"

> *You were right, dear aunt. What I have learned*
> *about my family is a "can of worms" indeed. And*
> *I look forward to telling you all about it when*
> *I have concluded my business here in Amherst,*
> *which I trust will be soon.*
> *Your loving niece,*
> *Anna*

She leaned back in her chair and smiled. Another white lie: she did not look forward to concluding her business, such as it was, and to departing Amherst in order to go—where? That was the question, and she was in no hurry to answer it.

❧

She had begun taking walks with Maud, who told her about the plans to open a woman's club in the town, as a kind of refuge for women who needed one. Anna asked: A refuge from what? Maud replied with spirit: From the cares of their lives. The tyranny of their husbands, the demands of their children. The oppression of simply being a woman in a world where men make all the decisions!

Anna could see that she would have to form an opinion about the question of votes for women. Maud was keen to convert her, and she felt ready to be converted—the experience of oppression and tyranny was not alien to her, though she had never looked at her life that way. There was much to think about.

But Maud in her zeal could herself become oppressive after a few turns around the Common. She had little of what was called "small talk"—hers was mostly big talk, and tended to bounce off almost any subject back to the issue of rights for women. She had given Anna a Rational Dress pamphlet with a picture on the front of an angular woman in pants and a loose jacket, hair bobbed to her chin. Maud had a particular interest in short hair. She swept off her hat—a sensible straw with a flat brim, from which her own hair escaped in curly tendrils. "Can you imagine how free we would feel, Anna, without this daily burden?" Anna said she could indeed—and, in truth, the thought of having hair as short as Davey's or George's or the postman's was not unappealing. The day of liberation would come, Maud said, and she would be first in line at the barber shop. Meanwhile, there was her friend Ida, whose solution was to wear a turban except on the hottest days. "Cut it off or cover it up!" Maud said, and when they passed the Bonnet Shop with its windowful of large, flowery chapeaux—very like the one Anna had pinned on for the walk—Maud turned her head away, as if from a scene of torture.

She wanted to introduce Anna to the interesting people of Amherst. Everyone would want to meet her! Mrs. Todd, the brilliant if sometimes overbearing woman who had helped with the publishing of Miss Dickinson's poems. The Reverend Morehouse, pastor of the Congregational Church, a progressive place where women had voting rights on church business and the sermons were all about justice for the downtrodden. And Maud's friend Ida Schmidt, she of the turban, a fellow crusader who was perhaps an even more ardent suffragist than Maud herself.

"I do hope you will come to one of our meetings. Every second Tuesday at noon. I will gladly call for you." Maud beamed at her, blue eyes alight.

They met Hazel for tea at the Green Valley Confectionary and Tea Room on Main Street. Inside, tiny tables, the scent of sweet things baking, waitresses in ruffled white aprons and caps, the confections written in a spidery script on a blackboard. Anna ordered a platter of cakes for the three of them.

Hazel, as Maud had said, did seem to need a pick-me-up: she was sitting alone when Anna and Maud entered, and, until she saw them and smiled and waved, her soft little face had been pinched with sadness. She had apparently been written off as unmarriageable, though it was hard to comprehend why. She was scarcely over thirty, with a delicate figure, fine eyes, a pretty mouth and chin. Anna supposed Hazel's shy reserve could be seen as aloof and her quiet loveliness overlooked. She had not inherited her mother's frank nature and easy ways and rather strenuous zest for ferment and for debate, no matter the subject. That good Italian word *gusto* was common in America (though mispronounced), and it was something Maud (and even George) had in abundance—Anna wondered if there was an Irish equivalent.

Hazel was quieter, but she had a dry humor and a lively curiosity. "I admire your daring," she said to Anna over her teacup. "What must it be like, to travel so far from everything you know?"

"It was not so much. I got on a boat and washed up at the home of my aunt."

When she smiled, Hazel resembled the statue of Persephone at Grandfather Prescott's Lake Como villa. "I'm a teacher of Latin, and the ancient poets write so eloquently about their love for Rome. Amor Romae! The most beautiful city in the world! You must miss many things."

Anna hesitated. It would be silly to deny Rome its wonders. The dome of St. Peter's, the misty hills, the winding streets, the sun on the old stone. And the grace of her father's house, with the long series of arches that led from sitting room to salon to music room to dining room to the tall doors out to the loggia, and the wide mosaic steps leading to the vast lawn and the pond with its coppery fish. The orange trees and the olives and the oleander. The summer pavilion with its four putti representing the seasons. From her balcony, the Tiber, a brilliant ribbon in the sun…

But amor Romae? When she thought about it, the only Roman thing she could truthfully say she loved was the coffee at Caffé Greco, a fact it might be tactless to admit when a steaming pot of Assam had just been set in front of her.

"I suppose I miss the gardens," she said finally. Through the tea shop window she looked out at the Common in its spring greenery, unadorned, the trees spaced to make way for the paths that crossed it. The leftover mountain of snow, she saw now, had finally melted away. "It is very different here," she said, but the differences only made her smile. They didn't make her nostalgic.

"And the ties that bind?" Maud asked. "You have lived there for so long. There must be many."

The ties that bind. Had she ever felt them? Not that she could recall. Was it because of her mother's early death? Because she was sent into the world so young? Because of something lacking in her character?

The answer to that particular conundrum was of no interest to her. "Fewer than you might expect," she said, and, reaching for a tiny cake, she changed the subject to the excellence of its cherry filling.

≈

Two days later, she drove to the Chillicks' anniversary celebration with Maud and George and Hazel in a rather grand carriage from Paige's: a fringed canopy over two seats, and Hazel up front with George behind a sleek horse named Nell. Anna offered to pay for it—"my treat," she had learned to say—but Maud shushed her. "George has been with Paige's a good twelve years, and those fellows give him whatever he wants, bless their hearts. So long as he comes to work sober."

George turned from the driver's seat and shot her a look. "Sometimes I do that, believe it or not."

Anna found their needling of each other curiously agreeable—the attachment palpable between brother and sister. They had had a grueling Irish childhood: the Mullens were impoverished and starving, they emigrated, their mother died on the ship, and Anna supposed there was worse that they had not told her. If she and Marcello—bound by the death of their own mother—had ever been able to talk to each other in such an easy and honest way, things might be very different. What a shame to rejoice that he was only half a brother. But rejoice she did.

The Chillicks' house was on the other side of the college, where the land stretched out to an orchard, a small pond, and then bright green pasture, where cows—not theirs—stood in clumps. The place had once been a working farm, and a barn and a haphazard collection of outbuildings remained—each of them with its peaked roof that, Anna now knew, was designed to shed snow in the winter.

They turned into the long drive and pulled up beside a carriage with high red wheels, a shiny black roof, a glimpse of yellow seats. "Archie's newest possession."

"It seems very fine."

"Lydia told me all about it," Maud said. "It was delivered from Kimball's not a week ago. Lydia says that to get your carriage from anyone but Kimball's is nothing short of madness, you might as well walk." She added, in an aside to Anna. "Though why I am telling you this nonsensical fact, I can't for the life of me say."

"I like to know such things."

"Well, then, I'll also tell you it's called a Rockaway, for reasons of its own. I suppose we are supposed to think of comfort. Though there's not much it can do about the ruts on the roads."

"I half expected to see the Wyatt monogram in gold on the doors." George jumped down. "You ladies go inside. I'll take Nell here out to the barn to have her supper beside Archie's matched pair. Maybe she'll learn some table manners."

The Chillicks—Tamsin and Samuel, their daughter Lydia and her husband, Archie Wyatt—welcomed Anna warmly as one of the family: it was the way Maud always referred to her and the way George had introduced her to Davey, as if there was logic to the idea that a connection forged by a kidnapping was as strong as the tie of blood.

The Chillicks' house was like her aunt Julia's in its singularly American combination of the homely (chickens, barn, woodpile) and the refined (good silver, paintings in elaborate frames). Dinner was a fat pink ham, new peas from the garden, a lobster salad with lettuces, and ice cream that Archie and Davey made themselves, taking turns cranking a contraption on the porch.

They drank George's rhubarb wine, a slightly fizzy concoction that Anna tried not to describe to herself as "surprisingly good"— she had decided by this point that nothing in Amherst could surprise her. Davey, at the end of the table, gave a brief, affectionate toast to his parents and their thirty-five years of marriage. Professor Chillick raised a glass to their children, to the grandchildren, and finally to Anna, the delightful addition to their company. You are too kind, she told him. We are lucky to have you, Anna, he said. First names all around: Maud had had her effect.

The conversation turned to Davey's professorial twin. The family had not laid eyes on Maddox since Christmas. It was not for want of badgering, Davey said: he had tried everything, from howls of anguish to promptings of guilt, but Maddox pleaded his reasons like the lawyer he was: a demanding schedule of classes, his book on the Fourteenth Amendment, and of course Caroline's pet cause, the Serbian refugees. It was thanks to one of her benefits—another blasted concert, Maddox called it—that they were unable to come to the party.

Professor Chillick—Anna knew she would have trouble with "Sam"—resembled pictures of Abraham Lincoln: tall, gaunt, serious, bearded, though with a pair of round steel spectacles perched midway on his nose. He was a professor of either astronomy or meteorology: Anna was confused, but it all had to do with weather and the skies. He would sail in a week for Brussels, where an international conference was convening to devise a sort of encyclopedia of cloud formations. The whole family, it seemed, could identify clouds by name. Even George, on the drive over, had pointed to the sky and said, "I hope we're not in for a storm. I don't like the look of that cumulonimbus," and Maud had countered with, "More of a stratocumulus, I'd say. No rain until morning, I'd bet money on it."

Tamsin Chillick, the family matriarch, was the age of Aunt Julia, but where Julia was short and fat and wheezing, Tamsin was tall and spry and brisk—no lace caps or perfume in evidence. Her snow-white hair wrapped around her head in braids, a style neither fashionable nor frumpish: she taught art at Smith College and was probably above all such considerations. Tamsin wanted to talk to Anna about music, about Rome, about her visit to New York, and when she heard that Anna had just finished *Great Expectations*, she jumped up from the table—"Ah! You're a reader!"—and left the room, returning with the novel *Roderick Hudson*, by the American writer Henry James, which Anna must read because it began in the town of Northampton, just over the river, and ended in Rome: "As if it were written with you in mind."

The jowly, freckled, amiable Archie Wyatt, a prosperous sheep farmer, explained to Anna how to tackle a 200-pound ram and shear it so that the fleece came off in one piece. He had a sideline in hogs and had not only raised the ham on the table—formerly a pig named Otto—but slaughtered it. "A happy animal makes for a succulent piece of meat," he informed Anna.

Across the table, Archie's wife, Lydia, in a dress with leg o'mutton sleeves big enough to hide a chicken, had to sit on the extreme edge of her chair to make room for her bustle. Lydia had Davey's rosy complexion and the same fullness around the jaw, but her hair was dark, like Sam's. Her conversation was all about fashion and jewelry: after a disquisition on shirtwaist brooches—whatever they might be—she complimented Anna on her pearls and asked her where they had come from. Ah, of course, Rome. Did they have good shops in Rome?

The Wyatts were the parents of a pair of small, badly behaved twins who never sat down to their dinner but chased each other in and out—Maisie and Matthew, dressed fussily in matching colors. Anna had been introduced as their new Italian auntie, and wasn't it nice of her to come all the way across the Atlantic Ocean to visit them? The question scarcely slowed them down, but when Anna called them by their Italian names, Margherita and Matteo, they stopped and gaped at her. "There's the secret to discipline," Archie said. "We all need to learn Italian. God knows, English has no effect."

There was also an older daughter, Valentine, aged fourteen, a young lady with a complicated hair arrangement, a dress almost as painfully fashionable as her mother's, and a rebellious attitude: when a forkful of lobster salad fell into Val's lap, Anna could have sworn it was deliberate. But after dinner, when they had moved into the parlor and Val was called upon to sing, her face lit up. Hazel went to the piano, and Valentine launched without self-consciousness into a bit of light opera.

It was a startling moment. The girl had a raw, powerful natural gift that cried out for good training, and Anna listened with something approaching pain, hearing herself, at the same age, in the process of having her own voice destroyed. The flutters at the high notes: she could sense Valentine pushing past them as she herself used to, purely by force. And the heaving of her flat little chest. And everything coming from the head, as if it were her only body part.

Valentine sang three lilting ditties and took her bows to applause. "Your voice is very lovely," Anna told her. Valentine's smile was cursory; she was used to praise. "Who is your teacher?"

Lydia broke in: "Miss Hortensia Finchett," as if Anna might have heard the name. Miss Finchett was teaching all the children piano and had begun giving Valentine singing lessons as well. The only music teacher in the town of Amherst, a cultivated woman who had fallen on hard times. Quite a competent pianist herself. She and her pupils performed an annual concert in the auditorium at the Amherst Town Hall.

Miss Finchett. Well. Anna took a deep breath. "I hope you will forgive me, Lydia, and I'm sure Miss Finchett is a fine pianist, but the two things—the two musical disciplines—are so very different. Is there not a real teacher of singing in Amherst? A professional who will not do harm to Valentine's voice?" Anna's words voice carried in a sudden silence, and she was conscious—as she often wasn't—of the hoarseness of her speech: You see what can happen? You see what your daughter is in for with your little pianist?

"A professional in some way Miss Finchett is not?" Lydia asked, with her kindest smile but an edge to her voice. "She has been teaching music in Amherst for two decades."

"It would be good for your daughter to work with someone who will discipline her. Choose her repertoire wisely. Teach her breath control and not push her voice too high."

"Well." Lydia's smile faded. "You seem to know a good deal about singing."

Anna had told a few people that she had once been a singer, giving no details. But she had not revealed to a soul the story of her rise and fall, not the opera-loving Hummerstons, not her doting aunt—or Flossie, who said that she and Gerald had gone to the Paris Opéra on their world tour. (And seen what? Oh—so long ago—Flossie would recognize the name of it if she heard it.) Her career was never something Anna had intended to talk about, but having heard Valentine's struggles—struggles the child did not even know she was having—she felt she must be candid.

"I was for many years a singer of opera, a soprano, until my voice gave way."

Conversation halted. Even Archie Wyatt stopped talking sheep barns with George. Valentine leaned forward in her chair. "Were you famous?"

Anna hesitated. How she hated this. "You might say so. Not in America, I never traveled here, but—well, in Europe I had—"

Could she really say that she had had twelve curtain calls at La Scala for Gilda? That she was paid one thousand pounds sterling to sing at Covent Garden? No: she found that she could not. "I had some successes."

It was Samuel Chillick who asked, peering over his glasses, "But your voice gave way, Anna? Does that mean you no longer sing?"

The room was a circle of friendly faces: concerned, sympathetic— American. *O Dio,* may I just sink into this? Let it all go. Why should I not? Here in this big, friendly house, with its barn and its chickens and its cloud formations and its beautiful children and its fat hams. Was she not one of the family? And was she perhaps getting tipsy on rhubarb wine?

She told them the story—or the outlines of it. The pretty little gift she was born with—like Valentine's. She too had been brought in to sing for her father's guests when she was young. Then came Signora Gismondi, who knew as much about teaching singing as Anna did about teaching needlework. Disastrous years of bad training, too much, too little, too early, Signora G wanting only to see her protégé onstage to prove that she was herself not a nobody, not merely—Anna glossed over this—the mistress of a rich man. The debut in *Lucia,* the worst possible mistake.

"The mad scene," Valentine breathed. "I have a book called *Great Operas of the European Repertoire.*"

Anna wanted to hug her. What a dear child, with her shining green eyes and her terrifying hopefulness. "Yes, the mad scene. Cadenza and all. I knew nothing of the world—" (Well, not quite nothing: another unspoken amendment.) "But I went mad onstage when I was sixteen, and the audience threw flowers."

And then: years of glory followed by years of panic, as her top notes turned unreliable. Throat sprays, foul-tasting lozenges, charlatan doctors, useless exercises, and then her collapse at La Fenice in *Faust,* as Marguerite, during the vocal leaps of the Jewel Song: getting through the trills, Lord only knew how, but then on the run up to the G-natural—"c'est la fille d'un roi"—gazing in wonder at her bejeweled self in the mirror and feeling the notes catch in her throat and die. The gasps of the audience. Abbadelli at the podium, his baton stuck in midair. The pain in her throat when she tried to recover. She had sunk to the stage in her finery as the curtain was brought down, knowing that if she uttered one more note it would be a croak.

"That was the end." She said the words without emotion. She had never told the story to anyone. Why would she? Everyone in Rome knew it. "I have not sung a note since. I cannot. My vocal cords have been too much damaged with little things—growths— *nodi, noduli*. Nodules, I think they would be called. Perhaps knots? It is what happens." Her hands were trembling. She folded them together in her lap and managed a smile. "My singing voice is now that of a crow, I think. Or a rusty gate."

Davey, from a chair in the corner—she had not been sure he was listening—said, "This could happen to Valentine?"

"Oh yes. It could happen to anyone, however beautiful the voice. It is all in the training."

Davey sat forward in his chair, his face as pink as Archie's ham. "I'm not the only one who's been telling you this for a year, Lydia. I know you hate to be wrong, but it's Valentine you need to think of, and I'm glad someone who knows something about it has said so outright. Hortensia Finchett is a quack."

Anna demurred—what kind of family squabble had she stepped into?—but Lydia heaved a loud sigh and sat back on her bustle. "You don't need to scold me, Davey. We have all had our doubts, and of course Val can go off to a conservatory someday to study seriously. But we didn't know we were doing her harm." She stretched her huge sleeves toward Anna—a gesture of supplication. "Could you teach her?"

Anna was not sure how to answer. The depth of Valentine Wyatt's talent remained unknown, and the amount of disciplined work she was capable of. Anna was not a professional either, but she would be leaps ahead of Miss Finchett. "I could try. We could have a few sessions, Valentine. I could show you some things, maybe correct a bad habit or two, and if you liked it we could go on. I would do nothing to damage your voice, I can at least promise you that. But it would be best to find a very, very good teacher in the next year

115

or two. If you really do wish to become a singer. Perhaps that is yet to be seen."

Valentine leaned across her mother and gripped Anna's hand. *Lucia di Lammermoor! Faust!* Both were in her book! Her face glowed. "I would rather sing than anything. Anything!"

The child's intensity was slightly terrifying. "We will do our best," Anna said. "We can have a lesson. But please do not come to it in a corset."

Before the party disbanded, Archie gave them a lively tune on the fiddle—a Scottish jig, he said, called "Devil's Dream"—unlike anything Anna had ever heard. Then Hazel sat at the piano and played a Chopin nocturne. She played well, and not without passion, but what interested Anna about her performance was Davey Chillick, who gazed at her from his chair in the corner with a look of—what to call it? Hunger. Craving. Adoration.

Gesumaria! Davey Chillick was in love with his cousin. Anna wondered if Hazel felt the same way. And, if she did, why was nothing done about it? None of the family appeared to notice what was so obvious to her, an outsider. Anna could only think that no one wished to see it because a union between cousins was probably against the law in America, as it was in Italy. Though who in Rome had not seen a half-dozen such marriages arranged—and within the Church—for one purpose only: to keep the money in the family. How much more scrupulous life was in America. Often a good thing, an improvement of the New World over the Old. But how much unhappiness could be the result.

The month of May was chillier in Amherst than in Rome. The nights were cold. One morning Anna awakened early to see footprints across the grass of the Common: there had been a frost overnight. But the day warmed up, and she wanted a longer walk than usual.

Hazel had taken her to Miss Beaman's Dress Shop on Main Street, where Anna had bought herself what was called a walking jacket: light wool, just right for a New England spring, Miss Beaman said with approval, and the pale green was ravishing with the signorina's auburn hair.

Under a canopy of trees in their yellowish spring leaves, Anna headed north on Pleasant Street, beneath a canopy of elms, toward what they called the aggie college. It was quite new, the second college in this small town. George had told her about it; he liked its practicality, the fact that it taught young men not Latin and Greek but better farming methods. It was, he said, devoted entirely to plants and animals, which struck Anna as a peculiarly American idea, both romantic and sensible. Someday, George said, the place would be the making of the town.

Now, it looked like Amherst College, its venerable cousin to the south: the usual white-pillared brick buildings lining a broad avenue. At the edge of it was an expanse of green, where, in the company of a boy and a dog, Anna watched as two draft horses pulled an ingenious piece of heavy machinery down into a pit which, a wooden sign revealed, would someday be the Campus Pond. A workman directed her to the Conservatory, a grand glass edifice ringed by rose bushes: in Rome they would have been in the first flush of bloom, here they were tight buds the size of seed pearls. Anna peered through the misty windows—damp, lavish green wherever she looked—and a man in a dark blue apron offered to let her in, the orchids were worth a visit. She thanked him but didn't stop. She had much to think about, and she had always thought clearly when she was on her feet, in motion. *La donna è mobile*, Umberto had once punned as she was setting out for a walk.

An idea had been floating in and out of her head, but today it stuck fast, like the tune of a song she was learning to sing: What would it be like to live in such a place as this?

On the ship coming over, after she stopped heaving and retching—it took four days—she would linger on deck before her dinner seating. New York, she fancied, was directly ahead, toward the setting sun, and she let herself daydream about transforming herself: settling in America, the home of her Prescott ancestors, far away from her bad memories. Then she arrived and decided she could never live in such a barbaric land.

Now she was wondering why she could not. What would it be like to settle down in a little farming town where, to see an orchid, you had to walk to the conservatory of an agricultural college? How Marcello would sneer. And not only Marcello. The supremacy of Rome over all other cities on earth was taken for granted by every Roman she knew: Nunzia Colluci had once turned down an offer of marriage to a man of fabulous wealth because she would have had to live in Florence!

But it was sailing back to Italy that now seemed an absurdity, returning to a city that, for all its flowers and marble, she had grown to dislike. And return why? For no reason except that she had lived there all her life. And that, she now knew, was not even true. She had begun her life in this corner of the world called New England. Maybe the air we breathe with our newborn squalls settles somewhere deep inside, waiting to blow us back to what we knew first.

She was thirty-six years old: no husband, no child, no family, no home that beckoned. Where was she to live? Sweden? Argentina? Tibet?

It was Amherst, Massachusetts, that was beginning to feel like home. That was the strange and improbable truth.

She made her way back toward the hotel by a roundabout route that took her down streets lined with houses set on broad lawns, past trees whose names she didn't know, and east again to Main Street. She passed the sawmill, the hat factory, the depot, the Dickinson houses, the Congregational Church, and back to the corner and the grim fortress that was the Town Hall. The chestnut trees on the Common, with their yellow-green leaves, were like those in Rome—but different too, less imposing, surrounded as they were by the compact and agreeable town. Everything was plain and simple. The finest dwellings were farmhouses made of wood and brick— foursquare, with many-paned windows and tall painted doors. Both George and Tamsin had told her with pride that the oldest building in town—one of the white houses on the hill of the college—was put up nearly 200 years ago, in 1700. A few weeks ago she would have considered this amusing. Now she thought: why are old things more admirable than new? Why should there be only one kind of beauty? Why should America try to look like Europe? Everywhere she had visited in this country was New: first York, then Haven, now England! These were people who were proud of their short history, and who lived in contentment among their newness. In this country of New This and New That, the buildings *should* be new! Rome was perfect as it was, but so was Amherst.

And the vital difference was this: here she had no history. Her mind could stretch out in a kind of freedom—that big American idea! In the window of Sanderson's Dry Goods on Merchants Row, as part of a display of straw hats and picnic baskets, was a banner: LET FREEDOM RING. She was not sure what it meant, but it seemed a noble sentiment, and the words stayed in her head.

She walked on, around the Common to Grace Church. The ivy that grew thick on the façade was alive with the chirpings of small birds, and on the church porch were pots of pink and blue flowers Anna did not recognize. The place reminded her of the medieval chapel of Santa Paulina in Florence. But of course it was not a medieval chapel, just a pleasing copy of one, a building possibly not as old as she was.

In the vestibule, she dropped a coin into a box marked OFFER-INGS and went through an ornately carved door to the church proper: pointed arches and Gothic vaulting, dusty light, the smell of candle wax. Someone was practicing on a superior organ: Palestrina? Only a red-bound stack of *The Book of Common Hymns* revealed that she was not in the fourteenth century.

She slipped into a pew and sat down to rest. She unlaced her boots, wrapped her walking jacket around herself, closed her eyes, and sank into a reverie: her own house, a shed and a hen coop behind it, vegetables growing in what was called a *patch*. Learning the names of alien trees and plants. Buying hats at the Bonnet Shop, dresses at Miss Beaman's, going to suffrage meetings with Maud. Attending this funny little church on a Sunday, maybe not to pray, but to listen to the music. To say good morning to people she would come to know. To be a citizen of the community. The Italian woman who had chosen to grace the town with her exotic presence. Wasn't her English surprisingly good? And she only looked foreign from certain angles. No husband, but friends who loved her. Her cats Stella and Salvatore waiting by the door.

A new, more *prudent* Anna Felice: was this not just the place for her?

Chapter 8

21 May 1892
My dear Maddox,

Yes, I gave the toast, since I had no choice. It seems unfair that you've gloated for nearly forty years that you beat me into the world by ten minutes but, when you should be fulfilling your duty as eldest child, you conveniently forget. My oration was short but seemed to do the job. Lydia (of course) reproached me for my failure to mention this and that. But who listens to Lydia?

The party was not unbearable. The merriment flowed like George's wine, and vice versa. Sam gave a tribute to you and Caroline and Tobias, with some grumbling at your absence but all glasses raised and a loud "Hear, hear!" Perhaps around five o'clock you felt a sudden flood of remorse and wished you were in Amherst, eating lobster and ham in the bosom of your family? But I hope Caroline's concert for the Serbians went off well and didn't require too much heroism of you.

Speaking of musical treats, Valentine sang for us. The Italian signorina was present. She was duly referred to as "one of the family" at least six times. Anna (yes, it's all first names now) was much taken with Val and has offered to give her singing lessons in lieu of the hopeless Miss Finchett, and Lydia was much taken with the suggestion because Anna would do it for free. Val is hypnotized by her, having learned that she was once an opera singer who performed in Italy and France and Germany. Not that Val had ever heard of La Scala, but, now that she has, she is enchanted, and wants to go to Italy, preferably tomorrow.

And here I would like to ask your advice—which is really what this letter is about. I am troubled, Maddox, by Hazel's intended, Stefan Dubrowsky. Who is this man? Yes, some of us have met him—for an hour or two—and some of us (Hazel especially, of course) found him agreeable. She says Calvin values him highly, but is that only because he knows his apricots? And what brought him from New York all the way to California? The family is in Poland except for a sister in New York—Brooklyn, I seem to recall—and that is all anyone knows. I can't bear to send Hazel off to such an uncertain future.

After much self-torture, I wrote to Calvin with a few questions, but we all know Cal is better at writing books than he is at writing letters. I wonder if you know someone from your New York days who could make discreet inquiries about Stefan Dubrowsky and his wife Kasia, or Katarzina (not sure how to spell that), immigrants from Poland. Kasia died giving birth to their son, Victor. Does Jack Truesdale still practice law there? He is a good man. At least, he was a good first baseman back in college. I may be harboring mistrust and apprehension because I have read too many Sherlock Holmes stories. Or because I am so full of love for Hazel I can't see things straight. Or because too much solitude has made me strange beyond all hope. This is very possible. And I know my suspicions are vague and unfounded: they are not even suspicions. But I'm willing to look foolish, and I know you will be honest with me, and I will value your advice.

A last note: Archie informed us that in fifty years every street in every city in this country will be buried nine feet deep in horse manure. One wonders if bicycles or even horseless carriages will eventually replace horses. Horseless carriages, I have learned, are called "automobiles," and no one seems to know on which syllable the stress of the word falls: Archie swears it's AUT and George MO. Archie is very keen on having one, however it's pronounced, and Lydia said (hands clasped under chin, eyes radiant, as if seeing a vision of paradise), "Wouldn't it be something to have the first one in Amherst?"
Your loving brother,
Davey

๛๑๑

28 May, 1892
My dear Maddox,

Caroline in Paris! I will not say I had no suspicion that you and your wife were not happy together. What astounds me is not the difficulties in your marriage—though perhaps their extent (and, I must confess, their nature) is a little unantici-pated—but the fact that you're terminating it. Do not think I disapprove. The world is full of unlucky and unloving couplings, and many of them go on for years and years, until the misery of it kills one of them off. I applaud your decision, and hope it will not have a bad effect on Tobias. As you say, to live in a house that is not wracked by discord cannot but be an improvement in his life. And the intrusion of this ridiculous Serbian poet is outrageous! Yes, you had mentioned him (and his black mustachios and his dueling pistols), but I had no idea it had gone so far. What is the woman thinking?

I'll take this opportunity, and hope you will not resent it, to say that I never understood why instead of that delightful girl Betsy (her surname escapes me: Linford? Linton? At any rate, I would have bet my best shirt on her) you chose Caroline Vandermeer.

But the past is past, carrying all our mistakes and stupidities with it as it flows along. For now, please tell me if I can be of assistance to you. I promise to say nothing to anyone in the family, until you tell me I may—though I suspect Mother, at least, may sense something is amiss. The two of you—and especially Caroline—have been so elusive this past year.

Here is a thought: Would it be helpful if Tobias spent the summer in Amherst? And another (imagine me gritting my teeth as I write this): If it would make your life easier in any way for me to come to Boston, I would do it.

As for Stefan Dubrowsky, I'm heartened that you don't think I'm being over-cautious. And I understand that it may be some time before Jack Truesdale can look into the question. Just knowing you've written to him eases my mind. Hazel hasn't confided in me lately, so I don't know what stage the negotiations have reached between her and Sacramento. She has still not told Maud about it, and so perhaps she hasn't yet given him a definite answer.

I suppose what I have lived with all these years is a kind of hope. The thing with feathers, as Miss Dickinson put it in her own curious way. If Hazel is off to California, it will fly there with her. And then where will I be?

Of course, the more immediate thing with feathers is Owosha, and her hopes are all for a rodent or a pigeon. So off I go to abet her and her filthy appetites.

Your devoted brother,

Davey

Chapter 9

I t took her more than a week to decide what she wanted to say, to get it right—first in her mind and then on paper. A week of bad sleeping, when she lay awake in her bed under the eaves in a kind of terror. Her mother's gentle snores from across the hall. Somewhere a coyote barking. George getting up in the night to visit the outhouse. The hazy morning light crept around her curtain as she considered phrases—*I look forward, I have decided, I do believe*—and rejected them. At the edge of her consciousness, an image stayed sharp: Davey sitting slumped with his legs stretched out before him, the cuffs of his shirt rolled to the elbow. "I wish you would not go," he had said over the sound of the pounding rain, and she had wanted to reach across the sleeping cat, take his hand, and tell him she would not, she would never, she couldn't.

Her apprehensions seemed boundless. The heat would make her ill. The child would be ungovernable. The well would run dry. How far was the ranch from a doctor? From shops and stores? Would she have to make everything herself: bread, aprons, blankets? She would be worked off her feet, like a frontier wife. And what about love?

Many nights, she gave up trying to sleep, went to her desk, lit the lamp, and took a fresh piece of paper. Composed a new draft, shredded it, began over again, pivoting between *Yes I will be your wife* and *I must give you a final answer that I fear you will not like.* Variations on her displeasure at being pressed. A whole page of *How can I leave this place, how can I leave the people I love*—scrawled over and over with something close to despair. Others that spoke about the passage of time, her loneliness. In one mad version, she wrote with longing about the hour they had spent together, now nearly a year ago. *I would not have objected if you had embraced me.* She wasn't sure that was true. What, in fact, would she have done if such an inconceivable thing had happened, there on her aunt's porch? *Or kissed me,* she wrote in her boldest handwriting. A shiver went through her, like the flicker of a candle flame. *You could have kissed me. That is how close I felt to you!*

Exclamation point. Oh, Hazel. She put down her pen with a kind of horror, and tore the paper into confetti. Her small wastepaper basket was half full.

Finally, one morning toward dawn, she settled on a plain statement of intent. She would travel to Sacramento in the fall. In September. October at the latest. She wanted very much to see him again, and to talk. To get to know Victor. To see the ranch, and his house with its new addition. To view a landscape that seemed so— she searched for the right word: alien, strange, foreign—*dissimilar* to the one she knew. It was difficult to promise anything, and she was not someone who acted on things quickly, but if they still liked each other as much as they had when they met last year she would be honored to become his wife.

Reading it over, she could see that it expressed what she felt, but it was not a warm letter. *I hope*, she wrote at the end, and then wasn't sure what should follow it. *I hope we can be happy.* She stared at the words for many long minutes before she signed her name.

All the next day, the letter in the pocket of her dress, she thought almost unceasingly of Stefan out there in California on the ranch. Doing what? How little she knew about this man who might become her husband. Calvin had described the suffocating heat of a Sacramento Valley summer—close to a hundred degrees, even in May—so when she pictured Stefan he was in shirtsleeves, sweating, mopping his forehead, looking forward to a cold glass of beer at the end of the day. To imagine herself there with him—fanning herself on a veranda, making apricot jam, teaching Latin to her stepson—was beyond her ability. But she did not need to imagine it, only to reach up to the shelf and do it.

It was not until after supper, when the sun was beginning its slow red decline behind the hills, that she walked down to the post box on the corner. This was the sixth letter she had written to Stefan Dubrowsky and, except for the very first one, by far the shortest. She stood there holding the letter—now slightly crumpled. Maybe she should rewrite it. She waited, her eyes shut tight, thinking: *I cannot, I cannot.* The bell on the Episcopal church began its slow series of clangs, and between the sixth and the seventh she stilled her mind, opened her eyes, and dropped the letter through the slot.

Chapter 10

O n Decoration Day, the odd name given to the remembrance of the men who were lost in the war, Anna went with Maud and Hazel and George to the cemetery where Maud's husband was buried. When she had walked there a month before, the place was abandoned and desolate. Now it was full of people arranging flags and flowers and plants and little tokens on the graves.

Charles Cooper lay under a stone with a handsome Civil War marker and his sad dates: 1830–1874. What a short life the poor man had had. Maud and Hazel stood arm in arm. Lydia, in voluminous black and carrying a frilly black parasol, laid an enormous wreath on the grave. George, somber and a little drunk, said, "A grand lad, he was, and that's the truth," and Anna was reminded again that, if Charles Cooper hadn't been such a grand lad, willing to dash through the streets of New Haven to free Prudence Ann Prescott from captivity, Anna Felice would not be standing at his grave.

And where would she be instead?

As they were leaving, Maud paused by the marker for Miss Dickinson, the poetess: a plain gray stone carved only with her initials. Anna was no longer surprised at the frugality of Americans. "Safe in their alabaster chambers," Maud murmured. A line from a poem, she explained, brushing off some pine needles, and, with her hat sitting crookedly on her cloud of gray hair, she closed her eyes and recited the whole thing: "untouched by morning, untouched by noon," and something about the sweet birds continuing to sing, and "what sagacity is buried there."

Maud spoke it beautifully: it was not difficult to imagine her on a stage before an audience. Then she sighed. "You may not know that Charles returned from the war with one arm missing—his writing arm. He dictated to Hazel and me, mostly letters to old comrades and to wives and mothers of those who did not come home. He used to laugh about it—his poor old arm, he would call it, lying out in the rain and the snow at Gettysburg, wishing it could hold a pen again. I can still hear his voice—still see his face."

How old could Maud have been when he died? Barely forty. And Hazel just emerging from childhood. "What a terrible thing for you."

"Yes. But I do not mean to exalt my own grief over anyone else's." Maud took her arm, and they walked on. "I try to remember that we have all felt this. We all know what it's like to love someone so much."

Anna was silent. No, we did not all know what it was like. The look in Maud's eyes as she stood by the grave. Anna had had that look only when she was on stage. Carmen, Norma, Violetta, Lucia. *Il dolce suono…. Al fin son tua, al fin sei mio….*

What nonsense.

She wondered sometimes if what she wished for was not an actual man to love, but just the feeling of it: the passion, the tenderness, the intensity. It came to her so easily on stage, when she was singing—pretending. But it never seemed like pretending. Maybe what she missed when people talked about love was simply her voice, and her life as a singer.

And yet she envied people who did know what it was like, even those who had lost the object of their love. Lately, they surrounded her. Maud and her wifely grief. Poor Davey with a hawk instead of a Hazel. Pip and the cold-hearted Estella. Even Mary Garland, the jilted young woman in *Roderick Hudson*, the novel Tamsin had lent her. The losses were unfortunate, but a kind of happiness had been theirs, a feeling Anna had never known. She asked herself: Who have

I loved? Her child when she was carrying her. Mamma, though she hardly remembered her. Little gray Tosca, killed by one of Papa's dogs.

Umberto? No, she had not loved Umberto. But, after her humiliation at La Fenice, his adoration had no longer wearied her: it was a solace. And he was as handsome as the statue of Hermes at the Vatican, with his broad shoulders and full lips and masses of reddish curls. She remembered how he would pick her up in his arms and carry her to bed. And how, for their first year or two, before pregnancy made her repulsive to him and his cruel stupidities made him hateful to her, their lovemaking was—

This was not something to dwell on.

Making her way through the densities of *Roderick Hudson* as if through mud, Anna conceived a desire to visit Northampton, described by Henry James as a "dull backwater." She told Hazel she had never seen a dull backwater: she pictured a smaller, more rustic Amherst, where cows still grazed on the Common. Hazel laughed. She had gone to the women's college in Northampton. It had no Common, she said, and in fact was no duller than Amherst—maybe less. As a young man, Henry James had spent a period of time there in search of a cure for the constipation from which he suffered for many years: an unsurprising ailment, to anyone who had read his constricted prose. He had described the town as not only a backwater but a stupid and vulgar one—his very words—maybe because his ailment hadn't been cured. But Northampton had its river, the longest in New England. And some good dress shops. And the dining room at the Hotel Northampton served peach tapioca!

Anna was intrigued by peach tapioca—another American mystery. She and Hazel would go to Northampton. Seeing the Connecticut River would be part of her American education. More practically, the weather was warming up, and she needed two or three simple, comfortable cotton dresses like the ones Hazel and Tamsin wore. She wanted to shop and see things, but she also wanted to give

Hazel a treat: the carriage ride, at least, and luncheon. And maybe Hazel would let Anna buy her a dress.

Anna was always conscious of the frugality Hazel lived by, and of her own wealth, which had just increased: after a series of cables, Signor Morelli had sold the apartment in Rome with such remarkable speed that she suspected the price should have been higher, or that Morelli himself had found a way to make a quick profit on it. But no matter: the important thing was that she no longer owned it.

While she was in the Western Union office, she also canceled her booking on the *Britannia*. The clerk was obliging: And did Madame wish to book passage on another ship? Thank you, no, Madame was not quite ready to do that.

She had not told anyone about her decision, if it was indeed a decision, to stay in Amherst—how long? Forever? Was there such a word as *forever* in her life? She had told no one because she feared it would be seen as a mad idea. Daft, Maud would say. And yet was Maud not herself an immigrant? And George? Living in a nation of immigrants? Why should Anna Felice not be one? It seemed daft only because she was fleeing not poverty and starvation but an apartment with ten rooms and views from every window, a villa in Tivoli that Morelli would also be disposing of, a safe deposit box that held her mother's jewelry and her father's gold. She was leaving behind a vast wedge of Felice family history, and she could not find within herself the tiniest shred of concern.

Anna and Hazel set off in one of Paige's best hansom cabs—Hazel appalled by the expense—an elegant black affair with narrow yellow wheels, pulled by a white horse and with gap-toothed Isaac Paige driving. They went at a good pace through the town of Hadley—corn fields, tobacco, onions, Anna was interested in it all—and over the bridge to Northampton, past a row of large and very fine houses, another thin-steepled church, the cemetery where Hazel said Archie Wyatt's people were buried. Isaac set them down at the corner of Market Street and would retrieve them at the hotel at three o'clock. He cast his eyes up to the heavens and said he'd pray the rain held off.

The town was unremarkable, Anna thought—very like Amherst, but not as pleasing. The Northampton town hall loomed even more gracelessly than Amherst's. The lack of a central Common was a grievous defect, as if the place was unfinished. And instead of being thronged with dashing young men the streets were full of hatless, uncorseted Smith College girls, striding along with book-bags slung over their shoulders.

Hazel had gone to a preparatory school in Amherst where the male students dominated—they were louder, more confident, unafraid of rudeness or sarcasm. In college it was restful, she said, to attend classes among women only, though there were male teachers—she pointed out to Anna the home of the Latin professor who used to invite the girls for tea, and the yellow brick building where she had had piano lessons with an elderly, irascible *musiklehrer* who had been a student of Czerny. When they came to the turreted rooming house she had lived in, Anna regarded it with something like envy, thinking how different their lives had been. At eighteen Hazel Cooper was studying Latin and literature in a quiet little river town, a few miles from her family; Anna Felice at the same age was touring the continent of Europe as a singer, living in hotels, evading the attentions of corpulent tenors and infatuated aficionados—and in the process ruining her voice, losing the part of her life that made her most happy.

She didn't speak of it: Hazel had heard enough about her troubles. And it was all water under the bridge, as she had heard someone say—meaning that those days had passed and would not come back, and thank the *buon Dio* for that.

She still found it a novelty to go into shops rather than having a milliner or a dressmaker come to her. Not since she was married to Umberto had she gone into a shop in Italy. Umberto (this she did not tell Hazel) liked to buy her jewelry on the Via Condotti—at Bertollini's, Lamberti's—not from generosity but from the need to show off his money and his taste—and his wife. Anna had left behind in Rome everything Umberto gave her, even though some pieces were very elegant. She disliked even thinking about them. Let Giovannina have them—her maid but also her closest relative: she would write to her attorney. He could arrange these things.

Anna and Hazel made their way up one side of Main Street and down the other. Anna came away with a pink seersucker dress and a shirtwaist—she had not known what they were called, the starchy blouses everyone wore, including the Smith girls. She also bought a straw hat trimmed with daisies. Hazel bought two of the simple frocks she invariably wore, called wash dresses: not only, Anna hoped, because they were cheap and practical. Hazel—like her mother—seemed without vanity, but surely she knew how well they looked on her. At Miss Fry's Fine Ladies Dresses, Anna urged Hazel to let her buy her a gift, something she would never think to get for herself: like a ravishing black-and-white-striped gown that Miss Fry informed them was made of "Hoboken silk" (could there really be such a word?) and would look very smart on the young lady.

Hazel said it was much too smart for her, and added, suddenly, "Though it might do for a wedding dress." Her voice trembled on the words. She took a ragged breath, as if barely keeping in check some wild desolation, and then, while Anna and Miss Fry watched in horror, her face crumpled and she burst into tears.

Which is how Miss Hazel Cooper imparted to Signorina Anna Felice the news that she was contemplating marriage with a fruit-grower in California—a man she hardly knew, who had gray eyes and a nine-year-old son!

They left the silk dress behind and walked two blocks to the Hotel Northampton, Hazel apologizing all the way, her arm through Anna's, her face blotched with the remnants of tears. They were shown to a table. Hazel asked for a glass of water and drank it down. Another glass was poured. Anna ordered chicken croquettes. Hazel was not hungry.

She told Anna more about the situation, which she insisted was not yet a true engagement: she had met this man once, he worked for her cousin Calvin on his ranch in Sacramento, taking care of the orchards. She had told him she needed to know him better before she could think of marrying him, and that she would make the trip to California in the fall to stay with Calvin and his family. She and Stefan would talk, they would—well, Hazel did not know what they would do. But she saw this as her last chance at some sort of happiness.

She had not talked about it with her mother. Why? Hazel could not explain. Or yes, she could. It was all so dreamlike: there were so many miles between them, she had spent an hour with him, he had probably forgotten how plain she was. She remembered him very well—no, in fact, she remembered him hardly at all, could hardly bring to mind his face, though she did remember his light gray eyes. And why would he want her—the tears threatened again—why would anyone want her?

Anna laid her hand on Hazel's wrist. How had this sweet young woman come to see herself as such small coinage? And why—Anna paused a moment to frame the question, abruptly conscious of being from a world where things were done differently—why had not this Stefan Dubrowsky written to Hazel's mother? Or perhaps her uncle George? And should Hazel not speak of this to someone she was directly related to? Or was this the informal way marriages were accomplished in America?

Food was put in front of them, water glasses refilled. Hazel looked exhausted: eyes damp, nose red, wisps of hair escaped from their moorings, but it was obvious that there was more she wanted to say. Anna asked the waiter to bring a glass of sherry for each of them—they did not have an Amontillado, they could bring an Oloroso. Had Hazel ever drunk such a thing? No matter: when it was set in front of her, she took a sip, then another. Yes, she said. She had spoken of it to someone: she had told her cousin Davey.

Ah. "And what did Davey have to say?" Anna stabbed at a croquette: rather dry. She dipped it into mayonnaise: better.

"He said he wished I would not leave Amherst and move to California."

"Well, yes, there is that to consider."

"And that we know so little about Stefan."

"That too."

135

"But, most of all," Hazel said, "he wants my happiness, and so he is resigned to my leaving. I'm sure this is the conclusion everyone will come to, finally, when I let it be known that I have accepted Stefan."

Anna thought of Aunt Julia and Flossie. "Your mother too?"

"Even my mother. She has said many times that she doesn't want me to have a life of loneliness…"

"I'm surprised the two of you have never made a match of it."

"The two of us?"

"You and Davey Chillick."

Hazel's cheekbones turned bright pink. "Davey!" The word came out in a squawk, as if Anna had stuck a knife into her bosom. "Cousins do not marry."

"Surely you know that Queen Victoria of England married her first cousin."

"I am not a queen."

An onlooker might call Anna's sigh exasperated. "First, have another sip of sherry. And then you may be able to tell me why the only reason you will not consider marrying the man you love is that you are not the queen of England."

"I did not say my cousin Davey is the man I love."

"You did not say it in words, but there it was, plain as afternoon."

Hazel sat silent, looking toward the window. Anna could almost hear her brain rattling around in her head as a new idea took hold. Anna let a minute go by, and then she picked up her glass. "To cousinly affection."

Hazel raised hers. "To common sense." She had collected herself; her voice was firm. "I have never allowed myself to think about such a thing."

"And yet you will allow yourself to think about going on the railway to California and throwing yourself into the arms of a stranger. When you have someone right here in Amherst who is dying of love for you."

Hazel stared at her. "How can you know that?"

"How can you not?"

"It is ridiculous."

L'amour est un oiseau rebelle. Anna wished she could sing a few bars. Hazel would not know the opera; *Carmen* would not have reached Northampton. They had passed the Academy of Music: a signboard advertised a revue, with scenes from *The Barber of Seville* and *Aida*, along with "dance numbers and juggling."

Anna had been Carmen in Paris—how many years ago? The role was never right for her voice, and yet, even now, the "Habañera" hovered closer to the edge of her memory than anything else she had sung, gorgeous and electrifying.

Hazel would never agree that love was a rebel bird, or a gypsy child, or anything but this last-chance desperation—as if she were on a rushing train and had to get off or perish, no matter what the station. But Anna felt she must try once more. "Surely," she said, "you have noticed how Davey feels. Why is that so ridiculous?"

"Davey Chillick the hermit in his cabin, and Hazel Cooper the Amity Street spinster."

"Could a pair be better suited?"

Hazel managed a laugh—it was admirable, heroic—and Anna rewarded it: Yes, let us call it a joke, a sherry-induced fancy of Signorina Felice. She changed the subject to the peach tapioca. The waiter brought two dishes—a strange concoction but delicious after one got used to it—and they had an amiable and very enlightening talk about the works of Henry James and the theme of naïve young Americans confronted with European decadence. Hazel asked Anna if reading about Italy was making her homesick, and Anna said a novel needed to be written about an Italian woman who flees the decadence of Rome for the peace and the safety and the plain white houses of New England!

Isaac retrieved them and their bundles at the hotel, and they drove back to Amherst as the sky paled and clouds gathered. Davey Chillick's name was not again mentioned, nor Stefan Dubrowsky's. They arrived at Amity Street rather late, in a cold drizzle that poor Isaac apologized for as if he had brought it down from the skies himself. George bustled out with an umbrella to help them inside. He had been watching for them: a telegram had come for Hazel.

Maud was huddled into her shawl by the fire, looking apprehensive and suddenly older, and the eternal pot of tea waited on the table.

Hazel sank into a chair. George, Maud, Anna—they all crowded around—and, when she tore it open, the words leapt out at them, stark black: ARRIVING FRIDAY. WILL EXPECT ANSWER. STEFAN.

Chapter 11

Maddox and Tobias got to Amherst on Wednesday, on the noon train from Boston. Archie and Lydia met them at the station: Tobias would spend the summer with the Wyatts, persuaded by the prospect of helping Uncle Archie on the farm, watching the new sheep barn go up, playing with the new litter of Scotch collies.

After Tobias was settled in, Maddox showed up on South Pleasant Street for supper. Sam had left for Brussels. Maddox kissed his mother, clasped Davey's hand, voiced the usual ritualized complaints about Lydia's officiousness. It was Tilda's day off, and Tamsin had made a chicken fricassee for Davey and Maddox.

"With carrots, I hope," Maddox said.

"Without carrots, I hope."

"Your brother is a guest, Davey. You can pick the carrots out."

"I wasn't being serious. It's just that twins are always trying to differentiate themselves."

"You two have differentiated yourselves so thoroughly I'd forget you were twins if I hadn't been present at your birth."

Maddox had still told no one but his brother about the flight of Caroline and the end of his marriage, but they talked about Hazel and the prospect of hers. Stefan would be arriving in two days.

Tamsin was of the firm opinion that a secret betrothal was wrong: Hazel should have told her mother.

"And Maud would have been the first to point out that Hazel is of an age to make her own decisions. If women are going to get the right to vote and choose politicians, surely they have a right to choose their own husbands." Maddox took a forkful of stew. As always, when he got excited, his eyes burned, his eyebrows bristled. He had never been a trial lawyer, but in a courtroom he would have been ferocious. Davey, beside him, seemed made of a softer substance entirely. He had spent his first twenty-odd years regretting that he wasn't more like Maddox. Now he knew that being his twin for only a day would exhaust him for the rest of the week.

"But Maud was hurt," Tamsin said. "Deeply. It's not that this man had to ask for her hand, or that Hazel had to get her mother's permission to marry. But it was cruel to keep it to herself."

Davey poured himself another glass of wine. "I suppose she had her reasons."

"If Hazel burned down the barn you would say she had her reasons."

"I'd put money on it."

After supper, Davey and Maddox walked to Mount Norwottuck, over the fields toward Granby to the pass called the Notch, and up the rugged western path—the one they called the Nonotuck: hard-trampled dirt, bordered by clusters of the delicately glowing bluets that always reminded Davey of Hazel. End-of-day sunlight dappled through the new leaves, casting long shadows. The valley spread out below them in the clear air: west and south, low hills stretching down to the river with its oxbow—to the north the colleges, farmland and woodland, and in the far distance the dark mountains of Vermont.

Maddox asked, "How many times have you walked up here with Billy Fox?"

"Four thousand nine hundred and eighty-two."

"You're positive?"

"Could be eighty-three, or eighty-one. I was drunk at least once."

"How is Billy? I haven't seen him in a year or more."

"Billy Fox is the way he always is and no different."

"May he ever be. I hope to stay long enough next time to see him."

"He would be glad of it."

They sat on an outcropping near the summit that looked out over the rock and the trees to the huge blue sky and the border of hills to the south. The chimneys and gables of the town lay below. Somewhere in that maze of green, Hazel would be in the kitchen, wearing her apron, washing up the supper dishes. It was a moment he wished could go on forever: the green world spread out before him, and Hazel in it.

After a minute, Maddox asked, "Do you want to talk more about it?"

"What is there to say?"

Davey had not seen Hazel since his parents' anniversary party. He had been doing well, he thought, proposing toasts and filling glasses and putting up with Lydia's nonsense and the children's shenanigans. Then, after dinner, Hazel sat down at the piano and began to play a Chopin nocturne. His mother was leaning forward eagerly, little Matthew had flopped down on the carpet in exhaustion, the sun slanted between two lace panels at the window—and then the room around him disappeared, nothing left but Hazel's small head bent in concentration over the keys. And the quiet pain of his love for her.

"I wish we would hear from Jack Truesdale. Even from Calvin." Maddox took his pipe from his pocket and struck a match against the rock. "I would like to know more about this man. Though I suppose his making the journey here shows that he loves her. That is something."

"Of course he loves her! If he doesn't now, if it's just that he wants a wife, then he soon will. How could he not?"

Beside him, Maddox drew on pipe and ground out the match beneath his boot sole, saying nothing. Davey sighed heavily. "Oh blast it, Maddox. I'm being a clod. It's you who are going through the real calamity—not some harebrained hankering but the upheaval of your entire life. It's your sea of troubles we should be talking about, not my tiny fishpond."

Maddox blew out a cloud of smoke and uttered a sound between a laugh and a groan. "I can bear the upheaval, believe me. I will not miss Caroline. Over the years she has revealed herself as someone I haven't the least understanding of. I suppose she would say that's the problem. But I don't really know what she would say, since we now communicate only by letter. An occasional telegram. The last one said: LEGRAND NEEDS COPIES ALL DEEDS WILLS ASSETS STATEMENTS CERTIFICATES. PLEASE PROVIDE BY 15 JUNE. Signed with her initials. Legrand is her Paris lawyer. The divorce is now an international phenomenon."

"Well, my brother, as someone who has known you all your life, I must say that Legrand knows not whom he is dealing with."

"My taste for ruthless negotiation was one of the reasons I decided not to practice law. I figured teaching would be better for my character." Maddox chuckled. "But the relish for it has not left me. Caroline will be provided for, but she will not get everything she wants. Her own income from the Vandermeers is enough to keep the poet in mustache wax and champagne."

"And then there is Tobias."

"It's not easy to be abandoned by your mother. But it's part of my ruthlessness that Caroline will not see him, except in my house. He is not going to be shipped off to Europe for his school vacations like some hapless child in a novel."

"Do you remember when Mother left Father? Spirited us away to the depot in the dark of night. We never saw him again."

"But we thought about him."

"Yes. And we survived it. Tobias will too."

"I hope so. I want him to be in Amherst as much as possible, with his grandparents and his cousins. His uncle Davey. If you hear about anything for sale, I'd like to know. I thought Tobias and I might spend our summers here."

"Archie wants to make a farmer of him."

"What a good idea. Nothing would horrify Caroline more."

They sat a while longer, Maddox quietly smoking, Davey watching a buzzard circle over the trees below, lazily zeroing in on something. *Oh, to be a buzzard,* Hazel had said. Nobody puts them in cages. He thought of Owosha on her perch, enclosed, constrained, and thought: how funny that his own life was not unlike the life of his hawk. And he had closed the door on it himself, by choice.

Oh, to be a buzzard....

Maddox stood up. "We should head home before it gets dark."

They started back down, the setting sun at their backs. Davey walked behind his brother's reassuring bulk. Having Maddox in town always brightened his existence. "Name the clouds," he said.

Maddox stopped on the trail. "What? Oh. Let me see." He spoke around his pipe stem, squinting into the sky. "Cirrocumulus? Just a guess. Unlike the system of writs, identifying cloud formations is a pocket of knowledge I've probably lost."

"Not a bad guess, but I think they're just good old altocumulus. Unexciting except for the sunset colors."

"Sam would have my head."

"What different things we learned from our two fathers. Clouds and weather and astronomy from one. And from the other—"

"The solace of crying ourselves to sleep after a beating."

"Ah, but music too, Maddox. Don't forget that. Also some Welsh." When the twins were little boys, their private language had been part English, part Welsh, part words of their own devising. They'd forgotten their father's language years ago, overwhelmed by a new life, a new father, a new lightness of heart in their mother. All they had left were bits of songs. "Owosha likes me to sing in Welsh," Davey said. "She can't tell when I'm faking. At least I don't think so." He broke into "Ar Hyd y Nos." Maddox joined him, laughing, but they soon gave up. "Val sings it. In English. 'All Through the Night,' of course. It's very effective."

"She should learn the Welsh."

"I would not be surprised if the formidable signorina knows the language and could teach it to her."

"I must meet this signorina."

"She has landed among us like a tanager in a nest of sparrows. I already have the two of you married off. You have much in common. She had a husband, but he was mysteriously annulled out of existence in Rome."

"So we know as little about her as we do about Stefan Dubrowsky."

143

"Ah, you're forgetting. Our family has known her since she was a baby."

"I'm always willing to meet an old family friend, especially if she's a pretty woman. Maybe Mother will invite her to lunch on my next visit."

"I believe few things would give Mother greater pleasure. She and Anna have become great chums. In fact, there has been chatter in the henhouse about inviting her to move into the back bedroom while Sam is away. You know how Mother hates to be alone in the house."

"She's always got you."

"Yes, brooding like a toad in my cabin. Not exactly a sparkling table companion, even for one's mother."

They took a shortcut across a tobacco field, walking single file between the young plants, then over the Fort River and past the gristmill toward home. A lamp shone in the window of Tamsin's bedroom, a smaller one in the kitchen to light the way.

Davey stopped before he went down the drive to the cabin. "You are going to tell Mother about Caroline, I hope. You saw how Hazel's secrecy disturbed her."

"I did, and I will, this very night." Maddox started up the steps, then turned. "And Davey? Are you going to be all right? Sometimes I think it's you I should be worried about. Your solitary existence."

"Your worry capital can be applied to more profitable ends. I thrive on being alone. Why else would I live in a cabin? Maybe I'll mind it more when I'm an old man. Maybe someday Ida and I will make a match of it. I would almost do it to see the look on Lydia's face."

"If you'd stop joking, you'd see that I meant this blasted Hazel situation. Knowing how much you'll miss her."

"That's different from solitude." Davey looked up at the night sky: quarter moon, wisps of cloud flitting across the darkening blue. "You know—I sometimes get pictures in my head of the simplest things. Myself sitting at the kitchen table, holding the baby while Hazel stirs something in a pot on the stove. Or sometimes—well—"

He broke off. "It's all nonsense. I would not tell it to anyone but my brother."

"It's Hazel you should tell it to. You've got until Friday."

Davey laughed and clapped his brother on the back. "Don't worry about me. Go talk to Mother and convince her that one of her sons, at least, is a rational human being."

He walked to his cabin, poured some whiskey, and went outside again to sit on the bench near Owosha's enclosure. The hawk stirred, a black shape in the darkness—like a football, Davey thought. Then she tucked her head under her wing; he couldn't see her do it, but he knew the whispering sound of feather on feather.

The night was absolutely still, the moon above the barn blurry at the edges. He closed his eyes, and Hazel was sitting on his lap, warm and nearly weightless, her head on his shoulder.

৵৵৽৽

A letter arrived next day from Calvin:

> *The story, what I know of it, is a sad one. Stefan's wife died in childbirth soon after they arrived from Poland. A devastating blow for a young man trying to make his way in the world. The little boy, Victor, was cared for by an aunt, I think. He is now eight years old, handsome, intelligent, and good-humored. They came out here from Brooklyn nearly three years ago. What brought him across the country? The need to escape bad memories, a sense of adventure, the lure of the balmy Santa Ana winds. He heard I needed a plantsman and a manager, and I hired him on the spot. His family were fruit growers in Poland, and in Brooklyn he worked on the landscaping of Prospect Park and was one of the planners of a small orchard. Stefan's knowledge is sound. He's a steady worker*

and a staunch friend. I don't see why he and Hazel
should not be happy together.

"Seal of approval. Admirable fellow all around." Absently, Davey folded the letter back into the envelope and looked at George Washington's purple face on the stamp. "I can't deny that I liked him myself."

"So you said."

"It's just that—" He crushed the envelope in his fist. "Damn it all, Maddox, I don't ask for much. I'm just so used to having her down the road. Dropping in when the whim takes her. Sitting with me by the fire talking about things no one else talks about. Making sketches of the teapot, or the hawk. I could bear anything, I could bear having her marry this man, if he wasn't taking her away."

"It's true that you don't ask for much." Maddox said dryly. "You should ask for more than that."

"Much good it would do me." He stood up. "It's time for Owosha's daily rodent. Do you want to walk across the meadow with us?"

"Are you not coming up to the house for lunch? Tilda has made that alarming cheese-and-spinach thing because, as she says, Master Davey likes it. Presumably she'll still be calling you Master Davey when you have no teeth left to chew it with."

"Please convey my regrets."

"Davey."

"Mother is used to me. Probably Tilda is too." Davey shook his head. "I can't do it, Maddox. I need to take the hawk out for a spin. You don't have to say it—she's my substitute for life."

"I wasn't going to say it."

"I wouldn't mind. I say it to myself often enough."

Chapter 12

"You should have told your mother. She is taking this hard."

"I didn't know she would take it hard."

"Or maybe you did. Maybe that's why you didn't tell her."

"It wasn't that at all!"

"Then what was it?"

"Oh, I don't know, Uncle." Hazel sipped at her tea. "Maybe it was that I couldn't believe in it."

"On Friday you will start to believe it, I suppose."

It was Wednesday, a warm morning. Hazel and George were having breakfast on the porch: tea, milk, scones. Maud had gone off early on her bicycle. "Where did Mother go?"

"The cemetery, I think." George finished a scone, washed it down. "She has spent more time there than usual this week."

"I'm going to walk over and meet her. Maybe she'll talk to me there, over Father's grave. She's hardly said a word to me."

"Leave her be, Hazel. She doesn't want company. She said yesterday she wished that ladies' club she's so keen on was a little further along so she could get away by herself."

"As if I were a houseful of screaming babies." Hazel rattled her cup into its saucer, her hand unsteady, tears in her eyes. "I don't know what to do."

"Hazel, Hazel." George's voice was a croon, as if he might suddenly break into one of his Irish ditties. "Calm yourself down. There's nothing to be done, lass. You can't live your life for your mother. Or your uncle either. Or any of your Amherst relations who don't want you to leave us. But just make sure it's worth it. That's all we're asking of you." He swallowed the last of his tea. "I was due at Paige's half an hour ago, so with those words of wisdom I'll be off. Do I look presentable enough to meet the Boston train? Not that there's damn-all I can do about it if I don't."

Hazel reached over and brushed the crumbs off his waistcoat. "You look very distinguished, Uncle. Thank you for not deserting me."

"Don't be a silly girl. This will all come right."

He shuffled off down the street, and Hazel went inside to wash the breakfast dishes. Ella would be there later, to make the supper that Maud would hardly touch. Hazel had never seen her mother in such a state—even when her husband died, all her efforts had gone toward easing Hazel's grief: her own had been private, invisible. And now, since the telegram arrived, Maud's cheerful high spirits had vanished, and she had folded herself into a quietness that was almost frightening.

When pressed, Maud said she could hardly bring Stefan Dubrowsky to mind: a dark-haired young man, very polite—that was as far as her memory went. Who were his people? And what was his position, exactly, out there at Calvin's? Ah yes. He managed the orchards. What did that mean, exactly? She listened to Hazel's answers with her eyes half-shut and her head back, as if the words exhausted her. The railroad journey to Sacramento: how many days? And how old was the little boy?

"I want you to be happy for me, Mother."

"Oh, I am, Hazel." Maud touched the locket she wore around her neck, with her husband's picture and a lock of his hair. "Of course I'm happy for you, my goodness, how could I not be happy for you?" It was painful to watch her try to smile.

⊷⥰⊷

On Thursday Hazel had a final tutoring session with Amy Osborne, who had been admitted to Smith College—not, Hazel suspected, because of her intellectual abilities but because her uncle was assistant rector at First Church in Northampton.

After lunch, there was nothing she wanted more than to walk out to Davey's, but Maddox had been visiting, leaving she knew not when. She did not want to see Maddox. Or Tamsin, or even Tilda. Everyone had heard the news about Stefan, and she was sure they all disapproved—even Owosha was probably sitting there stewing. *It's just as well I'll be going to California*, she thought, and then she spent the rest of the day in her bedroom.

Friday morning, at her session with young James, Hazel read to him from Virgil—not the *Aeneid*, where they had stopped with Book Three. It was a long way to the end, and James would not live long enough to see Aeneas attack Turnus in a fury and plunge his spirit into the gloom below: *sub umbras.* James did not need to think about such things.

Instead she turned to the *Georgics*, the poems about farming and the pleasures and pains of country life: cattle, shepherds, the heat of the sun, thorns and thistles. The boy lay propped on pillows, a damp cloth draped above his eyes. She knew he didn't understand all the Latin—nor, for that matter could she have translated much of it without a dictionary and a headache—but his little flushed face was peaceful as he listened. From time to time, she wrung out the cloth in the basin of cool water by his bedside. She would ask him if he wanted her to go on; he always said yes, and he smiled at her whenever she came to a passage they had worked on together.

Their sessions ended at noon, and, when the whistle from the hat factory sounded, Hazel looked up and said, *"Meridies est,"* as she always did, and closed the book. James clung to her hand. She removed the cloth and put her palm against his burning forehead, then wrung the cloth out again and replaced it. He closed his eyes. *"Vale, Jacobe."* His reply was faint. She knew she would most likely never see James Clay again.

❧❦

Out on Sunset Avenue, the noonday sun glared overhead. When she was halfway down the steps, Hazel stopped and squinted at a man standing on the sidewalk in the shade of a sycamore tree. He removed his hat and looked at her without smiling.

"Stefan?"

"Hazel."

"I thought you would come later this afternoon."

"The train was early. I arrived two hours ago. I took a room at Sisson's Hotel, across from the station. I remembered where the Chillicks live, so I walked out there, and your aunt directed me to your mother's house, and your mother told me I should find you here."

Hazel stayed where she was, her hand on the railing. His eyes were in shadow. She wished she wasn't wearing her old yellow gingham with the muddy hem. They looked at each other, maybe for as much as a full minute, before she continued down the steps and stood before him. Her eyes were level with his chin: she had forgotten he was that much taller, and that his hair was so dark. He bent to kiss her cheek. "You wouldn't come to me, Hazel, and so I came to you."

They walked up Amity Street and sat on Hazel's porch. Maud had disappeared but had left iced tea and stale gingersnaps on the table. Hazel and Stefan sat on the swing, inches away from each other. His face was a ruddy brown from the sun, and he had grown a small mustache—or had it been there a year ago? She could not remember. His eyes were the same, his mouth. She thought about drawing him: she would begin with the hollows of his cheeks and the line from his ear to his chin, then move to the soft tenderness of his lips.

She had to catch her breath. "It was in this very spot that I read your first letter."

He smiled at her, and patted the faded cushion between them. "Just here?"

"Yes. It was the tenth of April."

"I like knowing this. And what were your thoughts, Hazel?"

He had been in America since he was a very young man, and his Polish accent was barely noticeable, but it was there when he said her name, the buzz of the Z more like an S.

"That you had beautiful handwriting. That it was cold on the porch. That I was scared to death. That a door was pushed open an inch and through it I thought I could see something that might be happiness."

"That is exactly what it is." He removed her hand from her yellow gingham lap and held it tightly. "I know it. I don't know how I know such a thing, but I am sure we will find happiness together."

She liked it that he hadn't hesitated to kiss her cheek, to take her hand. How easy it was now that he sat beside her in his scuffed brown shoes and his striped jacket. A year ago he had not reminded her of her father—now he did. She wasn't sure why. She would figure it out another time. Something about his calm confidence, his kind eyes. Or was it just that she loved him? Was this, then, how love felt?

The agricultural college in northern Amherst, Stefan told her, was going to begin granting a new Bachelor of Science degree, in arboriculture. He had been recommended by a man he had worked for in Brooklyn, Jasper Kendall, to be a teacher there and possibly manage the orchards as well—not this year, he added hastily. Perhaps next, or the year after that. The program was still being planned. But they had showed interest in him.

Hazel had been staring at their entwined hands, glimpsing through the crack in the door not only her own happiness but her displacement to California: the weeping at the station, the long railroad journey, the house among fruit trees and monkey flowers where she would bear her children in the heat of perpetual summer. Now she looked at his face. His pale gray eyes under dark eyebrows, his smile.

"You mean, to teach here? In Amherst, Massachusetts?"

He laughed. "I will meet Mr. Henry Goodell, the president of the college, Wednesday morning, to talk about this possibility. They would hire me to teach pomology and agronomy. Because of your Latin, you will know that pomology is the growing of fruit. Agronomy is the science of growing plants for practical purposes besides food, a new discipline, and one in which this college intends to be a leader. I would feel fortunate to be part of it."

Even from happiness, thou shalt not weep.

"My plan is to return to Sacramento next week—it's not a good time of year for me to be gone. There is fertilizing to be done, and Calvin has just put in a new irrigation system that I know will need some adjusting. But I could come back to Amherst at the end of the summer, and you and I could be married then." His hand tightened around hers, and he raised it to his lips. "If you will, Hazel."

Amity Street was thick with noontime traffic: carriages and wagons and the Northampton stage. A shouting pack of boys from the grammar school ran by, and the Reverend Tilley hurried past the porch, tipping his hat and looking at them curiously. Hazel took no notice. She pulled Stefan to his feet, and they walked together around the side of the house to the back garden, where the lilacs were fading and the ancient hydrangea was just coming into bloom. In the dense shade under the old pear tree, she said, "I will." He put his arms around her, and she kissed him as she had dreamed of kissing him.

On Wednesday, while Stefan was at the college, Hazel walked to Davey's cabin. Crossing the Common, she was surprised when Ned Dickinson in his summer whites—the pale and handsome nephew of the poet—congratulated her on her betrothal. And Mrs. Wilcox called out from her front porch, "So you'll be off to California, Miss Cooper! I heard the news from my cook. She heard it from yours. He sounds like a fine young man."

Hazel found Davey on the bench by his garden: the lettuces were three inches high, beans were coming up, the mint she had given him was spreading its little leaves. The stand of Joe Pye weed in the corner was as high as her waist. Davey sat in the sun whittling a piece of wood, sleeves rolled up, hat on his knees, his hair a blaze of gold in need of a trim.

"I hoped you'd be here. Am I interrupting anything important?"

"I'm working on a leg for the footstool I promised to George. But mostly I'm watching that little cirrus cloud traveling over the barn toward the hills." He pointed. "The one that looks like a figure eight. Or—wait, now it's an alligator." He put his knife down and moved over. "Sit. You look agitated."

"Sometimes I can understand why you avoid town and prefer to be a hermit." She sat. "All of Amherst seems to know about Stefan and me."

"Small-town life. How we treasure it."

"I suppose, in fact, we do."

"What I treasure is the miraculous fact that my cousin Hazel is not abandoning this small town for the Wild West."

"Only for a year or two."

"A year or two that will fly as swiftly as Owosha swooping down on a field mouse."

The engagement had been formally announced two days before, at an impromptu party in the backyard on Amity Street. Hazel made lemonade, Lydia brought an angel-food cake, George and Archie played Irish tunes on harmonica and fiddle, and Stefan gave Hazel the sapphire ring he had hastily bought at Stackman's on Main Street. When they kissed under the green of the rose arbor, everyone applauded.

"The miraculous fact is that you went to the party. Thank you for that, Davey."

"I hope you noticed I wore not only a clean shirt but my best necktie."

"You looked wonderfully handsome." She could not see her cousin now without the echo of the words *he is dying of love for you*, and wondering if they were the truth or the product of Anna's romantic Italian imagination. "We should have had dancing. Anna would gladly have been your partner."

"The signorina will be a perfect second wife for my brother."

"What an intriguing idea. Your mother would be delighted, I think. She told me that my engagement takes some of the sting out of Maddox's divorce."

"Not that Caroline was ever a favorite of hers."

"No, but—" *Now both her sons are alone*, Hazel thought. "She seemed regretful."

"The important thing is that Maddox is not. If it weren't for Tobias, he'd be glad to see the last of that woman—which is what we now officially call her."

"Tobias seemed happy enough at the party. Lydia is doing her best to mother him."

"Smother him."

Hazel laughed. "He may thrive on smothering, at least for a while."

"Will you walk with me down to the tracks to poke in the dirt? Tobias and I found a spearhead there. Tobias was elated." Davey stood up and put on his hat. "Spearheads are, as you know—and if you don't you should—much older than arrowheads."

"Three days after I arrived in Amherst you showed me your collection and told me that very fact. That was the year 1873. I have stored it away all this time."

"You were Tobias's age."

"And you were a dashing young student at the college."

"I was not dashing!"

"To me you were dashing. And so was your collection of arrowheads and spear points."

She followed Davey across the yard to the meadow. The hawk was dozing on her perch in the sun—her wings fluttered when they passed, then stilled. The flowering fruit trees were thick with the buzzing of bees; the chickens squabbled in their yard. Hazel and Davey crossed the meadow, keeping to the narrow path Davey had made over the years simply by walking it. Davey carried what he called his digger—five feet of knobby apple wood, shaped to a point, that he claimed could sense an arrowhead the way pigs in France could find a truffle. Hazel stayed close behind him, concentrating on keeping her skirt free of burdock.

"Davey." She spoke to the back of his checkered shirt. "I need to know something. You like Stefan, don't you? It's important that you like each other."

"How could I not like him? He makes you happy. Even if I didn't like him, I would like him for that. And for the lucidity with which he described the operation of the rotating hamburger cooker in the grill car on the train. But I do like him." He banged the digger into the earth with every fourth step. "One question—has the word *love* now been properly uttered?"

"What a thing to ask me."

"I ask only because you were so concerned about it—when was that, now? Back in April, I think."

"Oh. I suppose I was. Well. As you might expect, the word has indeed been uttered."

"Ah." Davey walked with his head down—looking for arrowheads, she hoped, and not from despondence. Dying of love....

He stopped and turned, leaning on the digger. "I've been thinking about love lately."

Hazel sidestepped a rut and nearly tripped over a rock. Davey reached out to steady her. "I know it sounds unlike me. But one day when I was watching Owosha in flight, riding so high on the wind she almost disappeared, I was suddenly aware of how much of other creatures' worlds we can't know. She can see what is invisible to me, and of course nearly everything I know is alien to her. And we have no language to express any of this." In the sky above them, a flock of starlings wheeled toward the orchard. "A bird may be an extreme example, but it's true of people too, or so it seems to me. That inability to really know anyone. And that's where love comes in."

"Because love gives us the language?"

"I suppose it does, but what I mean is that this is the problem with love. It has to cross the gap, or else it's not love. And that's what I've always feared, Hazel—losing that distance."

She stood looking at him, and then she did what she felt she should have done years ago: stepped toward him on the path and embraced him. For a moment he was in her arms, smelling of sweat and hay. Then he pulled away. "Don't do that."

Her cheeks were burning. "I'm sorry."

"No—you needn't apologize. But that's what I meant. The gap threatened to close. I could hear the doors creaking shut."

She had to laugh. "You make it sound like a trap."

"Do I?" He laughed with her, took off his hat, and wiped his shirtsleeve across his brow. What a picture he made, with his golden-brown eyes and his shining curls. In spite of what he had said, she felt a gleam of hopefulness on his behalf. He had come to her engagement party, after all. And he said he had gone to a baseball game. He had even promised—she only half believed him—to put in an appearance at Archie's barn dance in August.

"Maybe you don't have to close the gap. Just build a bridge over it. Nothing fancy—you could devise something out of logs and bits of scrap lumber. So long as it's sturdy."

"Should the occasion arise, I'll remember your suggestion." He pounded his digger into the dirt. "Come on, then, Hazel. Enough love talk. Let's look for spearheads. If we find a nice one, you shall have it for a wedding present."

Chapter 13

When Anna Felice departed the Amherst House, Mr. Hatch, two hotel maids, Paddy the valet, and Mr. Otis the head-waiter stood in a line at the door to wish her a regretful farewell. Anna pressed silver dollars into their hands. She was able to tell Mr. Hatch with sincerity—not mentioning the snoring of the man in the room next to hers or the crying child and pacing parents above—that she had enjoyed her stay.

But she was happy enough to move to the Chillicks'. Tamsin had said, "I thought you might like to continue your study of the habits of Americans by actually living among them," and added with a smile, "But it will also be a favor to me. I hear things when I'm alone in the house. Polecats in the henhouse, burglars in the attic, ghosts in the linen press."

"Burglars and ghosts do not trouble me," Anna assured her. "And, since I don't know what polecats are, they do not either."

George stowed her trunks and cases and bundles in the back of a wagon with PAIGE'S RELIABLE TRANSPORT stenciled on the side. He swept off his hat and bowed before he helped her up to the seat. "Off to the next stop on your American journey, Miss Anna."

"Half a mile down the road. No one can say this signorina is not adventurous!"

He settled beside her and took the reins. "Life is best eaten in small bites."

"Is that a bit of Irish wisdom, George?"

"My mother used to swear by it."

"Oh, get on with you," she said in Maud's voice to make him smile.

It was the day after Hazel had seen Stefan off on the train. "Amity has descended again on Amity Street," George said to Anna. Hazel and Maud had "made it up," which meant they had apologized, wept in each other's arms, and made plans that Maud would visit Sacramento soon after the suffrage convention in Boston where she would be speaking. "Bless my sister's motherly soul," he added. "Still perking away under all that suffrage nonsense. I even heard her say the word *trousseau*."

Tamsin and Davey had cleared out the back bedroom at the Chillicks', where Sam had stored years of weather records in boxes and cartons. Tilda retrieved a quilt from the attic and pinned it to the clothesline for a whole day: now it carried the scent of the sweet Amherst wind. George helped Davey drag a maple bedstead from the barn loft. It was nearly 100 years old, Tamsin told Anna: her grandparents had slept on it as newlyweds. On warm afternoons it smelt faintly of manure. Anna thought of the carved walnut Cinquecento bed where she had slept in Rome—scented with, if anything, the corruption of the ages, and so high she had to climb two steps to get into it—and marveled at how she had learned to value what was new and rough and simple. I have fallen in love at last, she thought: not with a person but with a town.

But when she had been at the Chillicks' for nearly a week, she could see the glimmer of something she could not at first identify: some combination of restlessness and gloom. It took her another day to identify it as boredom.

It was not that she wasn't grateful for her relocation. She liked the comfortable farmhouse: the wide porch, the fields stretching into the distance, the hens and the cows and the big vegetable garden. And the drowsy gray cat so like her old affectionate Tosca. But time passed slowly. The evenings were pleasant: supper with Tamsin, and their quiet talks afterward, while Tamsin sewed on a chemise she was making for Hazel, and Anna tried without enthusiasm to work a bit of embroidery. But in the daytime she was on her own, while her hostess was teaching art classes and taking photography lessons at a local studio, and Davey did whatever Davey did out in his cabin out behind the barn. She hadn't laid eyes on him since the day she arrived.

In the face of Tamsin's industry, Anna felt more aimless than usual, and increasingly aware that she wanted to be more than a guest in this town, a small appendage of the large and interesting family who had taken her in. Should she learn to use a camera? Buy herself a bloomer suit and ride a bicycle?

She browsed in the shops, bought another shirtwaist—plaid—at Miss Beaman's, speculated with Hazel over tea about what kind of undergarments would be best in temperatures of 100 degrees. She went to one of Maud's suffrage meetings and sat through a talk about women and the poll tax by Mrs. Juno Pitts of South Granby. She wrote new words in her notebook—*sloppy, crush, awfully*—that she was unable to find in her Italian-English dictionary or even in the tattered green volume Tamsin had given her, amusingly titled *The American Dictionary of the English Language*. She continued to make her slow way through *Roderick Hudson*, following Mr. James's misguided sculptor to Rome, which was, so far, not doing well by him, as Anna certainly could have warned him it would not!

She wrote another short letter to her aunt Julia and a note to Mr. Banks: noncommittal, dull, uninformative. But what to say? She found herself wanting to chop vegetables with Tilda, or hang dish towels on the clothesline. Sweep the front steps! Pull weeds in the garden!

When Lydia brought Valentine over for the promised singing lesson, Anna's world became more interesting. Valentine arrived giddy with excitement, dressed in a pinafore, blessedly without a corset, her hair in a simple crown of braids like her grandmother Tamsin's. Anna suggested she begin the lesson by singing anything she liked. Valentine chose a song called "After the Ball Is Over" that she said was "all the rage." It was a sentimental waltz tune, which she performed without accompaniment, hands clasped at her waist, perfectly on pitch. The treacly emotion of the lyrics poured out of her with a poignancy that might have brought someone else to tears: not Anna, but she was stunned again by the potential of the child's voice. Someday Valentine must have better instruction—the best— but for now Anna would try to, at least, conserve her gift and undo her bad habits. And maybe even improve her taste in music.

They worked for an hour at the piano in the parlor, beginning with *solfeggio*, which Valentine approached with bemusement. Miss Finchett had not taught notes, she had taught songs. How? By playing them on the piano until Valentine had the tunes by heart. She knew the names of the notes from piano lessons, but had never sung a scale. Never? Never. Miss Finchett had not required it.

One afternoon, out on a walk, Anna and Maud had passed a sweet-faced wisp of a woman with a tiny dog on a lead: none other than the Miss Finchett who, out of a deep well of musical ignorance, had declared herself to be a teacher of singing—Amherst's own Signora Gismondi. But even the Signora had taught *solfeggio*! Anna was tempted to stop Miss Finchett on Main Street and harangue her about the damage that could be done by tampering with such a delicate instrument as the voice of Valentine Wyatt.

But now she only said, gently, "*Solfeggio*, Valentine dear, is the basis of all singing. If you don't learn to sight-read, and to sing scales, you are learning nothing. But you will find the scales tedious, I warn you."

Valentine shook her head vigorously. "You may not believe me, Miss Anna, but I assure you I will find nothing tedious if it has to do with singing."

"I do believe you," Anna said, thinking: *She is so like me at that age it's frightening.* But it was also exhilarating. How well she remembered the joy of pouring out your young heart and of pleasing people with nothing but the sound of your voice: like magic.

What was best about the hour at the piano with Valentine was the gratification Anna found in it. She had wanted to do the child a service, to correct a wrong; she had not known that she would love teaching for its own sake, that it would seem like the answer to a prayer she scarcely knew she was praying—a prayer disguised as a daydream of being useful. To do, not just be! Part of her suffering since she stopped singing was the sense that her life had no point.

When her marriage was annulled, Anna, like all good unattached Italian daughters, had taken care of the family home: the vast palazzo where she and her papa lived like gods, attended by the regiment of servants needed to keep the wheels turning. Anna sat every week with the *maggiordomo*, an amiable man called Giangrande, to go over the books to be sure he wasn't cheating them, though he probably was nonetheless. She approved the menus, tasted wines, agreed to the replacement of the broken statue of Pan and the repair of the Florentine tapestries in the salon. The work of keeping her father happy was exacting and not without its challenges: Basilio Felice required perfection, whether it was in a cut of meat or the silk ribbons on his daughter's hat, and Anna had learned how to keep a rich old man happy, or at least uncomplaining.

Sometimes she could laugh at what had become of her life, but the best way to live it, she had slowly taught herself, was not to think too much.

But to be a teacher of singers! To spend her days with the young and the gifted, helping them travel down a road that was—this was always in her mind—different from the road she had taken. Of course, she had no qualifications. Could she learn? What did one do: go to a conservatory? It was too late for that, especially with her blighted voice. In fact, to teach without being able to demonstrate the proper sounds was almost impossible—Miss Finchett's methods aside—and was one of the reasons she knew she could not take Valentine very far....

But, though she could not teach, might she bring other teachers to Amherst? Could she open a school of music and be its—what was it called?—*direttrice*. Director. She consulted the green dictionary. Headmistress. Principal. In Italy, she had never dreamed of such a thing. In America, she could dream it—that was what people in this country did—but how it could come about was the difficulty. The idea left her too excited to sleep. It was grandiose, presumptuous, outrageous. How did one go about founding a music school? How to decipher the ways of this new country so she could find a house to live in and a building to staff with teachers—and then find the teachers—and then find the students?

That, she thought, was what would set her to rights! If nothing else, it gave her something to think about besides needlework and the lives of characters in books. And Mrs. McAlmond in Connecticut, who, it seemed, had indeed gone to the angels, leaving George's letter to moulder somewhere under a heap of oyster shells.

⋘⋙

"I heard Valentine warbling her do-re-mi's," Davey said. "It sounded like a real singing lesson, not like one of the musical evenings they put on at Town Hall."

Anna had encountered Davey as she was returning from a hot walk into town, and he had invited her to have a lemonade on the porch of the big house. Tilda had left a pitcher in Tamsin's icebox. Anna sat down gladly and removed her hat, wishing she could kick her shoes off as well.

Davey also found a plate of shortbread. His gesture of friendliness surprised her. It seemed part of a small but unmistakable change in him, as if the loss of Hazel—now officially announced at the engagement party, where Davey had actually made an appearance—had pushed him out of some long trance and into the world.

The day was dreadfully hot. The Rational Dress Movement would have had her in a short skirt and nothing under it but a chemise and knickers. "Tell me this, Davey." She sipped the cold lemonade gratefully. "Have you ever been to a musical evening at Town Hall?"

"I don't have to go to them. They are easy enough to imagine. Hortensia Finchett and the *Moonlight Sonata*, and an army of children singing patriotic songs."

She laughed. "The trouble is that Valentine's voice is always a joy to listen to, even with bad instruction. So I don't blame Lydia for subjecting her to Miss Finchett."

"When you know my sister better, you will. Lydia always knows best—always has, even when she was a tiny girl bossing her big brothers around. We're all dumbstruck that she not only listened to your opinion but heeded it."

"I hope I can be a good teacher for Valentine, at least for a while."

"How long will that be, do you think? I mean—if you don't mind my asking—how much longer do you intend to stay in Amherst?"

It was an inquiry hardly anyone had made. Maybe it was impolite to put such questions to a guest. Even Tamsin, when she invited Anna to stay until Sam returned, had murmured, "If you think you might be in Amherst until then," and Anna had said, with equal vagueness, that she expected to be. The truth was she didn't know what to tell people. Her decision to settle herself in the town was firmly fixed; only the details were wobbly, and she had no idea how to begin.

Maybe the time had come to stop standing still and take a step forward—at least to reveal her plan to someone. And how to find things out except by asking? How to make major changes in your life without making minor ones first? *Life is best eaten in small bites*: the wisdom of George Mullen. "I have no plans to leave. I am someone who has no real home, and I am thinking of settling down."

Davey raised his eyebrows. "Here? In Amherst, Massachusetts?"

"I thought I might find myself a little house."

Just saying the words made her heart beat fast. She held the frigid glass against her hot cheek and turned her gaze out toward the barn, rosy red in the sun and, between two clumps of trees, the low mountains beyond. How peaceful it was. No matter what agitation life might bring, it would be easy in this place to find a measure of serenity: just look into the distance. The mountains were always there, and the vast sky, the clouds....

Anna realized Davey had been staring at her. "Davey?" It still unsettled her a bit, to use his first name. "Does it seem so preposterous?"

He blinked. "Preposterous? No. Not preposterous at all. It's a fine idea. I was just thinking." He told her that Maddox and his wife had separated—yes, she had heard all about it, from Tamsin—and it seemed best for young Tobias to be with his cousins in Amherst when school was not in session, so Maddox was looking for somewhere to spend the summers. "And what I thought was this," Davey said. "There is a house at the west end of Amity Street. I went to see it on the day of—" He took a sip of lemonade. "Of Hazel's engagement party."

"I noticed that you left early."

"Yes. For many reasons. But one of them was to walk by this house." He did not enumerate the others. The house belonged to Tom Paige, he told Anna—from the stables—but when his wife died last winter Tom moved in with his daughter in Hadley. The place was standing empty. "You might take a stroll past it," he said. "It's painted gray, with two dormers and a white fence. The fence needs a coat of paint, and you'd want to have a gardener come in and clear out the brush, put in a couple of flower beds. But it's a nice little house. I could see right away that it's not right for Maddox and Tobias—not enough land, for one thing. But I thought, just this minute, that it might be exactly the thing for you. If you like it, you should talk to George."

"George?"

"My sister Lydia thinks she knows everything, but it's really George who does. Whatever you need in the town of Amherst, whether a house or a carriage wheel or a case of Irish whiskey, George is your man."

"I will want a kitten or two."

"Name your color, long or short fur, length of whiskers, male or female—George will come up with what you need."

Anna laughed. "This is moving very fast. I don't know how to buy a house."

"I'm pretty sure it's not difficult if you have the cash."

"I have the cash."

"I thought you might."

Anna sat thinking. A small gray house at the end of Amity Street. Could anything be more different than the life she had led until now? And should she not be terrified at the prospect?

In a way, she was. But stronger than terror was the feeling that this was what she had been waiting for: here was the transformation she had sought when she boarded the *Britannia* in Naples on that rainy day in April.

A bird high in a tree gave a call—*teacher teacher*—answered by another. The noon train from Boston came rattling through: Anna could glimpse the flash of it through the green and black maze of trees. Once it passed, the quiet of the world around them was absolute. Was it too fanciful to believe that her soul had been longing for this new world since she was removed from it as an infant?

"Where is it on Amity Street?"

"The opposite end from Maud's, not far from the Hadley town line. On the right side as you go down the hill. I think it's number 21—you'll see it painted on the mailbox."

Chapter 14

The next afternoon, when Davey returned home with Owosha on his arm, Maddox was sitting on the bench by the cabin, hat off, jacket slung over his shoulder.

"Christ almighty, it's hot."

"I didn't expect to lay eyes on you again so soon." Davey opened the enclosure so Owosha could flutter to her perch. He stowed the sack and the gauntlet and fixed the latch in place. In the sack was a young rabbit, still warm, soon to be stinking. Hot weather presented a new problem: putridity. Not that Owosha minded. "But of course I'm glad you're here, whatever the reason."

Maddox looked not only hot but agitated: some new hell, no doubt, with Caroline at the center of it. "Is Mother not at home?"

"She's taken her camera up Mount Holyoke on the tram to photograph the oxbow from the summit."

"And has the signorina moved in?"

"A week ago." Davey looked at his brother curiously. "Is that why you're in town? Shall we go up to the house and see if she's there?"

"No. We should sit in the shade where we can have privacy. I have something to show you."

"Something not good."

"Something very much not good."

They walked to the row of maples on the north border of the property, Heloise the cat following them. The wild strawberries at the base of the stone wall were almost ready to pick. A warm wind blew the rich, rank smell of cow dung from Oakley's pasture. Davey hoisted himself up on the wall. Maddox sat beside his brother and took a letter from his pocket: two pages, typewritten. He handed Davey the top one. "From Jack Truesdale. It's a sorry document."

Davey took it gingerly. Since Stefan Dubrowsky had come and gone, the anguish of the kiss under the rose arbor had retreated. He had witnessed Hazel's happiness and come a long way toward accepting it. He had even begun to think he might build himself a new world to live in—that, at least, was the way he thought of it after two ballgames, a walk down to Blodgett's, and a stop at Jackson's to buy a handful of walnuts.

The letter had the look of something that would tip that world sideways and spill him out. "I suppose I have to read it."

"It was you who set this in motion, Davey."

"With the ominous feeling that I would live to regret it."

"You may or may not regret it. Just read the thing."

Davey unfolded the letter:

> *14 June 1892*
> *My dear Maddox,*
>
> *We have finally completed our inquiries in Manhattan and also in Brooklyn, as you requested, in search of information about one Stefan Dubrowsky, a wife (Katarzyna) and child (Victor), and possibly a sister, Polish immigrants. My clerk, William Lyman, has done much of the legwork, including a trip to Brooklyn on the ferry and a long conversation with a Catholic Sister who keeps the records at the church there. I have complete confidence in him. If anything, he is more dogged and meticulous than yours truly. He has summarized on a separate sheet what we've managed to find. You will see that much of*

*the information you looked for is missing or seems
to be mistaken, but city records are often incomplete or riddled with errors, and some surnames
are very common. Handwriting too is sometimes
misleading.*

*On a personal note, the Greenpoint addresses
brought to mind our excursions out that way during
our law school days, including a couple of evenings
at the Warsaw Tavern that I've not forgotten
(however hard I try!). And do you remember the
borscht at Szarlota's? William tells me the place
is still there, now called Jowita's, but that it's on
the skids—his Irish mother-in-law makes better
borscht! I'm glad we are old enough to have experienced Greenpoint, Brooklyn, in its prime.*

*My best regards to you, and please tell your
brother I send same. Many fond memories of our
time at Amherst. I hear they've built a new baseball field with all the latest improvements and
actually mow the grass there. What towering
giants of the game we would have been if we'd had
a decent field to play it on!*

I hope the enclosed will be helpful.
Yours sincerely,
John P. Truesdale, Esq.

Davey gave the letter back to his brother, feeling sick. "And the
enclosed, Maddox. What does it say?"

"It says a great deal. Do you want me to read it aloud?"

"No. But that would be preferable to having to read it myself."
Heloise leapt up onto the wall and elongated herself beside him.
Davey spread his hand on her hot flank, feeling the quick rise and
fall of the cat's breathing. "Go ahead."

"Mr. Lyman is an impressively organized young man. So. Here
goes. Passenger manifest *S.S. Edam* from Rotterdam, arrival at New
York 6 March 1883. Stefan Dubrowsky, age 24, laborer. Katarzyna

Rusnak, age 19, no occupation. Also Eva Rusnak, age 17. On 8 August 1883, at the city clerk's office, Brooklyn, marriage license issued to Stefan Dubrowsky of 166 India Street, Brooklyn, and Katarzyna Rusnak, same address. Wedding recorded St. Anthony of Padua Church—same people, same address, 17 August 1883. Witnesses Eva Rusnak and Marek Nowicki. Birth record: 22 December 1883, male child, Victor—born to Stefan and Katarzyna, address as above. No surprises there, we knew all this."

"But there's more."

"Quite a bit. Shall I go on?"

Davey waved his hand. Maddox read, "No death certificate found for Katarzyna Dubrowsky, or for Kasia Dubrowsky, either in December 1883 (i.e., in childbirth) or thereafter. And here's something odd. Petition to the Brooklyn Civil Court, dated 19 July 1882, by Katarzyna Dubrowsky for the restoration of her maiden name, Rusnak. Petition granted. Judge—illegible, possibly Henry—Garvey. Further searching found no divorce record."

"And so are we to understand from this that Kasia did not die, and nor did Stefan divorce her?"

"So it would seem."

"And this means what, Maddox? Always allowing for incomplete records and common surnames and bad handwriting. What are these lawyers saying?"

"It's not the lawyers. It's the Brooklyn City Directory for the year 1888. Listen to this. K. Rusnak, occupation shopkeeper, address 131 Greenpoint Avenue. E. Rusnak, occupation clerk, same address. And then at 166 India Street there is a boarder listed as S. Dubrowsky, occupation garden worker. Also—" Maddox looked up. "One moment. The heat is unbearable."

He took off his jacket, loosened his tie, pulled out a handkerchief and wiped his brow. Davey watched him, feeling sweat run down his own neck, not caring. "There is more?"

"Not much. One last thing. Mildly interesting." Maddox stowed his handkerchief and resumed. "At St. Anthony of Padua Church, the records list Victor Dubrowsky, age four, registered in the St. Stanislaus Infant School. Address 166 India Street. The signature on the enrollment form is Stefan Dubrowsky. And then there's one more item, maybe not relevant to anything except to demonstrate the persistence of Jack's clerk. Marek Nowicki was listed in the directory as the owner of a business. Lived at the Greenpoint Avenue address. William found a death certificate for him—died on 30 September 1889 of typhoid fever."

Davey's heart raced. "So. There it is." He stroked the cat, and she woke, rubbed her head against his hand, yawned, stretched. Oh, to be a cat. A hawk. A field mouse. "Well. You and I should go over to the pond for a swim."

"Davey?"

"Because you're right. It is really a very hot day."

"Davey? You see what this means."

"I don't want to think about it. What does it mean? It means unbearable suffering for Hazel, and I wish we hadn't found it out. I wish I had never doubted Stefan Dubrowsky. I wish you had never written to Jack Truesdale, and I wish he had never replied."

"The truth is always worth knowing."

"That's what lawyers have to say, I suppose. For me, the truth is that I have half a bottle of whiskey sitting on my table, and what I'd like to do is have a swim and then go home and drink it."

Maddox folded the two pieces of paper and tucked them back in their envelope, put the envelope into his jacket pocket, refolded the jacket and set it beside him, all in silence. Davey knew his brother was giving him time to think more clearly, and he tried to do so. He stared out at the weedy edge of the meadow. Here he and Hazel had sat on the cold spring day she told him about Stefan's marriage proposal. Her words had plunged him into misery, but it wasn't a completely unfamiliar feeling: his doomed love of his cousin was a sorrow he'd lived with so long it felt like his natural home. Tacking on a removal to California only deepened a chasm that had been dug years ago.

Now there was this new and confounding kind of grief, and at the center of it was not himself but Hazel's life and happiness. On her behalf, the truth would be worth knowing.

"No," he said suddenly. "That's not really what I want."

Maddox looked over at him, sweat glinting off his high, domed forehead. "And I was just thinking how what a tempting idea it is. A large whiskey with plenty of ice."

"What I'm really thinking is that we need to go to Brooklyn." Davey jumped down from the wall. "She could have died later. There could have been a divorce and the record lost. There could be a coincidence of names. There could be a dozen explanations for these—these ugly facts. Maybe they are not facts at all. Maybe Jack Truesdale's clerk is a fabulist like Edgar Allan Poe. At any rate, I won't believe any of it until this woman Katarzyna tells me it's true."

"I had hoped you would say all this. I had planned to go myself, and I'm pleased that you'll come with me." Maddox hesitated. "It was because of the hawk that I didn't suggest it."

"It will be only one night?"

"An afternoon in Brooklyn should take care of things. Then we can get ourselves a good steak dinner somewhere, put up at a hotel, and take a morning train back to Amherst."

"Owosha will be fine. I'll give her a rabbit head before we leave."

"And you?"

"I'm not fond of rabbit heads."

His brother gave him a look. "You know what I mean."

"Damn it, Maddox, I'm not a freak!" He slammed the stone wall with one palm. The cat leapt down and stalked back across the meadow. "I'm just someone who doesn't like to go places and who prefers to be alone. That doesn't mean I can't spend a night now and then doing something different."

Maddox raised both hands in what for the twins had always been a gesture of peace. "I'm sorry. I'm an idiot."

"So am I. Both of those things." He almost smiled. "And, in the interests of normalizing the conversation, here's something else you should know. I was talking with the signorina yesterday, and I told her a whopper."

"The signorina interests me more than your whopper does, but go ahead. What was it?"

171

"George told me about a house that's available, down on Amity Street at the bottom of the hill—old Tom Paige's place. He wondered if it might do for you and Tobias."

"Gray frame house? Dilapidated barn behind it?"

"Right. But the barn is gone—collapsed a couple of winters ago. There's a gazebo or something out there now."

"I'd like to find a house further out of town, since we would be inhabiting it in the summer only. Maybe with a brook or a pond. Tobias has an interest in frogs."

"And so he should at age twelve. I'll mention that to George."

"Where is your whopper?"

"Ah. Well, Anna has the idea that she might live in Amherst herself. Permanently. She likes it here, and says she has no other place to go. She doesn't want to return to Italy. So I told her George has been scouting out houses for you and Tobias." He smiled. "Same whopper I just told you."

"You did *not* ask George to find a house for me and Tobias?"

"That's right. I asked George to find a house for me. I'm figuring you and Tobias could stay with me in the summer months. I told Anna—this is not a whopper, this is the truth—that the Amity Street house, which is too small for the three of us, might be just right for her, and she is very interested."

Maddox stared at him. "At the risk of making you snap at me again—do you mean you would leave the cabin and move to a house?"

"It's by no means a sure thing."

"But you're considering it?"

The question of the cabin had been preoccupying him lately. He would soon be forty years old. Another year: buds, blossoms, wrens, finches, corn, the reddening of the hills, apples, frost, snow, muck, buds.... And what would Davey Chillick have to show for it all? He had lived by himself in a one-room cabin since he was twenty-two. For years, it had made sense—to him, if to nobody else. He hadn't thought much about the why of it; he thought about ways to stay warm in the winter and fight off the mice. Now something had jolted him awake: Hazel and her suitor, most likely. Or was it just that he was getting old?

"I've been weighing the benefits and drawbacks of joining the real world, and I'm as surprised as anyone that the real world seems to be winning." Davey looked out past the trees to the silhouette of hills. "And going to Brooklyn is part of the real world, God knows. Let's go down there tomorrow."

❧

They took the early train. "We'll be in New York by noon," Maddox said.

"If the train does not derail. Or fall into a ravine. Or get held up by bandits."

"You have read too many Alonzo Woodley books."

"Impossible to read too many Alonzo Woodley books." Davey could not take his eyes from the dusty window. He wouldn't admit it to his brother, but it was both exciting and alarming to watch the Pelham hills rush by, replaced by tobacco fields, a row of crooked houses, an apple orchard. "I've not been on a train since we went to Boston in 1871 to beat Harvard 24 runs to 6."

"The trains are faster now. Probably Harvard is too."

Two children waved at the train, but by the time Davey got his hand up they were gone, and he was waving at a stand of birches. "If I were not tormented by the purpose of this journey, I would be enjoying it."

"In the midst of the torment, is there not at least a morsel of hope?"

Hope. Davey had spent a bad night trying to keep hope at bay. Trying not to think about Hazel at all, or about Kasia Dubrowsky in Brooklyn, or Stefan in California—the pleasant fellow who had kissed Hazel under Maud's arbor and brought a light to her face that was new to everyone who loved her. Sleep had not come until he stumbled out of bed long past midnight and found the bottle of whiskey—brought to him by Ida the week before: a night when he told her that their long liaison had to come to an end and she had said: It's your cousin, isn't it? And wished him luck. It's not luck I need, he had told her. It's the ability to endure this. She had wished him luck with that too. *The world is a hard and stony place.* Also: *I will miss you.* She slipped out as soundlessly as she came in.

"Hope of what, exactly?" he asked Maddox.

"Hope of Hazel, obviously. You said you used to live with hope— that thing with feathers. And then it died. Can it not be revived? Under the circumstances? You talk about rejoining the real world. Well, there it is! If Hazel cannot be his, she could be yours."

"She has never thought of herself as someone who could be mine. I'm her brother: she has said it over and over."

"In my recollection, she said it once, maybe twice, when she was—what? Sixteen? You don't know how Hazel thinks of you. She is the most unforthcoming person who has ever lived, except perhaps for yourself. The two of you! I can imagine you sitting cozily in your quaint little homemade chairs by the hearth, not a foot apart, talking about hawks or Rattlesnake Dick or how you hate Horace and she loves Horace, but aching to reach across a space the width of a pencil case and clasp each other's hands."

"I'm in no mood to laugh, Maddox. But I suppose I have to say you have hit it exactly. Or almost exactly. Only one of us is wanting to reach over and clasp a hand."

"What if we find out that what seems to be true is in fact true? That the admirable Stefan Dubrowsky has a living wife."

"I can't contemplate something that would bring Hazel such devastation."

The conductor came for their tickets: Maddox produced his instantly, Davey had to hunt through all his pockets. "You see how far I am from Alonzo Woodley," he said. "If he were modeled on me, Rattlesnake Dick would have shot up the whole mining camp while Alonzo was out somewhere watching the geese migrate."

"Don't romanticize a simple case of absent-mindedness."

"Well, don't think I can't bear whatever we may turn up. But I hope more than anything that this will be a false alarm, and the wedding will go on. They will be in California for a year or two or three. Then the aggie school will tap Stefan on the shoulder, and my Hazel will return—yes, yes, babies in tow, adoring husband at her

174

side, but she and I can still talk to each other. I'll teach the babies to grow lettuce and make quaint little chairs. Nice old Cousin Davey."

"Sometimes it absolutely astonishes me that we're brothers." Maddox's voice was edged with impatience. "There we were in the womb, two nearly identical bubbles of protoplasm, kicking and punching each other—doing whatever protoplasm does—and then we emerged, and—how could we be more different?"

"You sound like Mother."

"I sound like someone in the pits of exasperation! Caroline has left me for this Serbian poet, and what do you think I will do? Retreat to a cabin and mourn the demise of my marriage to my one true love?"

"I am well aware that you are a practical man who doesn't do that sort of thing."

"However you may mean that, I'm taking it as a compliment."

Davey often thought their mother's teasing had truth in it. When they were boys, looking at his brother was like looking in a mirror, but at this point in their lives, he and Maddox no longer resembled each other much—in appearance or in character. Maddox was stouter, his voice louder, his face redder, his hair, what was left of it, a darker blond and not yet streaked with silver: a large, convivial, confident man who never lacked for an opinion and always knew exactly what he wanted. More like their sister Lydia than like Davey, who was mild, benign, odd, diffident, alternating between admiration for Maddox's accomplishments and annoyance at their extent: Maddox occupying the Belcher Chair of Jurisprudence at Harvard while Davey roamed the hills and watched his garden grow.

"Maybe Caroline was not your one true love."

"I certainly thought she was, when I danced with Miss Vandermeer at the Amherst College Harvest Ball and sank into the depths of her décolletage and her enormous green eyes."

"Her décolletage I cannot vouch for, but she does have fine eyes. Or did. I'm quite aware that at this juncture we can grant her nothing. Her eyes are now small, beady, and calculating."

"A perfect description. But my point was—"

Davey held up a hand. "I know what your point was. But no, I don't want to profit from the downfall of Stefan Dubrowsky, and I don't want to talk about it. Forgive me—what I would really like to do is pass the rest of this very interesting train journey looking out of the window and thinking my bleak thoughts."

"The prosecution rests. I brought a book—Harrison on the privileges-and-immunities clause. Maybe over our steak dinner we can talk about this house we're going to share."

Maddox took a fat tome from his bag and began to read it. Davey looked out the window, not seeing the countryside roll by but seeing the house: the bedroom: and Hazel, standing before him, and slowly, slowly taking the pins from her hair and letting it down.

They pulled into the Grand Central Depot on the stroke of noon and took a carriage down to East Tenth Street, where they caught the Greenpoint Ferry. "I'd forgotten it docked at India Street," Maddox said. "No wonder that sounded familiar." They disembarked at the pier: behind them the East River, greenish and calm out past the press of ships and boats that crowded the waterfront, to the south the towers and cables of the vast bridge, before them a street swarming with tramcars and horses and wagons. Beyond that, a looming factory building. And, everywhere, people.

Maddox surveyed it all with a smile. "Scene of many a debauch. I'm thinking we should stop at the Warsaw Tavern and fortify ourselves with a beer and a sandwich. It's not far from here, and Greenpoint Avenue is just past it."

Davey dodged what seemed to be a motorized velocipede and a wagon top-heavy with a mountain of bricks. The chaos of the streets, for someone who was overwhelmed by the crowds at an Amherst College baseball game, was—he admitted it to himself—terrifying: so many people, faces, each with a story, a destination, a complicated life, and half of them, it seemed, trying to run him down. He tried to keep the panic out of his voice. "I could use a beer. This is pretty far from the corner of Main and Pleasant."

"It is certainly more than your usual dose of the real world. I won't ask you how you're holding up because that would suggest that you're a—what was your word?"

"Freak? Troglodyte? I can't remember because I'm too busy trying to stay alive."

They made their way to the tavern in the hot noonday sun—hotter than the sun back home: Davey was convinced that everything in Brooklyn was bigger, hotter, louder, faster than anywhere else. The tavern was noisy with the Polish language and crowded with workmen in caps—Maddox declared it hardly changed since his law school days. They found seats at the bar, and Maddox engaged the barman in cheerful conversation about the sausage sandwiches, also unchanged. In the mirror behind rows of whiskey bottles, Davey watched himself take a bite of sandwich, chew without tasting, wash it down with beer. The image Maddox had conjured up was still in his mind, of Hazel sitting beside him in the cabin by the stove. *How often have we sat here like this? Not often enough.* He felt dazed, the result of sleeplessness, the tumult of Brooklyn, and the prospect of what they might discover.

"Maddox?" He pushed his plate away and drained his glass. "I can't stand it anymore. We need to go and find this woman."

◦෫෮෮

Number 131 Greenpoint Avenue was not even a block away, in the middle of a row of brownstones: a flight of steps, tall front windows, and a doorbell with a card above it that read RUSNAK.

"God help us," Maddox said. "These people are real."

The woman who answered the bell was thin-lipped and sharp-chinned, with a pointed nose and masses of coarse blonde hair piled high on her small head. She surveyed them with disapproval. "Yes."

Maddox removed his hat. "Good afternoon. I hope you will forgive us for disturbing you. My name is Maddox Chillick, this is my brother David Chillick, and we have come from Boston in search of a woman named Katarzyna Rusnak, who lives at this address."

The woman gave him a level stare, unsmiling, then looked at Davey and stared a little longer. Davey raised his hat and lowered it. "Perhaps you know her?" he asked encouragingly.

"Perhaps you can tell me why it is that you have come in search of her."

Davey glanced at Maddox. They had not prepared what they would say: a mistake. Maddox shrugged. What choice but to be honest? "We are in need of information about Mr. Stefan Dubrowsky, and we thought Miss Rusnak might be able to provide it."

She eyed them each in turn, lips pursed, for another half minute before she said, "You can come in."

The heavy door opened into an entryway painted pea-soup green: tiled floor, row of mailboxes, dark hall with stairs going up. She pointed to an open door on the left and ushered them into a sitting room: stifling, cluttered, and crowded with tables, chairs, a fancy sofa piled with pillows, a fringed ottoman, a tall carved cabinet, a ladies' desk with a gilt chair, a dog's basket on the floor, and a grandfather clock in one corner that bonged twice as they entered.

They all sat. "Yes, then." The woman spread out her skirts and folded her hands in her lap. "I am Eva Rusnak. You passed by the bakery up on the avenue? Well, I am manager there. Mrs. Gromada is the owner—Magda. Today is my day off, so you were lucky."

"And Katarzyna is your sister?"

"Yes. Kasia. Since last summer, she no longer lives here, and she wants no one to know where she has gone. For this she has her reasons. So do not ask."

Her face was stern, and she seemed to be waiting for an answer. Maddox said, "All right. Then maybe you can tell us about Mr. Dubrowsky."

"Oh—Stefan. Again you have come chasing a wild goose. He also no longer is in Brooklyn. He lives now in California." The hint of a smile flickered on her lips. "It seems he has at last given up." A dog yipped somewhere in the depths of the apartment. "That is Fredzio. He is dachshund. I have to shut him in the bedroom when visitors come or he will love you to death." Now Eva Rusnak did smile, and became suddenly pretty. "Fredzio!" She said something in Polish and the yipping stopped. "Obedient when he wants to be. Not always when I want. Such are the natures of dachshunds."

Davey made an impatient gesture. "What do you mean, he has given up?"

"For now. I said go back to sleep, crazy dog!"

"No—I mean Stefan Dubrowsky. You said he has given up."

"Oh." She laughed. The interval of the dog seemed to have relaxed her. "Stefan. Yes. Though you know, he is something like a dog, for digging in his teeth and hanging on when you tell him let go, let go!"

"But he has finally given up."

"Oh yes. He came here last summer, but I would not tell him where she is." She looked at their puzzled faces. "Kasia. He came to see her, he hoped to take her to California on the train."

The story gradually emerged. The two Rusnak sisters had not emigrated from Poland, Eva said—they had escaped: that was the accurate word. From what? From a family of twelve, in which they were the two oldest. Their mother died when the last baby was born, little Tadeusz, who himself died just before his first birthday. "We did our best, Kasia and I, but Tadeusz died from having no mother. We were too busy being the servants—baby-minders too, but also cooks and cleaners and growing the beans and shoveling the snow and the ones who were beaten by Papa when everything did not go as he liked." She spread her hands in a gesture of hopelessness. "So this is how it was. We ran away."

Stefan had arranged it. His father was a prosperous fruit grower, very different from Papa Rusnak, a blacksmith who could not read or write. Stefan's father was educated, his mother was a teacher at the school in their village. Stefan himself was a botanist—very skilled, Eva said. He could take a plum tree and grow peaches on it, or pears—anything you like! Stefan had accumulated enough money for the three of them. He came for them in the dark of night, and they drove to Rotterdam in a wagon pulled by two mules. Seven hundred miles. "No need to talk about this," she said. "It was ten years ago. Now you ask me to do this? I would say leave me be. But we were children, we would do anything."

Kasia and Stefan were married in New York. "Yes, she was already expecting a child. Kasia had not wanted this—no more taking care of children, she said. Ever ever ever. But these things happen. They were married. The baby was born. And then—"

Eva paused for half a minute, frowning down at her clasped hands. A cockroach appeared, from nowhere, on the wall high behind her head, and Davey watched with fascination as it made its way slowly down.

"And then?" Maddox prompted.

"Yes. Well, this is not the so nice part. Kasia, she would not live with them. She did not even want to see the little boy. Victor. When he saw her, he called her Ciotka Kasia. That is aunt." She pulled a handkerchief from somewhere and gave one eye a delicate wipe. "He didn't see her often. A very sweet child. Here."

From the table beside her, she took a framed photograph of a man, a woman, and a boy of perhaps two, dressed in rompers. The man was Stefan Dubrowsky, younger, without a mustache. The woman was very blond, very like Eva, with the same masses of light hair, but prettier. Much prettier. A beauty. The child, the blond image of his mother, was perched on his father's knee.

"Stefan had to pay her to sit for this! Yes. It is the truth. Pay her money!" Eva took the photo back, shaking her head. "Little Victor. So much like our Tadeusz. But Kasia did not care. Also, she did not care what anyone thought of her—that was Kasia. Here in Greenpoint we have a very close Polish community. You have seen? Everything is *Polskie*. Like being back in Gdansk. Kraków. Kasia was a bad mother, people did not like this. So she was—" She made loose circles with her left hand. "The proper word, I do not know in English."

"Ostracized?"

"Yes, very good, thank you. I think that is it. But—you know—she was so young, not even twenty when the boy was born. And where we had come from! I could tell you things. She could not help herself. Still, it was not good. Such a nice little boy." She sighed. "Well. Stefan cared for him, I helped when I was not at work. I am managing the bakery. And Mrs. Bukoski, on India Street, she helped too. Also the sisters at the church. And then—well, after a time, Marek and Kasia were as if married. Marek Nowicki. They lived here, upstairs. Marek was handyman, carpenter, those sorts of things. Very nice man. Older. Longtime friend." She looked down again at the photograph. "So Stefan took the boy and went to California when he saw that Marek was—what is the word? It doesn't matter. Stefan left, but he kept writing to Kasia, always hoping. He knew how she hated winter—she should come to California, land of no winters! Built her a house in the middle of an orchard. Sent her presents on her birthday. She hardly read the letters—some, she didn't even open them. Then last summer Stefan came here again because somebody told him Marek died."

"Typhoid," Maddox said. Eva looked at him sharply. "There are public records."

"Oh. Well, yes, it was typhoid. Very bad. My sister was—" She made the circles again, groping in the air, and said something in Polish. "Devastated, I think is the word. It was Marek Nowicki she loved. Stefan—he was of her youth. You know?" She shrugged her narrow shoulders. "Marek left everything to Kasia. More money than you would think. And so she went off—making a new life, she said. Where? I cannot say, but I will tell you it is someplace very, very nice. What is it called? Easy Street. She has always been lucky. So when Stefan came, she was gone. And he said to me, all right, at last I am done with it, I give up. And he left without hope to go back to California. And that is the end."

The cockroach paused above her chair and, at the last minute, disappeared behind the carved cabinet.

"They were never divorced?"

"Stefan and Kasia?" Eva gave a short laugh. "My sister, how she would have loved a divorce. He would not do it. You understand? He didn't want to let her go. Ever."

When they stood up to leave, the dog began barking again. "You see? He knows now he will be let out. We should all be as smart as dogs." Then she said, "Ah! Wait! One small thing!" and disappeared through a doorway into the back of the apartment.

Davey picked up the photograph: Stefan expressionless, the little boy with an uncertain smile, and Kasia Rusnak, who had not died in childbirth—one of the most alive-looking people he had ever seen.

Eva returned with a paper parcel tied with red string. "Khruchiki. Little cookies, from the bakery."

Maddox thanked her, for the cookies, for her time. She smiled and waved her hands. "No no no no," and, as she opened the door to let them out into the hot street, she added, "She is not a bad woman, Kasia. Just—you know—life is so hard. Isn't it not?"

∽ひ✑∾

On the train the next day, sitting across from each other, they argued. Davey insisted that Hazel should not be told: let the wedding proceed, and who would ever know the truth but the two of them and Jack Truesdale and his clerk?

"Just tell me this," Davey said. "What right do we have to destroy Hazel's happiness? A couple of meddling cousins who—believe me—will not be thanked for it."

"Davey!" Maddox looked at him goggle-eyed. "What right do we have to let her marry a bigamist and a cad? We'd not be destroying her happiness but ensuring it. Think about it." He spread his hands in a gesture of frustration. "His wife died giving birth to his little boy? What kind of scoundrel would tell such a falsehood?"

There was a long period of aggrieved muteness while the train chugged north through the Bronx toward Connecticut. The twins had argued all their lives, conflicts that never lasted long and usually ended in laughter. But Davey could find no humor in a situation that, however they twisted it, presented nothing but grief. Should they tell Hazel? Should they not? Should someone write to Stefan and give him the chance to explain and somehow make it right? How make it right? And why should they give Stefan this consideration? And what if Eva had lied to them? What if Kasia Rusnak had been behind the bedroom door with Fredzio the dog, listening to everything they said and plotting to wreck the life of a husband she no longer loved?

182

They approached the Hartford station, and the woman beside Davey—she had been eavesdropping so openly that Davey was tempted to ask her opinion—moved into the aisle, banging him on the knee with the sharp corner of her basket, as if her vote was with his brother. The train shuddered to a stop, and Davey said, "Maybe he's not a scoundrel at all but just a man who is no longer so young, who wants a wife, who can't get rid of this woman who has never been a wife to him, never been a mother, and he saw no other solution."

"There are other solutions. Who but a scoundrel would think lying to Hazel is the best one?"

"Or what about this? Can you bring a bill of divorcement against someone who's disappeared?"

Maddox frowned. "It's possible, for desertion. The law varies according to state."

"What if he's gone to court and done that? Sometime between his visit to Eva and his proposal to Hazel. What if he's no longer married?"

"You're playing devil's advocate."

"I'm not playing anything, Maddox. If I'm advocating, it's for the man Hazel truly loves. We can't forget that."

"*Truly loves*—what does that mean? Love is easy when you hardly know someone."

Maddox rummaged in his bag for the package of khruchiki and held it out to Davey, who shook his head. *Love is easy when you hardly know someone*: maybe his brother was really talking about his own quick courtship of Caroline. Davey thought: *I have known Hazel half my life: that is what makes love easy.*

Maddox ate a cookie, then another, and a third, crunching loudly over the sound of the train. Davey's stomach knotted; he pressed his eyes with his fingertips. His brother's energy could be wearying.

When the train stopped at Springfield, Maddox tapped him on the knee and said, "Davey. Listen. We need to tell her, and that's the end of it. If we do not, we're treating her like a child. Let her ruminate on all this. If she wants to marry him despite everything, so be it. But she has to know."

"Why? There is nothing preventing him from being a good husband. This Kasia woman has disappeared—forever. It's Hazel he wants. They will be happy together. There's no point in talking about it further. And your beard is full of crumbs."

Maddox made a strangled sound. "Why are you like this?" A man across the aisle turned to look at them, and Maddox lowered his voice. "You don't deserve this cousin of ours, and that's the truth. You may think you're wishing her happiness, but you are not. Think what you are wishing her."

Davey could feel himself sinking into the lake of perversity that he had swum in all his life. Of course, his brother was right. Why was it so hard for him to admit it? *The world is a hard and stony place.* Ida had said so. Eva had said so. Who in his right mind did not feel it to be true?

By the time the train pulled into the Amherst depot, his eyes were brimming with tears he had to wipe away before he could speak. "You're right. Hazel has to be told. And I will do it tomorrow."

He took Owosha out for her morning hunt—singing to her softly, more to calm himself than for her—and then stowed her back in her enclosure. He had been planning to walk into town and knock on Hazel's door, but she surprised him with a visit. Her basket—sketch pad, pencil case, and a rhubarb tart—almost made him lose heart. That and the expression on her face, Hazel's new look: of someone who is waiting to open a wonderful present.

Owosha was on her perch, satisfied, wiping her beak on her breast feathers. Heloise wandered through the vegetable garden and settled for a nap under a pepper plant. The scent of blossoms, of manure, of an early summer morning: everything as it always was. Davey and Hazel sat on the bench in the sun, the white sky above them promising heat, the grass thick with clover.

He told her about the trip to Brooklyn and what he and Maddox had found. When he was done, she asked no questions, she just sat quietly for a few moments, her lips tight, fists clenched in her lap.

Then, without warning, she leaned into his arms, shaking with sobs. He held her close. Her hair was soft against his cheek.

Thou shalt not weep, he thought, *except when thy heart is broken.*

Chapter 15

It did not take long for heartbreak to move aside and make room for anger.

Hazel walked home from Davey's. No, he need not accompany her, she was fine—though fine was not, exactly, what she was: she walked in a state of numb wretchedness. But she wanted to be alone. Halfway across the Common, she remembered she was wearing Stefan's sapphire ring: she pulled it off her finger and dropped it into her pocket—repressing the urge to throw it in the frog pond. Then, suddenly unsteady, she had to sit on the bench in front of Spear's and squeeze her eyes shut to stop the tears.

Enough, she thought. I will not cry for that person.

She spent the afternoon in the garden with her sketchbook, trying to think about anything but Stefan: either this new Stefan, with his living wife and his glib fabrications, or the old Stefan, to whom she had promised herself with both words and kisses—with exchanges of caresses that did not bear remembering. She wished for a magic concoction that would provide harmless, salubrious oblivion long enough for her to forget that she had been made a fool of. Failing that, she took out her pencil and concentrated on getting to the heart of the overripe peonies out by the shed.

By evening, she was able to talk about it, and she told the sorry tale to her mother and her uncle. Maud embraced her, held her hands, wept indignant tears. That her daughter's sweet and trusting nature had been trampled on by a rotter with no morals! A man who had seemed such a gentleman, who had charmed them all, turning out to be not only a cad but a posturing blackguard! George brought out the whiskey, sputtering about bigamy and deceit: the man should be horsewhipped.

Hazel had anticipated lectures about her recklessness and fool-hardiness, but found only sympathy and indignation. The immediate, outraged kindness of the people who loved her was a comfort. Tamsin stopped by with Sam, who was back from Brussels and talking about legal action. Ella, covering her face with her apron, wept bitter tears at the perfidy of men and thanked the Lord that Miss Hazel was not to be spirited off to that heathen land out west. Lydia folded Hazel in her arms, and said, "I will give thanks every day that my brothers showed some sense for once and found this out before it was too late!" Anna sent a gift, delivered from the Bonnet Shop: a straw hat trimmed with a band of bright red roses. The card read: "When you are ready to wear this, I'll take you to tea."

Hazel was surprised at how soon even the anger wore off, replaced by a kind of cool detachment—surprised that such a rabbit as herself had not retreated to her burrow, whimpering, huddled in a fog of humiliation. She kept a handkerchief in her pocket, always expecting tears. But the tears seldom came, and she greeted each day with gratitude that she had been delivered from catastrophe.

Life went on. She attended James Clay's funeral and joined the procession to the cemetery on Triangle Street. She had her last tutoring session with Selina Harper, who claimed, not unconvincingly, that she would miss Caesar and his troops over the summer. She returned her library books, took her boots to be re-soled, did the marketing. Of course the news, such as it was, had spread, and people might regard her with pity, but she smiled and said her cordial good-mornings as if she had never been betrothed to a promising young man from California.

There were bad moments: passing the Clays' house on Sunset Avenue, remembering the shudder of joy she had felt to see Stefan on the sidewalk waiting for her—that was one. But those moments were few, and her resilience was somewhat amazing to her, and puzzling.

More than anything, she was occupied with trying to decide what action to take. Maddox wrote to say he was willing to communicate to Stefan Dubrowsky a summary of the revelations of Eva Rusnak, the City Directory, and the Brooklyn Civil Court, and to officially break the engagement on Hazel's behalf. Kind-hearted Tamsin thought Hazel should write a tender message, ending the engagement but sympathizing at least a little with Stefan's predicament. Maud said he was beneath her notice and favored freezing him out with a dignified silence: send no letters and respond to none. George recommended a blistering letter telling him in plain language what Hazel thought of him. No, better yet—this was on another whiskey-drinking evening around the kitchen table—do it with a telegram to Calvin: HAVE CHANGED MIND STOP. CANNOT MARRY YOUR BIGAMIST SCOUNDREL CAD VILLAIN ORCHARD MANAGER STOP.

For three days, Hazel moved between her bedroom and the back garden, trying to think clearly. Contemplating what she now knew to be Stefan's long, troubled marriage was a kind of agony—long years not of mourning his dead wife but of trying to persuade the woman to overcome her coldness toward him. Kasia Dubrowsky must have her own story, and Hazel almost wished she could hear it.

Maddox wrote again to say he felt obliged to let her know that in the state of California Stefan might be able to obtain a divorce, even in absentia, on the grounds of desertion. Hazel tried to imagine demanding that he do this, then marrying a belatedly divorced man who, however the legal situation might change, had lied to her with apparent ease for many months. She also asked herself what she would have done if Stefan had simply been honest about his wife's existence and asked Hazel to live with him in spite of it.

It was a question she was unable to answer, and after letting it plague her for a long day and a sleepless night, she put it from her mind.

In the end, she decided to write a letter ending the engagement, and to return the ring, which sat on her dresser in its velvet box like a nugget of poison. She had the vague notion that she owed Stefan as few words as possible and spent a bitter hour at her desk trying to compress what she wanted to say into one short sentence. Finally, in her firmest script, on a scrap of paper, she wrote: *I have learned the truth about your wife, and therefore this marriage cannot take place.* No need to sign her name.

She folded it into a tiny square, tucked it into the box with the ring, and wrapped the box in a piece of a paper sack from the grocery tied with string from the butcher. Hattie Graves at the post office said she could send her parcel to California via Special Delivery for twenty cents.

Hazel marveled at how cheap self-respect could be, and handed over two dimes.

❧⚭

Anna had stopped lamenting the coffee houses of Rome—the only things about that city she had ever admitted she missed—and developed an affection for the Green Valley Tea Room. She liked the pastries, the striped wallpaper, even the ironstone teapots and thick white cups: all so sensible and American.

She and Hazel went to tea in the middle of a heat wave. Amherst was sweltering: the day lilies lasted only hours, the grass on the Common had turned the color of hay, the sky was the relentless bright blue George liked to complain about. Rev. Tilley, Lydia said, had asked his congregation to pray for rain.

Hazel wore the new hat, with its lavish crown of red roses— Anna's choice, and Anna's taste, but it told the world, as it was meant to, that Miss Cooper had risen above her recent misfortune. The tea room was crowded, noisy with chatter. Hazel held her head high as she entered, but, if the women of Amherst stared at anyone, it was

Anna, with her bright hair and vivid coloring—always regal, always cordial, with a wave across the room at Mrs. Mackey, the postman's wife, and a cheerful *buon giorno!* from Mrs. Todd. Hazel was not sorry to pale into insignificance beside her.

They were given a table by the window: the waitresses knew the signorina liked to look out. "It's like George at Blodgett's Tavern," Hazel observed. "They practically cheer when you come in."

Anything that marked Anna out as a citizen of Amherst made her smile. "They always know exactly what I want. A pot of Assam with a pitcher of milk, not cream. And a platter of tiny cakes, which I think are just what you need. Sweet things to help you recover from such heartlessness, such—" Anna frowned, searching for the right word. "Perfidiousness."

On the table were two cardboard fans printed with advertisements. Hazel picked one up—F. P. BEEBY. DENTIST. PAINLESS EXTRACTIONS. ALL WORK GUARANTEED—and slowly fanned herself. "I will tell you the truth, Anna. I have hardly shed a tear, and I don't know why. Maybe, in my own way, I'm as heartless as he is."

Anna laughed. "I doubt it. But I'm glad you are bearing it so well. You did not deserve this treatment."

"It's probably time I learned to be less trusting and more cautious."

"But why should you not expect goodness? There has been an enviable absence of scoundrels in your life. You've known only decent people."

"You have a wonderfully rosy view of this part of the world. I hope we won't disappoint you."

"I have made up my mind, and I do not intend to change it." Anna made a sweeping gesture that took in the tabletop, the tea room, the window and the street beyond. "My new world is a paradise on earth."

"It's a very small paradise."

"The smallness is what I like. You know who you are and where you belong. I have had enough of big places where you can get lost."

Hazel had heard something of Anna's life in Rome: remote father, brutal husband, lost child, the glittering career and the devastating loss of it—all in a golden world of palazzos and summer houses and opulent villas, tended by others and taken for granted. Could the lives of any two women be more different? It was a wonder to them both that they had become friends.

Anna reached over and squeezed her arm. "I hope you appreciate how lucky you are to call such a place your home."

"I suppose I must, because I so desperately didn't want to give it up." The tea arrived, and Hazel waited for the waitress to leave before she continued. "But there's no excuse for my foolishness—for walking straight into disaster. I keep having visions of that woman turning up on my doorstep and demanding her husband back, like someone in a dime novel."

"You will have to tell me what a dime novel is."

"They sell them at the depot newsstand. Cheap and lurid books with sensational plots. I've borrowed one or two that Ella left in the kitchen—they're hard to resist. I stayed up half the night reading one called *Mrs. Templeton's Trial*, about a woman who bludgeoned her husband to death with a frying pan."

"Good for her. I might very well have done the same if the pope had not intervened with an annulment. In Italy, of course, your young man could have had his marriage annulled. His wife was not doing her duties." Anna hesitated over the cakes and chose a chocolate one not much larger than a half-dollar. She paused before taking a bite. "But you have no need of a pope to rescue you when you have such admirable cousins."

"My mother says they shouldn't have just gone off to investigate. Like Sherlock Holmes and what's his name. Watson. They should have talked to me first. Indignation doesn't come as readily to me as it does to my mother, but maybe she's right."

"I suppose they wanted to make sure of it before they caused you distress."

"It's not so simple. The truth is—" She thought back to the men in her life: a parade of fiascos. Edward Fletcher, and Bessie Bell's caution: *Don't throw yourself at him, Hazel!* Douglas McGill, whom she'd barely found the courage to talk to. Merwin Booth, whom she had led on shamelessly because, however repellent, he was at least willing to take her to the Commencement Dance. The theology student from Yale who—oh, none of them bore thinking about. She picked up the fan again to cool her hot cheeks. "The truth is that they were not wrong to treat me like a ninny. Because I am a ninny."

"Ninny."

"A silly and irresponsible person, famous for her bad judgment when it comes to men."

"You are harsh with yourself." Anna sat forward, her elbows on the table. "Hazel. Here is what I have been wanting to say about all this, and it may be—I think the word is presumptuous. Because what do I know about such things? But I speak as an observer of people, and I hope you will not be offended."

"Be as presumptuous as you like."

"I don't believe you ever loved that young man. That is why you are taking this so calmly."

"Oh." Hazel looked out the window at Pleasant Street, dusty in the sun. Ella passed with her shopping basket, returning from Jackson's. Young Mrs. Greeley pushing a baby carriage. "Well." She sighed and set down the fan: PAINLESS EXTRACTIONS indeed. "I certainly thought I loved him."

"You loved marriage and a home and babies. A place in the world, maybe. But real love, Hazel—only in operas can it come so fast."

Hazel turned from the window. "You want to say something about Davey, but you're afraid I'll scream and change the subject."

Anna's laugh—throaty, with a crack in it—made people turn and look at her. "Don't say you have not thought of it." She lowered her voice. "That now you are free. That you still want to marry. That Davey Chillick is here, and he loves you."

"And that ending one engagement and in the next breath contracting another with my first cousin would be preposterous even in a dime novel."

"Truth is always allowed to be more preposterous than novels. And besides—" Anna paused to stir the pot and pour tea. "Think of your parents."

"My parents?"

"George has told me their history. That Charles Cooper was in love with my mother, but when she went back to Italy he was married three months later to Miss Maud Mullen. And I believe one might say they lived happily ever after."

Hazel had to laugh. "That's an ingenious argument. You would make an excellent lawyer." Then she sat back in her chair, shaking her head. "If it's true that he loves me, why doesn't he say so?"

"He doesn't say so because he is Davey Chillick. He would be less peculiar if he knew you loved him. If you wait for him, you will wait forever." Anna dropped a lump of sugar into her tea. "Here is my advice, *carissima*." She looked at Hazel with her slyest smile. "Don't be a ninny. Give him his heart's desire, and the spell will be broken."

Chapter 16

Anna went with the Chillicks to the Independence Day festivities on the Common, wearing a white shirtwaist, blue skirt, and red cummerbund, a tricolor ribbon on her hat. The day was pleasantly warm; the heat wave had subsided. In the parade down Main Street, Maud marched with a purple-and-green VOTES FOR WOMEN sash pinned across her chest; Ida Schmidt, in turban and bloomers, carried a sign that read: WE DEMAND UNIVERSAL SUFFRAGE. A group of war veterans straggled under a regimental banner. A woman in the flowing robes of the Statue of Liberty, carrying a torch, was wheeled by on a platform, to loud cheers.

The Common was a sea of parasols and straw hats. Folding chairs were set up, the bandstand decorated with bunting. Lydia and Tamsin had packed picnic baskets and spread a quilt on the grass. Mr. Austin Dickinson gave a stirring recitation of Lincoln's Gettysburg address. There were speeches by President Gates of Amherst College and the Reverend Morehouse of the First Congregational Church. The elderly daughter of a Revolutionary War general quavered out a poem written for the occasion. Whenever there was a lull, the firehouse band blasted away.

The whole town seemed to know that Signorina Anna Felice of Rome, Italy, had taken Tom Paige's house at the bottom of Amity

Street. She was introduced to the editor of the local newspaper, the dean of the college, a slew of Dickinsons. The little twins took her by the hands to meet their kindergarten teacher, Miss Miller. When Hazel introduced her to Mr. Jenkins, the organist at Grace Church, Anna recalled the day when she sat in a pew there, listening to Palestrina and surprising herself with the determination to call this town her home. Not even two months ago—and here she was, with a house, a library card, and a checking account at the First National Bank!

When a group of schoolchildren, Valentine among them, assembled on the bandstand to sing "The Battle Hymn of the Republic," Anna had to wipe away tears.

♧

She moved to Amity Street a week later. The house was no longer gray: after a crew of painters had come and gone, it was now the same egg-yolk yellow as Aunt Julia's house in New Haven and the Dickinsons' on Main Street, a color Anna had decided was particularly sunny, optimistic, and American.

She had gladly accepted an offer of guidance from Lydia, who knew that vinegar made windows sparkle, a kitchen floor needed linoleum put on it, cayenne pepper will discourage ants. Her brothers might laugh at Lydia's formidable competence, but Anna watched gratefully as her house became daily more livable. There was plenty of coal in the cellar, Lydia said: no need for a delivery until the autumn. She brought in Mr. Hunt to find the blockage in the water pipes and Mr. Kellogg to repair the back steps. She had a Wilton carpet laid in the sitting room. She found a girl—Gertie Potts, daughter of Archie's head sheepman—who would come in every day to lay the fires and cook two meals, do the washing and keep the dust down. She arranged for the delivery of an icebox and a block of ice to go into it: when more ice was needed, Lydia said, Gertie would put a card in the window and Cadwell's would deliver it.

Lydia also brought over the Montgomery Ward mail-order catalog, from whose astonishing pages Anna ordered a pair of lamps,

195

a revolving bookcase, a set of iron pans, two summer nightdresses, a coffee pot, and a Currier & Ives print of a snowy scene to hang over the fireplace. When she mailed the order form, she felt the last shreds of her Roman identity being sloughed away.

On her first night in the house, Anna sat up late: she had seen Roderick Hudson off to his unhappy end and was reading *The Woman in White*, borrowed from Tamsin's library—a family saga even more complicated than her own. She fell asleep as Count Fosco—how familiar that wily Italian seemed!—was insinuating his way into the plot, but she slept restlessly and, in the early dawn, went downstairs, struck by the absolute quiet, remembering Tamsin's polecats and ghosts. She had never before slept in a house alone, or lived in a place that didn't have a staff of servants in their own invisible quarters. Had never made her own breakfast. She had no idea how to cook an egg, but Lydia had helped her master the coal stove, and after she got it going she put on the kettle.

She had been warned that water does not boil quickly. While she waited Anna went around the first floor looking out through every window: white-curtained at her own insistence. Drapes, even from Montgomery Ward, even the very nice ones Lydia urged on her, with a pattern of doves and blossoms, were all wrong for her house. Where she had gotten the confidence to choose yellow paint and simple white curtains she did not know. But there it was: her practical American roots, watered now by the kindness of her new Amherst family, had pushed through the soil and grown and flowered.

To the east, the sun was rising on another modest, dormered place, where an old couple kept a large, amiable pig in a pen; to the west a field of corn stretched into the town of Hadley; on the shady north side was her backyard, with two cane chairs from Tamsin's barn; and, on the south, past the cobblestone path and her dewy front garden, Amity Street, under its sheltering elms, was at this early hour almost deserted, though, as Anna watched, a wagon piled with logs clopped by. From somewhere nearby, she heard a rooster crow.

The kettle boiled. Her coffee pot had not yet arrived, so she measured tea leaves into the new ceramic teapot, cut a slice of bread, opened a jar of Tilda's strawberry jam. She had bought a checkered tablecloth at Sanderson's on Merchants Row, along with a set of napkins and some dishcloths and two potholders. It was like playing house. Had she played house as a child? She must have, and what she must have pretended—she knew nothing else—was living in a palazzo like Papa's, with marble floors and views of the seven hills and her own maid to put away the toys when she was tired of them. A pampered child, prone to tantrums, who had grown up to be the owner of a yellow house with two dormers and a whitewashed fence in Amherst, Massachusetts.

The day before, she had stood in her backyard and looked up with pride at her chimney—a mason named Ben had done things to the mortar that, he assured her, made it the best-pointed chimney in the county—and realized that she had never really looked at a chimney before. It was a wonderful mechanism: You built a fire with wood or with coal so your house could be heated or your dinner cooked, and the smoke was diverted—how? who knew?—up the chimney and into the clouds. How simple life was!

Tamsin had asked her, on the evening before Anna transferred herself to Amity Street, if she thought she might regret her decision to make her home in such an unlikely spot. Her answer—it was impossible for Anna not to be honest with herself—was that she did not know. But she did know that, even if she had regrets, she would never go back. Things were possible here that in Rome were not even daydreams. She was not ready to specify what those things were. She thought of herself, she told Tamsin, as a flower—a very ordinary one, she hastened to add—that had been wrenched long ago from its natural habitat, struggled to survive, and needed to be pulled up by the roots and returned. Taken from the desert to a verdant forest. Or from a forest to an open field in the sun.

The two of them laughed about it. *I am a ridiculous woman,* Anna said, and Tamsin said, *You are a brave and admirable one, and I'm glad you've chosen our town in which to plant yourself.*

She was pouring a second cup of tea and wondering how one cleaned dishes—or should she just leave everything for Gertie?—when George knocked on the back door.

197

He advised her to let Gertie do the washing up. She offered him tea, proud that she had successfully made a pot of it, but he said he'd just finished his breakfast and had stopped by to see how she was settling in. Anna said she was settling in very well, and did he know where she might get a cookery book? He said they must have such items at Spear's. Hazel swore by Mrs. Beecher's book; Anna made a note of it. And why did she want a cookery book? She thought she might teach herself to cook—just simple things, like eggs.

Commendable, said George. Meanwhile, he had come with two items of interest. There was a litter of kittens at Blodgett's, and if she'd like a couple, she could have them in a month or so. Also, he had had a letter from Fair Haven.

Anna had given up on Mrs. McAlmond and, with her, the story of the mad aunt. She had more urgent things to think about: the furnishing of a house, the gazebo that needed rebuilding, where to put the piano that was being delivered from Boston. She was preoccupied with making herself over into an American, and the truth about Elena Zanetti seemed less vital with every potholder she bought.

And yet, when George pulled an envelope from his waistcoat pocket, her curiosity was piqued. "So you were right about those old Irishwomen."

Alas, no, he said. Maggie McAlmond had gone to her reward a few years ago. But that was not the end of the story. On the envelope was George's name and address in firm black script. George gazed at it, beaming at the sight of his name written with such magnificence. "It seems that wee letter I sent to Maggie made the rounds, traveling through Fair Haven to Boston and back again, and finally, after much travail, arriving at the residence of your uncle."

"My uncle."

"By which I mean that Irishman who married your aunt. Liam Whelan by name—I knew it was something like that. Quite the fine fellow he seems to have become. He wrote me a very civil note, even claims he remembers me from that day so many years ago. And he enclosed this for you." George set a fat envelope on the table before her—same creamy paper, elegant script: *Signorina Anna Felice*. "I'll let you read it in peace, Miss Anna. I'm off to work. I hope you'll stop by Blodgett's and see those kittens. One cunning little girl has a white muzzle and a black nose, her brother just the opposite." He put his hat back on. "And I will say it's good to see you here on Amity Street in your comfortable house, drinking tea at your own kitchen table, hand-me-down though it be."

⁂

Dear Signorina Felice,

By a roundabout route, I have received George Mullen's letter to Mrs. Maggie McAlmond, who I am sorry to say has been deceased for seven years. Her daughter, Colleen, who lives in Boston, patiently tracked me down and sent it to me because she felt it was too important to be ignored. I am grateful to her, and to Mr. Mullen for writing. How astonishing it is to find that the baby who once lived under my roof—however briefly—has returned to New England in search of her aunt, my dear wife Elena.

Elena died in 1874, just before her fortieth birthday. She had gone out on a sleigh ride with the children on a cold winter day, she came down with pneumonia, and a week later she was dead.

Our children are Helen and William— English renderings of their parents' Italian and Irish names. They were twelve and fourteen when Elena died. I cannot imagine a closer family than we were. We were sunk in grieving for a very long time.

Mr. Mullen in his letter says you have learned some of your family history, so you know that Elena's brother Tomasso—your father—was killed before your mother was sent to America. He was seventeen, by all accounts a handsome and charm-

*ing young man, beloved by many and greatly
missed. Elena never ceased to mourn him.*

*You may not know much about what I suppose
has to be called the abduction. What Elena did was
wrong, but I will tell you why she stole that baby.
She felt that Lily Prescott was too young and irresponsible to be a good mother, and that her child—a
Zanetti as much as a Prescott—would be better off
with the sister of her dead father: herself.*

*But it was only later that she told me this.
When I met Elena Zanetti, she presented herself
as a widow with a six-month-old baby. Her
husband, she said, had died on the crossing from
Italy. She had gone into service with a wealthy
woman in New Haven, and said that at first she
was allowed to keep the baby with her. But when
I met her she had been told she must put her out to
nurse. Once we were married she was able to give
up her position, and she and the baby came to live
with my sister Mary and me in Fair Haven.*

*Elena was dark, and the baby was fair, but
I never doubted her claim because she was so
devoted. The baby, she said, was all she had. She
never called you Prudence Ann. You were always
her little Anna. She loved you with what I can
only call desperation, mixed with her grief for her
dead brother, and her loneliness in America, and
her passionate desire for a child of her own. But
when George Mullen and Charles Cooper showed
up, she broke down and told me the truth.*

*It was a difficult moment. We had not been
married long, and were still getting used to each
other. I can remember when they took you away,
and hearing the wagon clatter away up the street,
and how my wife wept. In the end, I forgave her
the lies. We had a great love for each other, and that*

lamentable episode brought us closer. Time went by. I worked for the New Haven Railroad, and we moved to New York City. A son and daughter were born. The New Haven moved its headquarters to the city it was named for, and so we returned. I still live in our house—much too big for me now—built by a sea captain on the Heights, across the river from the oyster-shell streets and the boats and the packing houses. Your aunt Elena is alive for me in every room.

My long letter must go on a little longer, because here is what may be the strangest part of this strange story. As of course you know, Elena's sister Lorenza became a cook in your father's house. She was passed on to him by your grandfather Prescott after Signor Felice married your mother. Lorenza could read and write—not well, but well enough to send us news from time to time of little Anna—reborn as a Felice—a little princess who begged Lorenza for sweets, who lost her mother at six, who left home at fourteen to train as a singer. Of course all the Zanettis knew who you were, but—also of course—no one in that enormous and good-hearted family ever told a soul.

In 1879, some years after Elena died, I sailed to Italy with the children—by then almost grown. We went as tourists and sight-seers, but we also arranged to visit their aunt Lorenza in Rome. Signor Felice was away from home, and Lorenza was able to take us into his library to see the portrait over the fireplace of you and your brother—two beautiful children. I recognized you instantly!

And here is the last and perhaps the most wonderful part of the story. The three of us went on to Milan, and heard Anna Felice sing at La Scala. You must have been twenty-three, and you sang Violetta with such beauty and intensity I have seldom been so moved. I remember the long chorus of "bravas" after "Sempre libera," and at the end you were ankle-deep in flowers. Helen wanted to go backstage and throw her arms around her lost cousin. I told her this was not possible, and she cried all the way back to the hotel.

    Here I will close. And add a revision to what I just wrote: I hope this story isn't over. I have recently retired from the railroad after many years—I began as a ticket clerk and rose in the ranks to become an officer of the company—my history is as American as something from a book. I left sooner than I had planned because I don't like what is happening to the railroad indus-try. Maybe this was a mistake—I have too many hours to fill. But I am now thinking to fill a few of them by taking a trip to Amherst one day soon to make the acquaintance of my new niece. And to see Mr. Mullen too. I leave tomorrow for Chicago, where my son Will is a cellist, just hired to play with the Chicago Symphony, the newest orchestra in America, and it promises to be a very fine one. Helen is a violin teacher in New Haven. I hope the three of you can meet someday—three cousins who are also musicians! I'll be staying with Will and his family for a week, but then I will be in Amherst, and hope to see you there.
With best wishes to you and Mr. Mullen,
Liam Whelan

ൟ

Anna met her uncle Liam—for so she must call him—at the Amherst House, where he had checked in.

The day was overcast, threatening rain, so Anna had George pick her up and drive her to the hotel. He had fetched Liam Whelan from the station the day before, and they were already on good terms—two old Irishmen, George said, who hadn't seen each other since a kidnapped baby named Prudence Ann was handed over from one to the other. "Now don't tell me life isn't strange!" George laughed and slapped his knee. Then—this was George Mullen after a late afternoon ounce or two of whiskey—he reached over and slapped Anna's.

When he dropped her at the Amherst House, he said, "Don't be apprehensive, Miss Anna. Liam Whelan is a lad and a half, and you'll find yourself at ease with him from the start." Anna said she wasn't in the least apprehensive—perhaps not entirely true—at which George looked at her sideways. "Well, but don't you be underestimating him, either. He's quite the impressive fellow, our Liam."

And so he was. What struck Anna first about her uncle was that he had a very good tailor. He was a tall man, and stout, with white hair, jet-black eyebrows, and a short black beard shot with white. He had the clear blue eyes of the Irish, a strong chin, and an air of easy authority.

Mr. Otis showed them to Anna's favorite table, at the corner overlooking the Common. The rain had held off, but once they were seated it came down in a torrent. Mr. Otis himself brought them a bottle of Veuve Clicquot, on ice in a silver bucket. Anna was startled to see such a champagne at the Amherst House until she realized that Liam Whelan must have brought it with him on the train—and perhaps the silver bucket as well.

"You have not changed at all," he told her.

"Nor have you."

He had an easy laugh. The wine was poured. Her uncle said, "Sláinte." Having heard George utter this word many times with a glass of whiskey in his hand, Anna knew what it meant. She raised her glass: "Libiamo!"

Another laugh—of delight. "*Traviata*. My favorite of Verdi's operas. To hear you sing Violetta was a great joy for me and my children."

She was grateful for the champagne. How strange to sit there with her mother's lover's sister's widowed husband, who had once been part of the great faceless audience listening to her sing. She had no memory of the performance—she had sung more than a dozen Violettas. Back in Rome, somewhere at the Palazzo Felice—perhaps in the garret over the kitchens, perhaps thrown on the rubbish heap by Marcello—was a trunk full of programs, opera scores, dried nosegays, clippings from newspapers. She wanted none of them. She cared for nothing she had left behind—not her jewels, not her fur-trimmed cloak, not the paintings that she rightfully owned, not even the photograph of her mother the year before she died. Her banker, Signor Morelli, had his instructions. Let Giovannina do what she liked with the lot.

Liam spoke of Elena with deep affection. It was not easy to banish the image of a creature with staring eyes and wild hair behind the bars of an asylum—to replace her with a woman who had stolen a baby simply because she loved her and saw her as a daughter. And then a beloved wife and mother who could play the piano by ear, who learned to make Irish stew and bannock bread, who went sleigh-riding with her children....

Eventually, Liam asked Anna about herself: had she really given up Rome entirely to settle in town in Massachusetts?

Like everyone, he said the word *Rome* with the kind of reverence Anna thought of as the Roderick Hudson reaction: that ancient and magnificent city—who would not want to live in it?

"Many people might see my decision as misguided," she said. "Or worse. But I am giving up nothing that's important to me. Yes, the ancient beauties of the city, but—that does not seem to me a reason to live somewhere." Anna looked out the window at the dark sky, the rain beating down, the mud. "I suppose it seems a great leap."

Liam shook his head. "I left Ireland for the same reason. There was nothing there to keep me, and I've never regretted coming to America. Once a year—maybe twice—I miss that misty Irish countryside. A friend of my youth who has passed on. Maybe Joe Ginley's pub by the river in Killaloe. The taverns in America aren't a patch on the grand pubs of Ireland." He grinned. "George Mullen and I had a bit of a nostalgic blather about them."

"George seems to make do quite well with Blodgett's."

"He says he'll take me down there if I stay in town for a while." Liam poured more champagne. Anna noted his ebony cufflinks, each with its small diamond. "But you, Miss Prudence Ann. You're no immigrant from the old country. You were born in this part of the world, after all. In a way, it's a homecoming for you."

"That remarkable fact is in my mind every day." A thought came to her: what if Charles Cooper and George Mullen had searched the streets of Fair Haven and never found that baby? What if she had grown up Anna Whelan, Elena's first child? What if this Irish railway executive had adopted her? Helen and Will would be her siblings. They would all have traveled to Italy after Elena's death, gone to an opera and heard some soprano or other, and visited Aunt Lorenza in the Felice kitchen—not one of them aware that Anna was in fact the daughter of Lorenza's late mistress, Signora Lily, who had, sadly, died of the mal'aria and left behind a little son....

It was dizzying.

Liam ordered deviled oysters—how fitting—and another bottle. Anna told him—she had to tell someone—about her vague wish to open a music school in Amherst, and Liam listened carefully, his alert, intelligent face sharpened with interest, eyes narrowed under his heavy black brows. Now that he was retired, he too was seeking a new enterprise, something that would absorb him. He had an adventurous side, he said, that had drawn him to work for the railroad but that had been left unsatisfied by his years behind a desk. A school could be a practical scheme if there was a need for one, and if there were no competing institutions. There were the colleges, of course, and Boston had a good conservatory—his son, Will, had gone to it—but Boston was a hundred-mile ride on the turnpike.

Anna told him the story of Valentine's sufferings with Miss Finchett: if there was decent training to be had in this part of the world, she said, Val's mother would have discovered it. The colleges, however fine their teaching might be, were no help to a fourteen-year-old, or to an adult who might wish to study. That deficiency was a gap that could be filled by a school where people could be taught to play an instrument, to sing, to love good music. It would have to include rehearsal areas, practice rooms with pianos, an auditorium for performances—Amherst now had nothing but an airless room on the second floor of the Town Hall. Faculty concerts, student recitals, a library of musical scores, a resident orchestra....

"The school exists in my mind with perhaps alarming clarity," Anna smiled. "It is built of red brick, as all schools here seem to be. *Amherst Academy of Music* is chiseled over the front door. When you walk in, you hear scraps of music—a lesson, a rehearsal—always music, and the sounds of happy children. Down a hallway is an office with a bronze name plate: *Signorina Anna Felice, Director*, where I sit at a desk, wearing a black dress and looking severe."

Liam threw his head back and laughed. "I applaud your leap of imagination, which is where all great ideas begin. And, oddly enough, when I took a walk around town this morning after breakfast, I went past a building site on—I think—East Street, just where it crosses Main. Let me throw that into our flight of fancy. Which, you know, with some careful planning and a few machinations, could become reality." He raised his glass. "Let us drink to the Amherst Academy of Music."

He said he would stay in town for a few days and make inquiries. He and Anna would talk further. When he got home, he would broach the idea to his musician friends at Yale College, to his lawyer, to his daughter Helen, who was both sensible and musical. It might be a wild-eyed idea—but it could equally well be a very sound one.

It was apparent from the cut of his suit and the quality of the champagne that Liam Whelan, during his years behind a desk, had amassed a great deal of money. He did not say so explicitly; nor did Anna talk of her own finances. Such a conversation was premature. But they managed to understand each other: a mutual investment in such a venture was possible.

She found the word *investment* intoxicating—a term she had always associated with Signor Rat, Papa's advisor about his wealth, or with Marcello and his depressing list of sordid properties. Or with Umberto's collection of dirty pictures, which he liked even better than his gems. Anna had a general idea of what Signor Morelli did with her own money, but she had never thought of investing it in anything directly—anything substantial and real.

But to invest in music! To bring to life her daydream of giving young musicians the training she herself had never been given! This magical Irish railroading uncle who had allowed her to slam the door on her past—he might help her open one into the future.

Chapter 17

Sunday, 17 July
My dear Maddox,

It's a great pity that you missed the latest family party, and Tamsin's strawberry ice cream and Lydia's chocolate cake, all for the purpose of introducing the family to Anna's lost uncle, Liam Whelan, a large Irishman with a humble and what seemed to be genuine interest in just about everything: singing, hawking, cloud-spotting, ice cream making, the suffrage movement, the toy theater I made for the twins. Liam seems never to travel without cases of good French champagne, but he is so genial he would have been a big hit, as Valentine would say, even if he had brought ginger beer.

Hazel was there, in a new hat trimmed with bright red flowers. She ate a large piece of cake. Nor was the champagne lost on her. I suppose she has returned to her old self, and certainly she seems cheerful enough. She didn't talk to me much, but Maud told me she wrote to Stefan and returned the ring he gave her. It has been almost a month, *and she has not heard from him, but I admit to some apprehension every time a train pulls into the depot: that he will leap to the platform with some plausible explanation for all this—that he's the heir to the throne of Poland, in exile under threat of assassination, forced to live a life of lies and evasions....*

Maddox, I have changed—you know I have. I got a shave and a haircut at Plumb's last week. I went down to the Common and watched the fireworks on the Fourth of July. I've borrowed books from the public library. I am planning to buy a house. I eat supper with the parents almost every night. Why haven't I been able to say to Hazel what I want to say?

Don't think I am unaware of what a disappointment I am to you. And to myself.
With love from your brother,
Davey

When he finished the letter, he sat for a while with his head in his hands. All through the picnic, he had told himself he would walk Hazel home and, somewhere along the way, take her hand and tell her what was in his heart. Instead, he watched her climb into the cart with Maud and George, and, when they had disappeared down the road, he went back inside to help Sam dismantle the ice-cream maker.

He was putting the kettle on for tea when there was a knock at the door: Hazel, wearing her new red-flowered hat. His heart gave a leap. She handed him her basket. "It's Sunday morning. You are my church."

"I don't have the sermonizing skills of Reverend Tilley."

"Good." She pushed past him. "I didn't come here for a sermon."

"Maybe you came for a cup of tea."

"Nor did I come for tea. But you can give me a cup anyway."

He looked into the basket. "Shortbread to go with it."

"It's from Ella."

Hazel took off her hat and sat down. She folded her arms and looked at him with what seemed like belligerence. For several long minutes, no one spoke. Outside, two crows squawked back and forth, a sound he and Hazel had always found cheering—the wild energy, the passionate fussing over whatever it was. Today neither of them mentioned the crows, and the silence was like a thick fog in the room.

Davey measured tea into the pot, took their mugs off the shelf, arranged the shortbread on the cracked green plate. "Ah. Good. It has raisins in it."

"Currants."

The silence continued. He could hear her breathing. He looked at her soft hair, the curve of her cheek. The closeness of Hazel made him happy, as it always did, but her gaze was disconcerting. Belligerent? No—accusatory, maybe. Angry at him for being the bearer of the bad news from Brooklyn? He looked out the window: not a cloud in the sky, his beans climbing up their poles, Owosha on her perch. From the corner of his eye he could see Hazel's feet, crossed at the ankles, the buckles on her shoes, the hem of her striped skirt.

When the kettle boiled, he sloshed water into the teapot and said, with desperation, "You look well. I hope the turmoil is passing."

"It passed some time ago, thank you."

He set the kettle on the hearth and forced himself to turn and look into her eyes. "Hazel, what is it?"

"You got your hair cut!"

He touched his hair, puzzled. It had never been so short. "Yes. Thanks to Frank Plumb, I look like a convict."

She made a sound of exasperation and clenched her hands into fists. "You went down to Blodgett's with George!"

He stared at her. "Hazel—"

"Ella saw you buying walnuts and oatmeal at the grocery. You and Sam carried that old kitchen table over to Anna's. You took Tobias out to look at the new pond. This new Davey person, this former troglodyte—he has gone everywhere!" She drew a shaky breath, her eyes blazing and then softening as she looked at him. "Everywhere except number 7 Amity Street."

He shook his head, at a loss. "I thought you might want to be alone."

"It's been a month! It's I who have always come to visit you, trudging up Pleasant Street because you wouldn't trudge down. But now you—you go to Blodgett's, but you haven't knocked on my door. Didn't you want to see me?"

"I always want to see you." He pulled a chair around so that it faced her. They sat knee to knee. She closed her eyes, and he looked at her lashes, dark against the swell of her cheek. Her arms were smooth, bare from the elbow. He reached over and put his hands on hers. "I didn't come because I was afraid."

"And why was that?"

"Because—the day that I told you. And you—my arms around you." He blundered on. "I was afraid that—I don't know. That you couldn't—"

Her eyes opened: blue, direct. "I think we should talk to each other, Davey."

"We always talk. Why would we not talk as we always do?"

"I want us to talk as we do not always do."

"And how is that?"

"With honesty. Saying things that have remained unsaid." She unclasped her hands and turned them so that her palms touched his. "I want to know: do you love me?"

"Of course I love you. I've never not loved you. You're my cousin. You're my friend." His voice caught on the last word.

She looked at him steadily. "Davey."

"You mean—do I love you."

"You know what I mean."

"Yes. I do." He saw the way her face changed, lightened, showed the beginning of a smile, and the words poured out of him in a rush. "You're everything to me, Hazel, you always have been, and I love you so much it's going to kill me."

"No, it isn't. It's going to bring us both back to life." Her smile emerged. Her hands tightened around his. "My darling Davey. This is what we have to talk about."

The next morning, Davey went outside with a hunk of bread and sat on the bench, watching Owosha in her enclosure. She shifted from one foot to another, her wild stare unblinking. Tobias wanted to know how he had tamed her, and he had explained to the boy about the long days and nights, the Welsh songs and the whistle, the endless walking—but you can't call it taming, he was quick to add. She is as wild today as when Billy Fox trapped her for her feathers.

He had hardly slept, his mind filled with Hazel: the downy back of her neck, her tiny wrists. The moon rose and shone through the window and then disappeared again behind the trees. Who could sleep when life was so full of sweetness? He got out of bed and walked around the cabin in a passion of happiness. He would never sleep again. The time was not far off—they would marry in September, they had decided—when he could spend his nights gazing down at Hazel's face as she slept beside him. When he would watch for her to wake so he could hear her voice and see the blue of her eyes.

He had kissed her—how many times? And picked her up and carried her to his bed and kissed her there. *We shall have to buy a real bed,* she murmured, her lips curved into a smile when she pulled back to look at him. *I cannot sleep on this ridiculous cot.* She put her arms around his neck and drew him down.

He finished the bread and drank some water. Then, before the day was too far advanced, he put the glove on his arm. Owosha hopped to it. How rank and dirty and tough that glove had become, stained with blood and cut with the marks of her talons. Davey gave her the mourning dove she had caught a few days ago—the whole stinking thing. He made himself watch as she held it down with one strong

212

foot and dispatched it in her methodical way, eyes to tail, feathers and feet and all. When she was done she ducked her head and wiped her beak on her breast, and sat on his arm looking fat and satisfied.

Because that was the trick of it. He knew this from Billy Fox: she mustn't be hungry.

They set off over the meadow. It was another blistering hot day, the sky cloudless and pure blue. Any breeze there might be stayed high in the branches of the trees, where he knew Owosha would find it. They crossed the tracks and took the path, not quite as far as the pond, to a clearing bounded by birch and swamp maple.

From here he could look back and see the roof of his cabin and part of the north end of it. He hadn't noticed how weathered it had become, badly in need of painting, the roof shingles beginning to buckle. He would devote a week or two to sprucing it up. Maybe Tobias would find it an adventure to stay there sometimes. Or Sam and Tam could rent it out to a student who admired Thoreau. Davey had thought of it as a refuge, as a boat on a stormy sea. Now they could store apples in it for all he cared. He imagined packing up his arrowhead collection and his books, retrieving the antlers from over the door. The two chairs he had made would go to the new house, wherever it might be, and he and Hazel would sit on them by the fire on cold days....

He had thought of bringing Hazel with him, so that the event could set some sort of seal on his love for her: as if he were an acolyte taking up a new religion and letting go the trappings of his old fidelities. But in the end, he knew his bond with the hawk was not something he could share with anyone—or even properly explain, even to Hazel.

The hawk stirred on his arm. She raised up on her legs, her head forward; her wings quivered once, and again. He unhitched her from the jesses. No ceremony, no last song, no words at all; she was a hawk, and didn't care for such things.

It took her a moment to know she was free. Then with a great rush of wings she flew up and perched on the low branch of a maple, as if choosing her direction or feeling for the best breeze. The dove she had eaten had filled her gut, and she was heavier than she'd ever flown. Her tiny heart would be beating hard beneath the speckled feathers, she'd be trembling with the excitement of it, aware that something was different: the urgency of her need was no longer with her, the tie was broken. Davey thought back to the early days of her training, when he'd almost felt he and the hawk were one: he didn't have wings, but he had, sometimes, fleetingly, the *sensation* of having wings, of wanting to fly....

Suddenly, before he was ready, she took off, caught the wind, and soared east, toward the hills.

It was impossible not to weep. The hawk didn't love him, but he couldn't say he didn't love her: there were so many kinds of love. He had memorized her particular outline, the fringe of her wings. He would know her anywhere, he thought, though that couldn't be true. For how long—days? weeks?—would he would fancy that a hawk in the sky was Owosha, looking down at him, thinking—what? And then after a while a hawk would just be a hawk.

He watched until she was a speck, then a dot, and then there was only the blank blue sky.

Epilogue

4 August 1892

Cara Nunzia,

I hope this finds you well. And not furious at me! There is no good word, in Italian or English or, probably, any other language, to describe my compunction for not having yet written to you after all these months in America. To say I've been busy is not quite true, though, intermittently, I have been. Disoriented at first, and overwhelmed, and then gradually clear-headed and tranquil—these good English words describe my state accurately, I think. And I write in English because yours was always superior to mine and I have no doubt of your comprehension.

But to tell you of everything that has happened is quite an impossibility in a letter! The best thing would be for you to take passage on some large, fast, comfortable steamer and pay me a visit. Unless by now you have married some conte or other and settled into his palazzo grande on the Capitoline. (I am thinking of Alessandro Agnelli—non ridere, Nunzia! Admit he was mad about you!) I know how you shudder at the thought of leaving Rome, but what a joy it would be for me to see you here in Amherst, Massachusetts, where—take a deep breath, and sit down—I am preparing to spend the rest of my life.

I have purchased a yellow house, made of wood and as small as a peasant cottage. Because that is what houses are like here, and I have developed a strong affection for them. Especially for my own, which is as beautiful and simple as a new loaf of bread. And I have found friends here and—this is the part that is so difficult to put in a letter—also a family. You did not know—no one knew—I did not know! That I was born in America. Yes, it is true. I was born here, I am one year older than I thought I was, and Marcello is my half-brother. Have you digested this? There is more. I have an uncle, with whom I am hoping to embark on a business venture, and at a barn dance (I will leave "barn dance" to your imagination) I have met the first man to intrigue me since—well, since a very long time ago.

Here I will stop. But I urge you again to come for a visit and stay as long as you like. My house is not large, but I would welcome you to it, and there is also a good hotel. I miss you, carissima.
With many more apologies and with love,
Your friend,
Anna Felice

7 August
My dear Maddox,
I have found the right house—the old Armstrong place on the South Common. It sits on two acres and backs up to the pond where we used to go skating with

the boys from the poor farm. Tobias has pronounced the pond to be crackerjack—I don't know the exact meaning, but I recognize it as a superlative—and Hazel has inspected the kitchen, the bedrooms, the garden, and pronounced them, more soberly, suitable in every way. There is a separate wing for you and Tobias, a chicken coop of advanced design, and a carriage barn with two stalls, much too big, but the extra space means I can have a proper workshop. If you are serious about wanting to invest in this as a joint venture, you must come to see it soon—but I find that I can manage it with a bit of scrimping, and I wouldn't mind taking it on.

Life without a hawk feels pleasantly emancipated, but I can't deny there's a bit of a hole in it. Billy Fox and I went up Norwottuck to the Horse Caves and took the long loop back. He commended me for seeing Owosha through her first year, during which more hawks perish than survive. And then for releasing her, strong and healthy, to mate and breed. I had thought of none of this, but it was good to hear him say it.

We were all glad to see you at the Wyatts' barn dance. Your skills on the dance floor are the talk of the county. I for one was relieved that my Hazel didn't actually expect me to dance with her. She is a dear girl, and willing to take me as I am—to me, this is a miracle that is renewed every day. She tells me that you and the signorina have exchanged letters. I know it's too early to gloat, but let it be stated here that I was the first to predict it.

The news from Paris is most welcome, and the knowledge that you will soon be a free man. And here is something unexpected: a letter arrived yesterday from Calvin, with the rather startling report that Stefan Dubrowsky has left his employ

and gone off to work as a foreman on a coffee plantation in Costa Rica. So there are two chapters closed. I showed Cal's letter to Hazel. She was quiet a minute, then smiled, almost absently, said, "What a funny world it is," and then—ah, Maddox, I am a lucky man—she jumped up and kissed me.
With love from your brother,
Davey

৵৽

12 August 1892
Dear Bess,

    I was happy to get your letter about the new baby. I have no doubt he is as darling as Jonathan. How lucky you are to have two beautiful boys! Reading about the fullness of your life is almost as satisfying as telling you about my own.

    For I have news at last—an abundance of news, after all these quiet years. Since I last wrote, I have been engaged to be married, broken the engagement, and—this will make me sound flighty and most unlike myself, but I assure you that is not the case!—become engaged again, this time to David Chillick, my cousin. He is the handsomest man in Massachusetts, and the dearest person in the world.

    We have found a lovely, big house here in Amherst, on the South Common across from the church—not far from where Dana Manning's parents used to live. Our wedding will be in September, and then we will take a short trip. There are aunts and cousins to visit in Wethersfield, and we want to go to Old Lyme, where "our" river pours into Long Island Sound—and from there it is only the shortest hop to New London. So I will hope to see you then.

Sometimes, with great fondness, I remember those nights when we silly girls sat up late in our nightgowns, crying into our cocoa and lamenting the state of the world and the failings of the people in it—namely, Eddie Fletcher and Albert Leroy. Oh, Bessie, if only we could have known what happiness awaited us!
With best love to all,
Hazel

Acknowledgements

I'm deeply indebted to Sara Kane, Susan Snively, Richard Randall, Jane Schwartz, and Patricia O'Donnell for their close and thoughtful readings of the manuscript and for their unfailing support.

Thanks also to Katherine Florey for advice about things in general and the law in particular; to Carl Rubino for correcting my Latin yet again; to Sara ("Kandy") Kane for invaluable insight into voice training; to Chris Benfey for the view from Mt. Norwottuck; to Taylor Wise (*mille grazie!*) for her hawk-eyed copy editing; and to Linda Roghaar for expertly guiding the book through publication.

T.H. White's classic 1951 work, *The Goshawk*, supplied essential information about the way a hawk might have been trained in 1892. Thanks again to Jane Schwartz for a vintage copy of Mrs. Henry Ward Beecher's *All Around the House: or, How to Make Homes Happy*, source of much domestic detail. I'm also grateful to Julie Collier for sharing her vast library and her hands-on knowledge of raptors; to Stan Madyda and the Danbury Railway Museum Archives; and to Jenna Woginrich and her blog, coldantlerfarm.blogspot.com.

The Special Collections librarians at the Jones Library in Amherst have been a vital resource, especially Cynthia Harbeson, who provided images, scans, and research guidance. Many thanks also to Marianne Curling, curator of the Amherst History Museum, for both photography and historical perspective.

A special thank-you to Susan Snively and Peter Czap not only for allowing some of my characters to inhabit their house, but also for permission to construct a cabin behind it.

I took a few liberties with history and, in addition to some educated guesses, made a couple of wild ones as well. Railroad buffs, fans of early college baseball, suffrage experts, sheep farmers, and falconers may wince at the occasional glitch, and Amherst historians will find, along with much that's true and documented, some bits of pure invention. I've tried to stay as faithful as possible to time and place; any blatant errors or horrifying anachronisms are inadvertent and all my own.

Note: In the early years of Mass Aggie—now the University of Massachusetts at Amherst—a variety of Bachelor of Science degrees were inaugurated, with courses in pomology, floriculture, olericulture (edible plants), and agronomy (the use of plants for practical purposes). The arboriculture degree was added in 1893 and was the first of its kind in the United States.

Kitty Burns Florey is the author of twelve novels, most recently *The Writing Master* and *Solos*. She has also written two acclaimed works of nonfiction: *Sister Bernadette's Barking Dog: The Quirky History and Lost Art of Diagramming Sentences* and *Script and Scribble: The Rise and Fall of Handwriting*. Born in Syracuse, she has been a resident of Boston, Brooklyn, and New Haven. She now lives in Amherst, Massachusetts.

www.kittyburnsflorey.com